"You didn't take advantage of me," Christine said

Clay scowled. "Are you sure? Last night you were half out of your mind. I should have exercised more self-control, no matter how much I wanted you."

Christine sighed and confessed, "It wasn't all hysteria, you know. I wanted you, too."

Her candor seemed to startle him. He leaned forward as if to speak, but Christine waved him to silence. "What happened last night was a mistake," she announced baldly. "My mistake, not yours. It would be easy to pretend that it only happened because I was so distraught I didn't know what I was doing, but that simply isn't true. I made love with you because I wanted to."

She paused. "Are you ready for a little more honesty? I still want you, Clay McMurphy. You're the sexiest man I've ever met. The only problem is, right now you're the last thing I need in my life."

ABOUT THE AUTHOR

Lynda Ward is a familiar name to romance readers. With *Morning Has Broken*, Lynda's eleventh Superromance novel, this popular author once again introduces unforgettable characters whose love enables them to confront and conquer real-life problems. *Morning Has Broken* is set in Lynda's home state of California.

Books by Lynda Ward

HARLEQUIN SUPERROMANCE

Don't miss any of our special offers. Write to us at the following address for information on our newest releases.

Harlequin Reader Service
P.O. Box 1397, Buffalo, NY 14240
Canadian address: P.O. Box 603,
Fort Erie, Ont. L2A 5X3

Morning Has Broken

LYNDA WARD

Harlequin Books

TORONTO • NEW YORK • LONDON
AMSTERDAM • PARIS • SYDNEY • HAMBURG
STOCKHOLM • ATHENS • TOKYO • MILAN
MADRID • WARSAW • BUDAPEST • AUCKLAND

Published March 1992

ISBN 0-373-70491-7

MORNING HAS BROKEN

CHAPTER ONE

"YOUR WAITRESS will be with you in just a moment," Christine Dryden told the two couples as she led them through the crowded restaurant to a table beside the panoramic window overlooking the Pacific. A fog bank crouched on the horizon, obscuring the ocean vista, but on the Marin headlands the morning mist had burned away, and overhead the sky was a clean, clear blue. To the southeast, peeping above rolling hills made verdant by recent rain, the towers of the Golden Gate Bridge blazed orange-red in the bright noon light.

One couple, Southerners by their accent, paused at the window. "What a breathtaking view," the woman declared.

Her husband observed, "Well, honey, people did tell us that even though this place is a little out of the way, it's worth the drive just to be able to look at the scenery." As soon as the words were spoken, he glanced uneasily at Christine, obviously wondering if he'd been tactless.

She smiled reassuringly. While her hands moved quickly over the table, sharpening the pleats in an ornately folded napkin, smoothing an invisible crease in the linen tablecloth, she murmured, "I do hope that in the future you'll find our food as great an attraction as the view." She seated the guests and passed out menus with a stylized squash vine embossed in gold leaf on the cover.

A server walked past, headed for another table with orders of one of the house specialties, ratatouille served in shells of freshly baked sourdough bread, and Christine noticed the Southern man sniff appreciatively at the warm, spicy aroma. His wife continued to study her bill of fare dubiously. "Is it true that you don't serve anything but vegetables?" she asked.

Christine was used to the question. She explained, "I think you'll find that here at La Courgette we serve almost everything—except meat or fish. For example, you might want to consider today's luncheon special. Our chef has prepared a very nice fettuccine primavera with—"

She broke off her litany abruptly when the second woman at the table suddenly gasped in shock. "My God," she tittered nervously, clutching her companion's arm, "look over there by the door—it's the Hell's Angels!"

Christine's suave smile did not falter. At some almost subliminal level she observed that conversation in the dining area had halted, along with the usual clink of crystal and cutlery. All at once the room was so quite that the David Benoit tape playing over the sound system seemed to boom. She could hear Amir, the head cook, and his cousin the sous-chef back in the kitchen bickering in Farsi. Slowly she turned.

Her movements were deliberate, without haste, as silkily graceful as her soft challis dress and the blond hair that fell sleekly to her shoulders, but her grayish blue eyes swept the area comprehensively, missing nothing. When her gaze reached the foyer, Christine understood why the woman had gasped.

The man staggering down La Courgette's pastel entryway looked like a refugee from *Easy Rider,* his dark hair long and wild, a tie-dyed T-shirt visible beneath his scarred black leather jacket. He dabbed at his face with a bloodstained bandanna, and even from across the width of the restaurant Christine could see that his steel-toed cycling boots were leaving streaks of grease and mud on the shiny terrazzo. She watched him stumble to a halt and jerk his head back and forth in confusion. Then he scowled fiercely at Tish, the young waitress cowering behind the reservation desk. He lurched toward the girl.

Christine gulped. Reese Cagney, her partner, was out of the restaurant at the moment, and it was up to her to prevent a scene and protect the customers. "Excuse me, please," she murmured to the people she'd just seated. Squaring her shoulders, she glided resolutely across the dining room to confront the intruder.

As she approached him, Christine considered her options. She supposed it was entirely possible that despite his menacing appearance the man meant no harm. Maybe he was just hungry, she told herself bracingly—although she doubted the average biker often had a craving for vegetable paté or leek-and-mushroom quiche. Besides, his battered face seemed to make that prospect more than a little unlikely. Whatever he was after, it probably wasn't lunch.

Ten years in the restaurant business had given Christine plenty of experience sizing up people. Quickly she surveyed the man, who was tugging off his riding gloves and shoving them into a hip pocket of his jeans. He appeared to be alone, and she noted at once that there were no club emblems on his leather jacket, no insignias visible anywhere—including tattoos. Despite her customer's shocked assumption to the contrary, the interloper did not look as if he were part of some motorcycle gang. He was a little older than she was, Christine gauged, somewhere in his mid-thirties, and in good shape for his age. If she allowed for his thick-soled boots, she judged him to be slightly under six feet tall, lanky and athletic, but not so athletic that the two burly Iranians in the kitchen couldn't subdue him if he tried to cause trouble.

Assuming he's not strung out on something, Christine added parenthetically. Or armed. Nowadays one couldn't be too careful. In the office was a pistol Reese kept "for emergencies." To date the weapon had never been out of his desk drawer, thank God, but there was always a first time—not that it'd do much good with Reese away from the restaurant. Christine hated guns and knew she'd let thieves walk off with every penny in the place before she could bring herself to shoot somebody. She eyed the man in the leather jacket with grim humor. If he had burst into La Courgette intent on robbery, she thought mordantly, he was going to be disappointed. Despite elevated prices and a constant stream of customers, there was hardly ever much cash in the till. The sort of clientele who patronized trendy Marin eateries invariably paid with plastic.

Reaching the podium, Christine draped her arm across it with feigned casualness, forming a frail barrier between Tish and the biker. "Take care of table six," she told the quaking waitress.

The girl hesitated. She nodded imperceptibly toward the kitchen and muttered under her breath, "Shall I get—"

Christine shook her head. "Not yet." Her grayish eyes locked with the man's bluer ones.

He wasn't high on something, she saw at once. He stared at her with an intensity she found unsettling, his gaze bright and unclouded. She broke eye contact, studying his face, which was bronzed and leathery, as if he spent most of his time exposed to the elements. Close up the gory scrapes looked even more alarming than they had from a distance, streaks of fresh blood mixed with grit, vermillion and black. He smelled of gasoline and sweat, yet Christine couldn't help noticing that regardless of his unkempt hair and weather-beaten complexion, his square jaw was clean-shaven and the blunt fingertips holding the bandanna were neatly manicured. When he touched the cloth to his cheek, he winced. His thick, straight brows came together over the bridge of his strong nose, and his thin lips twisted, revealing good teeth, white and well cared for. Despite his tough appearance, Christine realized, he wasn't a bum.

"Ms. Dryden?" the waitress ventured again.

Exhaling carefully, Christine murmured, "Thank you, Tish, I'll take charge here. Please go to your station, your guests are waiting." The girl bolted.

Christine continued to stare at the dangerous-looking stranger. Seeking refuge in ritual pleasantries, she curved her mouth into a gracious smile and intoned politely, "Welcome to La Courgette. How may I help you?"

He grimaced. "Well, for starters," he grated, "you could quit gaping as if you expect me to whip out an Uzi and lay waste to this upscale little hash house of yours."

Christine recoiled. The man paused, shaking his head to clear it. "I'm sorry," he apologized gruffly. "You'll have to forgive me, but I'm not exactly at my best right this minute." His voice was deep and surprisingly cultured, the tone roughened by his obvious discomfort. He swallowed and tried again. "Look, lady—Ms. Dreyfuss, I think the girl called you—"

"Dryden, Christine Dryden," she corrected him.

He nodded. "Clay McMurphy," he identified himself. He repeated, "Look, Ms. Dryden, I'm not here to cause trouble. I can see I'm upsetting your staff and your customers, and I promise I'll clear out as quickly as possible. But I dropped my Harley on that hairpin curve a quarter mile up the road, and I need to call for help—"

"And we have the nearest telephone," Christine finished, relaxing. "Of course, I should have realized."

The one thing Christine had never liked about La Courgette was its location. The restaurant was positioned in the center of a particularly treacherous stretch of highway, whose steep turns and numerous switchbacks contributed to several mishaps annually. When Christine and her partner were scouting out sites for their new business, Reese had discovered the vacant building on a hillside overlooking the ocean in the distance. Christine had been skeptical, arguing that the isolation and difficult access would discourage potential customers, but Reese insisted that the spot's spec-

tacular scenery would attract more people than the
bad road kept away. Because Reese was the person financing their endeavor, Christine had felt compelled
to acquiesce, and in the years since, she was forced to
concede, his prediction had proved accurate. Business flourished.

Still, Christine's qualms about the road had not
been unfounded. In all the time since the restaurant
opened she had yet to witness a serious accident, but
sooner or later each year, usually during the rainy
season when the pavement was slick and the embank-
ment unstable, inevitably some driver would skid out
on one of the bends and wind up with his car against
a guardrail or in a ditch. And just as inevitably, those
drivers hobbled into La Courgette to call for help.

Christine assured Clay, "Believe me, you're not the
first person who's needed—" She broke off with a
shiver as she finally realized the significance of his
bloodied face and his limp. "You had an accident on
your motorcycle?" she mumbled idiotically. She considered herself a reasonably courageous woman, but
as a teenager she'd witnessed a collision between a
moped and a pickup, and the memory had never left
her. Motorcycles—of all sizes—scared her almost as
much as guns did. She tried not to imagine this man's
strong, attractive body tangling with white-hot steel
and whirring wheels, or the searing pain he must have
felt when his skin was abraded viciously by the unfor-
giving surface of the road. "My God," she choked,
"are you all right?"

Clay shrugged, the movement stiff and labored.
"My bike's in worse shape than I am," he said tersely.
"I can repair it, but it's going to take a truck to get it

home." He waited. Christine continued to stare at him. After a moment he pressed, "Well, if you don't mind me using your phone, would you please tell me where it is? I looked but I didn't spot one when I came in."

Dragging her eyes away from him, Christine felt herself grow warm. *You'd think I'd never seen a biker before,* she chided herself, discomfited by her reaction. To cover her embarrassment, she half turned to gesture toward an alcove near the kitchen and began airily, "Oh, the public telephones are back by..." Her voice faded.

Behind her, activity in the restaurant remained at a standstill while employees and diners alike continued to gawk at Clay with the same wary fascination Christine had displayed. Quickly she made a decision. "Come into my office," she said.

Clay's gaze flicked around the room before returning to her. He smiled ironically. "Are you sure you trust me to be alone with you?"

"Don't let the rarefied atmosphere of this place fool you," Christine told him with an impatient sniff. "Not everybody here is a wimp."

His unmarred cheek twitched. "I can see that," he murmured.

She glanced away. "Over there," she said, indicating an unmarked door across the lobby. "I'll be with you in a moment." Clay disappeared into the office. Behind him Christine checked the dining room. For the benefit of the customers her lips remained tilted in a bland curve, but her employees recognized her stern glare and reacted accordingly. Christine sensed a collective gulp, followed rather comically by a sudden piping chorus of voices. She almost laughed aloud. The people who worked at La Courgette were all well trained, entirely capable of caring for their patrons' needs without constant supervision, but every now and then a good, hard frown did wonders.

When the staff began bustling around the room again and the background noise returned to its normal level, Christine nodded her approval. Then she quietly beckoned for a busboy to mop up the mud Clay had tracked into the foyer, and she signaled for one of the waitresses to spell her as hostess. Once she saw that all was in order, she went into the office she shared with Reese.

Two large golden-oak desks filled the room. On one a Laurel Burch mug full of pens and freshly sharpened pencils stood next to a magazine cover in a silver frame, and menus, correspondence, and printouts were arranged in tidy piles between the telephone and a small Tiffany-style lamp; the other workstation housed a computer terminal, with invoices and travel brochures scattered haphazardly among diskettes and back issues of *Gourmet*. Clay stood between them, waiting patiently for Christine. "You can use my phone—that one," she said, pointing to the desk with the stained-glass lamp. Clay nodded, but Christine thought she saw his blue eyes glint. Unaccountably she found herself defending the absent Reese. She said, "You'll have to excuse my partner, he's getting ready to leave for Europe in the morning. His desk may not look like it at the moment, but actually he's a very well-organized person."

"You ought to see my place," Clay commented. He started to pull out her swivel chair, then glanced down at his stained jeans and changed his mind. He remained standing as he carefully tapped out a number on Christine's white telephone. "Hi, Lib, it's me," he announced when the other party answered. "Is that husband of yours around someplace handy? I need to borrow him and the truck for a while. No, don't bother Denny if he's busy with Dr. Berlinger, but as soon as they finish, if you can pass on a message—"

Christine tried not to eavesdrop, but in the small room it was impossible to avoid overhearing Clay's conversation, the warmth and affection in his voice as he chatted with the other woman, the rich humor of his chuckle. "Don't worry, darlin', I promise I'll be as good as new in a couple of days. Yes, you've warned me many times about my reckless driving, but haven't I convinced you yet that this mangy head of mine is too tough to crack? I know, Lib, I know, but just think what fun you'll have saying *I told you so*—" The instant he replaced the receiver in its cradle, the amusement faded from his expression, and he swayed unsteadily.

Watching him with concern, Christine said, "You'd better sit down."

Clay shook his head. "I'm filthy. I'll ruin your furniture."

"The furniture is my problem," Christine snapped. "Now sit down before you fall down."

"Yes, ma'am," Clay replied meekly. He flashed a grin at her, but when he half collapsed into the soft leather chair, she could see his clenched jaw grow white under the tan.

"It sounds as if it's going to be some time before your ride arrives," Christine noted. "Can I get you anything while you wait? A glass of water? Wine? Would you like something to eat?"

Clay said, "No, thanks, nothing—unless, of course, you're offering something along the lines of a nice juicy, rare T-bone with all the trimmings."

From his tone Christine could tell he was joking. "Sorry," she rejoined, encouraged that he felt well enough to tease her, "we're fresh out of steaks to-day—and every day, for that matter. Here at La Courgette salads are more our style."

"So I've heard." He cocked his head, but the slight movement made him flinch. Laboriously he dragged the wadded bandanna from his pocket and started once again to wipe his cheek with it. Instead, he paused, regarding the bloodstained cloth with distaste. "I don't suppose there's someplace I could wash my face, is there?" he asked. "These scrapes are kind of sore."

With compunction Christine exclaimed, "I have a first-aid kit in my bathroom, I don't know why I didn't remember it sooner—" When Clay tried to push himself up from the chair, she continued hastily, "No, please, stay there, I think you're still a little dizzy." She ducked into the lavatory adjoining the office and rummaged beneath the sink. When she returned a moment later with a small plastic box marked with a red cross, Clay was holding the silver picture frame in his fingertips, studying the magazine cover.

It was the front page from a three-year-old issue of a slick Marin gourmet guide. The photo was an artful portrait of Christine and Reese, shot through a yellow filter to impart gilded highlights to the couple hugging each other affectionately among baskets of fruits and vegetables. Despite a too-precious banner that blared, "Gold in the garden! How this savvy duo has turned carrots into carats..." Christine had always treasured that magazine cover. She loved it not just for the photo but for what it symbolized. Only the most eminent local restaurateurs were ever profiled in the magazine, and for her and Reese actually to appear on the cover meant that La Courgette had succeeded far beyond anything they'd ever envisioned in the days when they were students together at the University of Southern California. Reese had been pleased by the recognition, of course, but Reese, the son of a prominent Beverly Hills surgeon, was used to recognition and success. Christine had spent most of her life struggling against poverty and despair. For her, public acclaim meant she'd finally won the battle.

Frowning thoughtfully at the magazine cover, Clay asked, "You run this place with your brother?"

Christine shook her head. "Reese isn't my brother."

Clay's quizzical glance dropped to her ringless left hand. "You two look a lot alike," he observed.

"So I've been told." Christine smiled blandly at the portrait of herself and her fiancé. Yes, she and Reese did look alike; in fact, in college they'd been introduced by a mutual friend who claimed they must be long-lost cousins, if not twins separated at birth. Reese was a year older than Christine, and at six foot four he topped her by ten inches, but both of them were very fair and very slim, with straight blond hair and relentlessly patrician features. Although in her case the sharp nose and firm but feminine jaw were a happy genetic accident rather than the result of generations of good breeding, Christine felt certain that when she and Reese finally did get married, the two of them were bound to produce the blondest children this side of a hair bleach commercial.

Returning the silver picture frame to its spot on the desk, Clay glanced one last time at the magazine cover. "Interesting," he murmured.

"Coincidence," Christine countered, dismissing the subject. She opened the plastic box and took out a sterile wipe and a tube of antiseptic. "That scrape on your face will have to be cleaned before we put anything on it," she told Clay. "It's bound to sting. Do you want to try to wash it yourself, or shall I?"

He grimaced. "You'd probably be able to see what you're doing better than I could."

"I suppose." Christine pursed her lips as she tried to study his injured cheek. The wound was obscured by the upturned collar of his jacket and his heavy mane. "Your hair's in the way," she complained. Clay raked his fingers through the wavy brown locks at his temple and tucked them back behind his ear, exposing the raw-looking scrapes and contusions discoloring his hard jaw. A long tendril must have been adhering to the scab, because one of the cuts opened and Christine could see fresh blood. She shuddered. "It's going to be painful," she reiterated.

"I promise not to holler," Clay said.

Taking a deep breath to steady herself, Christine set aside the first-aid supplies and reached for his jacket zipper. "Here, maybe it'll help if we get you out of this coat first," she told him, trying to sound nonchalant. "If you'll lean forward a little..." She tugged on the pull tab, but it would not budge. "Damn, it seems to be snagged on something," she muttered.

Clay laid his hands over hers. "Let me get it," he said, jerking hard. Suddenly the slide broke loose from the zipper teeth. The abrupt movement caught Christine off balance.

She fell against Clay, causing him to rock backward in her swivel chair. She tried to brace herself with her arms, one palm pressed flat against the worn leather of his jacket, the other hand slipped inside the gaping lapels. Her fingers splayed over his rainbow-colored T-shirt. Through the thin fabric she could feel the crisp hair overlaying the hard muscles of his chest; she could feel his heartbeat. Beneath the petroleum tang that she'd noticed when he first entered the restaurant, he smelled hot and musky and vibrantly alive.

Clay caught her wrists to steady her. His callused fingers were inescapable yet surprisingly gentle. Christine waited. Clay's intense blue eyes glinted. "Lady," he teased, "I asked you to help me with a few bandages. You don't have to rip my clothes off."

Christine refused to cringe. "Too bad about the zipper," she said evenly. "I'll have better luck with the bandages if you take your hands off me."

He released her at once. Christine stepped back, blinking. She picked up the silvery pouch containing a cleansing wipe and busied herself opening it. For some reason her hands were trembling, and it was difficult to tear the perforations neatly. By the time she was able to remove the folded cloth, bits of shredded aluminum foil littered the polished surface of her desk.

Shaking out the wipe, which perfumed the air with lemon-scented antiseptic, Christine glanced sidelong at Clay. The leather jacket lay at his side in a heap on the floor, and he was lounging back in her chair, his broad shoulders and sinewy torso outlined explicitly through the garish cotton knit of the short-sleeved shirt. His arms were as brown as his face and throat, and fine hairs sun-bleached almost white dusted his dark skin. Christine lowered her lashes. "Nice T-shirt," she murmured, "very sixties."

"Some people I work with picked it up for me at a Grateful Dead concert," Clay commented. He crossed his legs, making Christine all too aware of the heavily muscled thighs beneath his tight jeans, the long, strong calves encased in high boots. Something about the hooded intensity with which he watched her made her strangely conscious of her body, as well. All at once she could feel her challis skirt swing lightly against her legs, the teasing slide of undergarments satin-soft against her skin, the swell and thrust of her high, firm breasts.

Christine swallowed dryly. The air in the office felt hot, stuffy; she wondered if somebody had meddled with the thermostat. Avoiding Clay's eyes, she looked at the cloth clutched in her fingers, the tube of first-aid cream lying on the desk. She looked at Clay's mouth. He had a beautiful mouth, wide and expressive, with thin, sensual lips stretched over fine white teeth. For the first time she noticed that one of his lower teeth was slightly crooked. She wondered why that small imperfection stirred her. "I'm almost afraid to touch you," she whispered. "I don't want to hurt you."

Through the shirt she could see his chest lift. "I hurt already," he said. He rocked forward in the chair.

The office door flew open and Reese barged in.

Christine jumped away from Clay. Jerking her head in her fiancé's direction, she beamed with relief—relief from what, she wasn't quite certain. "Hi, dear. Back already?" she said, her voice high and breathless.

Despite the disarray in which he worked, Reese Cagney was a fastidious dresser. He filled the doorway, tall and elegantly casual in Italian slacks and a silk sweater the same pale wheat color as his hair. Christine knew he'd spent most of the day dashing around Marin County making final preparations for his trip to Paris, but as always, he looked unruffled and impeccable. His hazel eyes scanned the room coolly. Christine had always admired Reese's self-control. Although she realized he must be agog at the sight of the grimy-looking intruder seated at her pristine desk, his manner remained reserved almost to the point of indifference.

When he did not speak at once, Christine gushed, "Everything's taken care of? There were no unexpected hassles about your passport or tickets?"

"There's nothing left to do but board the plane," Reese murmured. He closed the office door and sauntered to Christine's side. Wrapping his arm around her, he kissed her lightly, filling her nostrils with the oriental spice of his cologne. "No, darling," he told her, "there were no hassles, just the usual tedious, time-consuming, last-minute errands." Reese's gaze darted toward Clay. When he addressed Christine again, his tone was carefully neutral. "Judging from the state the staff was in when I got back here," he observed, "I understand your afternoon has been a little more interesting than mine."

Before Christine could respond, Clay levered himself out of the swivel chair and declared, "I'm afraid that's all my fault. I had an accident on my bike, and your partner here was kind enough to play Good Samaritan.''

Reese nodded. Without releasing his fiancée, he faced Clay and flashed a facile, winning smile that reminded Christine of the expression Reese used when explaining to disgruntled patrons why they couldn't order a hamburger at La Courgette. ''I don't believe we've met,'' he said, extending his free hand. ''I'm Reese Cagney—no relation to the actor.''

''Pleased to meet you. My name's McMurphy,'' Clay intoned, returning the salute. His solemn formality seemed so incongruous with his appearance that Christine wondered if Clay was deliberately mocking Reese.

The same thought must have occurred to the man at her side, Christine realized, because she felt the arm draped across her shoulders stiffen. ''McMurphy?'' Reese mused aloud. ''You mean like the nut in *One Flew Over the Cuckoo's Nest?*''

Clay shrugged. ''As you say,'' he drawled, ''no relation.''

He paused. Christine watched in bewilderment while the men stared stonily at each other. The office seemed to vibrate with tension. She had a weird suspicion that Reese and Clay were testing one another, sizing up each other as potential rivals—rivals for what, she couldn't imagine. Her polished, urbane lover and the uncouth-looking motorcycle bum were such disparate types that it was hard to conceive of them being in competition for anything.

The silence stretched on. Christine noticed that the David Benoit piano tape had finished, and now the fluid jazz of Mannheim Steamroller was playing softly over the sound system. The music reminded her that she had a business to run, customers to attend to. She felt herself growing annoyed. Whatever childish masculine game the two men were playing at, she wanted no part of it.

She tried to slip from Reese's proprietary grip, but to her amazement his fingers tightened, digging painfully into her skin through the fabric of her dress, anchoring her against him. Out of the corner of her eye Christine saw Clay's mouth thin. With him watching, she refused to squirm. Lifting her chin, she hissed impatiently, ''Reese, I have work to—'' but her words were interrupted by a light knock at the door.

Tish poked her head into the office. ''Uh, Ms. Dryden?'' the girl apologized diffidently. ''Excuse me for bothering you, but there's somebody here from the Berlinger Institute.''

The interruption broke the mood. Reese's arm fell away from Christine's shoulders, and he shoved his hands into his pockets while he scowled in surprise. The Berlinger Institute was a small, privately funded marine-mammal research facility a few miles up the Marin coast from the restaurant, the pet project of an eccentric millionaire who'd made a fortune selling plumbing fixtures before he shifted his interest to environmental concerns. Over the years Christine had spotted Dr. Berlinger in La Courgette a few times, but he'd never been a regular customer.

''The Berlinger Institute?'' Reese echoed blankly. ''What on earth do they want?''

Clay cleared his throat. ''That's my ride,'' he said. ''Apparently my friend was able to get away from work sooner than I expected." He glanced at Tish. "Would you please tell Denny I'll be there in just a minute?" The waitress withdrew, and Clay bent stiffly to scoop up his jacket from the floor by the chair. When he stood again, his expression was polite but unreadable. Shaking his hair back out of his face, he said, "Well, I guess I'd better head on. Thank you both for all you've done for me. I know it was inconvenient having me underfoot, but I'm really grateful for your help."

"No problem," Reese murmured automatically.

Christine glanced at the first-aid kit on her desk. "Are you sure you're going to be all right?" she asked anxiously. "We never did put any medicine on those scrapes."

Clay shrugged wryly. "I appreciate the concern, but you don't have to worry about this beat-up hide of mine. I'll doctor it when I get home." He paused. His blue gaze locked with Christine's. His smile was cryptic. "Don't fret, lady," he said deeply. "I know where I don't belong. Just be glad you're getting rid of me with a minimum of fuss." He pivoted on his boot heel and followed Tish out of the office.

The instant the door closed behind Clay, Reese whirled on Christine and demanded, "What the hell was that all about?"

Despite the fact that he loomed over her, Christine stood her ground. "I don't know," she replied quietly, recalling that perplexing moment when Reese and Clay had squared off like two stags ready to lock horns. "I was about to ask you the same question. You were very rude." She rubbed her shoulder. "I didn't appreciate the caveman tactics, either."

Reese was instantly contrite. "I'm sorry, I didn't mean to hurt you—but, honestly, Chris, do you have any idea how I felt? I mean, a bum like that—"

"If he has some connection with the Berlinger Institute, he's probably not a bum," Christine pointed out.

"I wouldn't be so sure," Reese countered scornfully. "I've seen some of the space cadets who work at that place. But in any case, you never should have let that guy into the restaurant, much less the office."

His caviling tone irked her. Christine asked tightly, "What was I supposed to do, leave him bleeding in the street?"

All at once Reese broke off his harangue. "God, listen to us bicker," he muttered, shaking his head. "I'm taking off for Europe in the morning. Is this any way to spend our last few hours together?" His mouth crooked into a winsome, self-mocking grin, the same grin that had beguiled Christine ever since USC, when she'd been a shy scholarship student and Reese was one of the golden boys, rich and smart and charming. Although over the years Christine had learned that Reese's charm was something he could turn on and off like a switch, she still wasn't altogether immune to it. Reluctantly she smiled back.

Slipping his hands around her waist, Reese soothed, "Forgive me, darling, I didn't mean to bark at you. I was just upset. I know you meant well, but sometimes you're too softhearted for your own good. I get chills thinking about you alone with a character like that. Anything could have happened."

"I'm a big girl, Reese," Christine reminded him.

"I've noticed," he said thickly, pulling her close. With a purr of pleasure she sank against him and nuzzled her face in his sweater, savoring the clean, heady fragrance of his cologne, the feel of his long, slim body hard on hers, familiar and comforting. Reese caught her chin with his fingertips and tilted her face upward. "Hey you, this is the first chance I've had all day to kiss you," he growled.

"Oh, dear, we'd better do something about that," Christine giggled, and stretching on tiptoe, she wrapped her arms around his neck and pressed her mouth firmly against his.

When the kiss finally ended, Christine asked Reese, "Will you stay at my place tonight?"

He hesitated. "I didn't know whether you'd want me to. In order to catch my plane, I'm going to have to get up at four in the morning."

"That's okay. I always intended going with you to the airport to see you off."

Reese said, "I'd rather you were going with me, period."

Christine grew very still. "Please, dear, we've been through all this before. I can't leave the restaurant right now. There are a dozen pressing things I have to take care of while you're gone."

"So you keep telling me," Reese said, an edge to his voice. "I don't know how many times you've reminded me about the contract you have to finalize with our produce supplier, or the new kitchen equipment you have to decide on, or your annual checkup—"

Christine insisted, "But I do have all those things to do, and more."

"You could have rescheduled your doctor's appointment," Reese said dismissively. "There's not a single item on that agenda you couldn't have delayed if you'd really wanted to—and if you had delayed them, then we could have hired a manager to oversee the day-to-day running of this place for the short while we'd be gone. There's a guy in Berkeley who comes highly recommended—"

"You know how much I hate the idea of bringing in an outsider, no matter how good he is," Christine reminded Reese. "Where La Courgette is concerned, I'm like a doting mother."

"Even overprotective mothers usually entrust their children to baby-sitters once in a while," Reese said darkly. "Do you have any idea how long it's been since the two of us had time off together?"

Christine agreed with a sigh. "I realize it's been too long, but that's the price we pay for going into business together."

Reese shook his head testily. "No, it's more than that. My God, Chris, I know you're a workaholic, but how any woman could prefer buying a stove to going to Paris..."

She tried to vindicate herself. "I'd love to go to Paris, just not for something as crowded and hectic as a convention. I hate conventions."

"Then how about going there for a honeymoon?"

At the quiet question, Christine's blue gray eyes grew round and reproachful, but before she could speak, Reese released her and turned away, hunching his shoulders in frustration. "Oh, hell," he grumbled, "forget I said anything. Right now I'm not in the mood to listen to your excuses."

Biting her lip, Christine gazed at the dejected slope of his spine and tried to suppress a twinge of guilt. Poor Reese. He had a right to be annoyed with her. He was a good man, intelligent and witty and charming, a patient, considerate lover, a cherished friend, and after all the years they'd been engaged, there was no earthly reason why Christine should still harbor any qualms about actually getting married. And yet...

"I'm sorry," she whispered.

He didn't seem to hear her. Exhaling raggedly, Reese declared, "I never realized before what a romantic I am at heart. These past few weeks I've been telling myself that if I could just talk you into going to Paris with me, everything would work out. I'd take you off for a moonlight cruise along the Seine, and there in a *bateau mouche,* with violins playing in the background, finally, finally you'd agree to set the date. We could be married at the American consulate, and your family could drive down from Frankfurt to witness the ceremony. I figured you'd like that, having your mom and the colonel and Adam there for the wedding."

Christine gulped. "Yes, I'd like that very much," she said hoarsely, her eyes growing moist at the thought of the family she saw so rarely, especially her adored younger half brother. She tried to smile. "Can you imagine how much Adam must have grown since the last time we were together? By now he's probably as tall as I am."

Rounding on Christine, Reese pressed, "Has it ever occurred to you that if we'd gotten married when we first started talking about it, we could have a child of our own almost as old as your little brother?"

"I want children," Christine asserted softly.

Reese said, "I'm glad to hear that, darling, because so do I—but first I want a wife. I'm tired of people snickering when I say the word *fiancée*." He gazed down at her, his hazel eyes sober. "We've waited long enough, Chris. In the beginning, when you told me you needed your independence, a chance to prove you could take care of yourself, I understood your reasons for delaying the wedding and I accepted them. But you made your point years ago. Now it's time for the two of us to make a life, a real life with a real family, together."

It would be so easy to say yes, Christine thought wistfully, so easy to allow herself to be seduced by this man's cajolery. She loved Reese, and he loved her. They worked together well and were compatible sexually. Their families liked and respected each other, and any children they might be blessed with were bound to be beautiful. If Christine legalized her relationship with Reese, she'd only be doing the logical, the expected thing, something that he and seemingly everybody else in the world agreed was long overdue.

Why wasn't *she* equally sure?

Christine sighed. "Please, Reese, let me think it over while you're away. You have a good time in Paris, and after you get back, we'll settle things once and for all, I promise."

Reese eyed her suspiciously. "You're a stubborn woman, Christine Dryden," he accused, shaking his head in exasperation. "A stubborn woman—and a strong one."

"Maybe that's why you love me," she said.

CHAPTER TWO

"I'M SORRY, Clay," Henry Berlinger told the younger man gravely, shaking his head as he studied the typewritten pages lying before him on his desk. "I can't possibly let you send out these press releases, not on the Institute's letterhead."

"Why not?" Clay asked. "You know we've been receiving inquiries daily about the elephant seal. Even though it's a month since he was beached, there still seems to be public interest in his condition, so I thought it was time to issue some sort of update."

Dr. Berlinger said, "But there's more in this notice than a simple update on the animal's condition. You've conjectured about causes, as well."

Clay clenched his fists in the pockets of his leather jacket. "I thought the Institute—I thought *you*—supported my conclusions."

"These aren't conclusions, they're only educated guesses," Dr. Berlinger countered in that quiet philosopher's voice that sounded so disconcerting coming from a stocky, ruddy-faced man who'd once dug cesspools for a living. "You have no proof." With an old-fashioned fountain pen he drew a slash across the top sheet and scrawled his initials on it. Tucking the papers back into a manila folder, he repeated, "I'm sorry. I know how much this means to you."

"I hope so," Clay muttered.

Studying his associate's mulish expression, Dr. Berlinger sighed. "Your feelings do you credit, son," he admonished him. "As a human being, it's right and natural to be disturbed by the suffering of another living creature—but as a scientist, it's wrong to lose your objectivity, because then you lose your credibility, as well." His tone hardened. "And if your credibility is challenged, so is the Institute's."

Clay shifted restlessly. He felt like a naughty schoolboy facing the principal. Knowing the lecture was justified didn't make it any easier to hear.

He admired Henry Berlinger more than anybody else in the world. While still a young teenager the man had begun working as a manual laborer, and eventually, through sheer determination and hard work, he had built up a multi-million dollar business in plumbing and industrial supplies. Then, following the untimely death of his beloved wife, who contracted cholera from contaminated water during a South American vacation, Henry's life changed direction. At forty-one he started college; at fifty he earned a doctorate in biology. After selling his plumbing-supply business he founded the Anna M. Berlinger Institute for Marine Mammal Studies and began a second career as an ecologist. At seventy he was a recognized leader in the field—and Clay hated the thought of disappointing him.

"Yes, sir," Clay muttered. "I'll try to keep that in mind in the future."

"See that you do." Picking up the folder, Henry Berlinger rose from his chair and rounded his desk to where Clay was standing. As he handed back the papers, he said, "Put these away for now. When you've collected the proof you need, we'll call a conference and you can release your statement to the media with my blessing—in fact, I'll buy air time for you, if necessary. I realize the waiting's hard, but you have to take things in order. There's too much at stake for you to go off half-cocked." He paused. "Clay, you mustn't be seduced by self-righteousness. I know how tempting it is to picture yourself as an ecological David facing the evil Goliath industrial polluters, but believe me, if you start making accusations without first arming yourself with good, concrete evidence, the confrontation is going to be more like Bambi versus Godzilla."

Clay's lips twitched reluctantly. "Yes, sir," he murmured again.

Dr. Berlinger clapped a work-toughened hand on the younger man's shoulder. "I do know what I'm talking about," he reminded him sympathetically. "Remember, I used to be on the side of the Philistines, myself."

Clay was still smarting from his mentor's reproachful words when he stopped by the pen where the elephant seal, a young bull, was caged. Clay gazed down at the animal, who was both magnificent and alarming. Even though the creature was far short of the three to four tons he would weigh at maturity, his huge brown wrinkled body was already over fifteen feet long. It was no wonder he'd caused such a stir when he washed ashore at Half Moon Bay....

The elephant seal lifted its massive head and stared at Clay with opaque black eyes. "Hi, guy," Clay crooned, leaning forward over the rim of the enclosure. The animal grumbled and inflated his pendulous snout in warning. Clay did not retreat. Suddenly the seal swept his foreflippers across the floor of the pen in a defensive motion that, in his natural habitat, should have sent up a sharp spray of sand and pebbles. On the smooth, damp concrete, nothing happened. Sensing the creature's confusion, Clay murmured, "Listen, fella, is that any way to behave toward the man who's trying to save your life?"

After a moment the seal apparently concluded that Clay was not a threat. Settling back lethargically, the animal closed his eyes and deflated his snout with a blubbery snort. Only when he tried to roll onto his side did it become obvious that he could not move his hindquarters.

Clay watched sadly as the seal struggled to shift his massive bulk, using only his powerful foreflippers. Even after a month the seal seemed bewildered by his disability—and his surroundings. Sometimes Clay wondered what that pinniped brain made of the strange land mammals who had abducted him from his familiar world of sand and water. Was there any awareness at all that the puny, jabbering creatures who swarmed around, feeding and poking and scraping with those odd flipperless extremities, were trying to *help*—or did the sick animal know only pain and panic and fear? After the elephant seal was transported to the Institute for study, there had been those who suggested that the most merciful course of action would be to administer a lethal injection and then perform a thorough necropsy. Clay had balked. His job was preserving wildlife, not killing it, he'd insisted. Now, watching the half-paralyzed animal struggle in his prison of cold gray stone, Clay wondered if his protests hadn't been just another example of the scientist losing his objectivity.

A scientist who loses his objectivity loses his credibility, as well. Dr. Berlinger's reprimand, mildly delivered but painful, replayed in Clay's mind, and he knew he had to get away. He could feel his frustration growing. He was tired, he was cranky and discouraged and upset—not fit company for man nor beast. He needed to go home.

At the compound gate, Clay stalked past Denny and Lib Abrams, who stood in the shade of a cypress tree, chatting with one of the volunteers. Denny called Clay's name, but Clay mumbled a curt good-night and strode by them without stopping. He made a beeline for his motorcycle on the far side of the parking lot, his heavy boots splashing heedlessly through puddles on the asphalt. He could feel his colleagues' worried gaze trained on his back. Their concern shamed him almost as much as his deliberate rudeness. Clay realized he was acting like a dope, taking out his anger and disappointment on his friends, but at the moment he didn't trust himself to be polite to anyone.

Belinda would call it a classic case of displacement, he thought ironically as he tugged on his riding gloves and straddled the Harley. His ex-wife would say that his surly, antisocial behavior was only a manifestation of his real problem—and she'd be right, of course. Clay had never faulted Belinda's skills as a psychologist. Where the two of them differed would be in their interpretation of exactly what Clay's real problem was. He told himself he was justifiably disillusioned with the powers-that-be for failing to take action in an environmental crisis. Belinda would probably say he was just suffering from a bad case of wounded vanity because people refused to do things his way.

Clay revved the engine of his motorcycle and watched the tachometer, while he listened for signs of slippage in the new chain he'd installed after his accident earlier in the week. He still felt like a fool whenever he thought of that spill, which never should have happened. Served him right for letting his attention wander. He'd been traveling that stretch of highway too many years to be surprised by adverse conditions during the rainy season. If he'd kept his mind focused where it belonged, instead of fuming over problems at the Institute...

But Clay had always had difficulty leaving his work behind him at the end of the day, he admitted as he cut back on the throttle and released the clutch, and the motorcycle proceeded at a relatively sedate pace out of the parking lot. Even at the university, his job had intruded on his personal life. At the entrance to the main road, while Clay paused, waiting for a line of cars to pass, Belinda's parting words taunted him. "I can't talk to you anymore," she had sobbed as she threw her clothes into a suitcase. "I don't understand you. What's so wrong about playing the game and advancing your career? Think of the grants you could earn, the research you could do if you were a tenured professor. But no, the only thing that matters to you is your pride—and your precious seals and walruses. You certainly don't care about me. Sometimes I think this marriage would have stood a better chance of success if I'd had flippers!"

After five years the accusation still stung. He'd always cared very much about people—some people. He idolized Dr. Berlinger, he liked his coworkers at the Institute, and he was genuinely fond of Dennis and Liberty Abrams. In his teaching days, he had cared about his students; it was the infighting and the sucking up that seemed to be necessary for success in the academic world that he'd never been able to stomach. And despite Belinda's denials, he had loved her, although in retrospect he could see that their differing goals and philosophies had doomed their union from the start.

A break in the traffic appeared, and Clay surged forward, the explosive roar of his engine echoing off the pavement. The Institute's private driveway joined the main road at a point where the highway narrowed and snaked through the woods around the base of Mount Tamalpais, and invariably progress slowed, especially during the evening rush. Clay forced himself to be patient, inhaling exhaust fumes while he dawdled behind an ill-tuned Chevy and resisted the impulse to drive down the center stripe between the opposing lines of automobiles. At the beach the road forked. The cars all turned inland, presumably aiming for 101, the freeway that crossed the Golden Gate Bridge and was the main north-south artery along the Marin peninsula. Clay gunned the Harley and headed west, along the shoreline.

The sun was sinking, and the salty wind that whipped through his long hair felt cool and moist. Clay remained agitated, but as always, speed and solitude began to alleviate his tension. He inhaled deeply, clearing his lungs, washing away the miasma of half-burned gasoline that clung to him. He loved the rush of the ocean air against his weather-beaten skin. Its clean caress soothed his still-tender cheek and made him think suddenly of slim white hands, perfumed and incredibly soft....

The distracting image made him smile. In one respect, at least, Belinda had been wrong about him. Marine mammals were not the *only* creatures that attracted him.

Although it was true that Clay lived circumspectly and for months at a time was able to channel his energies into his work, nothing, not even a painful divorce, had ever diminished his healthy appreciation of women—and the stunning blonde from the vegetarian restaurant had certainly warranted his appreciation. The first couple of nights after the accident, she had tripped tormentingly through his dreams, gazing at him with those smoky azure eyes that had flashed with reluctant awareness, her genteel image a far cry from the more earthy houris who usually populated his fantasies. He'd slept badly anyway, too bruised and sore to relax, but after endless hours wrestling with her misty, tantalizing specter, he'd wakened to find himself aching in ways that had nothing at all to do with his injuries.

Which served him right, Clay concluded mockingly. Even though Lady Christine of La Courgette was beautiful, sexy, sophisticated, and maybe, just maybe, a tiny bit attracted to him, she was also obviously every bit as wrong for him as his ex-wife had been.

Belinda had been wrong in so many ways—not just *for* him but *about* him, Clay reassured himself bracingly. Although his area of special interest was marine mammals, he did care deeply about people, just as he cared about the earth and all its creatures. He reserved his contempt and rage for those whose greed and shortsightedness raped the land and fouled the oceans, hunters who slaughtered with soulless efficiency until whole species were threatened with extinction, industrial polluters whose oil spills and toxic wastes turned the seas into open sewers. And Dr. Berlinger was wrong, too. Even though Clay was certain that his cause was righteous, never once had he fantasized himself as some sort of biblical hero singlehandedly felling the corporate giants. He was far too pragmatic to imagine that individual effort would ever be sufficient to rescue the world from its folly. Clay's goals were less exalted. He'd settle for improving the quality of life for the denizens of his own small corner of the universe. He'd settle for tracking down the cause of the elephant seal's affliction.

As he rode Clay whistled tunelessly, and the notes blew away from him, dissolving into the air that was growing noticeably chillier as the sun set. He glanced warily at the sky over the ocean. Another storm was moving in across the water, and judging by the clouds that lowered, dark and eerie looking in the sulfurous twilight, the rain would probably commence again before he reached home. He'd been planning on grabbing a quick bite and then heading down to the marina to work on the scuba gear he kept stowed in the Institute's boathouse, but suddenly the prospect of a solitary night run through wet, cheerless streets was singularly unappealing. He knew that before he went diving again he needed to replace his regulator and perform routine maintenance on the rest of the equipment, but he supposed there was no real hurry. Even though he was eager to resume his exploration, he wasn't a complete fool. Given how changeable the weather had been lately, it might be days before he and Denny could think about taking out the boat again.

A raindrop smacked his forehead like a cold bullet. Clay flinched. No, he decided all at once, tonight he was going to stay home. He'd done everything humanly possible for the seal, and now it was time to take a stab at improving the quality of his own life for a change. He'd been working too hard lately—undoubtedly the reason he'd been in such a rotten mood. He needed a break. First he'd call Denny and Lib and apologize for his insufferable behavior earlier, but once that was done, he was going to kick back and relax. He'd light a fire in the Buck stove, broil that steak that was englaciated in his freezer, maybe see if there was anything worth watching on cable. If nothing on TV caught his eye, he'd listen to CDs, *Les Miz* or maybe something by Andrew Lloyd Webber. His friends, who felt that real music had died with Jimi Hendrix, might consider Clay's preference for overblown operettas to be maudlin and self-indulgent, but in his opinion there was nothing like storming the barricades with Jean Valjean or prowling through underground caverns with the Phantom of the Opera to take one's mind off the problems of the real world—at least for a little while.

The shoreline curved inward on the lee side of the rocky promontory, and for several hundred yards the road was sheltered from the prevailing winds, giving an illusion of warmth, but as soon as Clay rounded the point and left the protection of the granite hillside, a barrage of raindrops splattered him. Although the scrapes on his cheek were almost healed, his skin remained sensitive, and he recoiled with pain. He could feel the wheels of the motorcycle fishtail ominously on the slick pavement. Cursing himself for letting his mind wander, he eased back on the accelerator and averted his face from the cold nip of the wind. In doing so, he nearly missed seeing the solitary car parked on the deserted headland overlooking the ocean.

Vehicles stopped in remote spots were hardly a rare sight along the Marin coast, where the spectacular ocean panorama invited admiration and every turnout provided a photo opportunity. Each day as Clay drove along the winding coast road he passed teenage lovers seeking seclusion, tourists pausing for snapshots, local residents simply meditating on a particularly impressive sunset. Ordinarily he scarcely noticed them—but tonight, for some reason something glimpsed in his peripheral vision made him pause. He pulled off onto the shoulder of the highway and stared back across the pavement.

The car was parked at a vista point about fifty yards behind him, and as clearly as Clay could make out in the murky, fading light, it appeared to be a late-model Japanese sedan, well kept but unremarkable. Brushing his hair out of his eyes, he squinted, trying to discern what it was that had attracted his attention. Suddenly he spied the shadowy figure of a woman silhouetted against the ruddy glow that marked the spot where the sun had sunk beneath the horizon. She was sitting on the hood of her car, gazing out to sea. She seemed unnaturally still, oblivious to the dusk and the storm, and as Clay gazed at her, he thought he'd never before seen anybody who looked so utterly alone.

He surveyed the empty road up and down while he considered his options. Whatever impression the woman's behavior gave, in all likelihood she was perfectly all right, someone who'd simply driven to the headland in quest of solitude, someone who'd resent having her private ruminations interrupted. Given the knee-jerk alarm that his appearance seemed to rouse in so many people, if he approached her, he stood a chance of being cussed out—or maced. Good Samaritans operated at their own risk these days. Hell, given the temperament of the times, he'd probably be lucky not to get shot! A man with any sense would clear out and forget he'd even noticed her.

Clay's fingers tightened on the clutch lever, then released it again. He couldn't simply ride away. There was always the faint possibility that the woman's little Nissan had a flat tire or engine trouble, or maybe it was out of gas. Common charity demanded that he at least ask the woman whether she wanted assistance. He knew he was no menace to her, but if he just took off and left her stranded in the dark, the next passerby might not be so...altruistic. With a sigh Clay wheeled his bike around and putted back down the highway to the turnout.

He pulled onto the gravel parking area and stopped about thirty feet from the car, deliberately racing his engine to announce his presence. She did not react. Clay scowled. Turning his handlebars so that the headlight aimed directly at the woman, he studied her slim figure limned in the watery beam. She was perched on the spattered hood of her car, her heels hooked over the bumper, her clenched hands resting on her knees. Her shoulders were slumped forward, bowing her long spine into a dejected arc. Clay had no idea how long she'd been hunched in that awkward position, but obviously she'd been there when the rain resumed a few minutes before. He could see dark splotches of wetness on her thin shirt and light-colored slacks, and the fair hair framing her delicate profile looked damp and stringy. In his heavy jacket, Clay shivered.

Clearing his throat, he called hoarsely, "Hey, lady, are you all right?" Still there was no response. Clay wondered if she was ill, or in shock. He came to a decision. He switched off his ignition.

The Harley engine faded with a last explosive pop, and for a moment silence reverberated in Clay's ears. Then he heard the scraping cry of a sea gull somewhere nearby, the crash and murmur of waves against the rocks at the foot of the cliff. The woman said nothing, did nothing. Leaving the key in position so that the headlight would continue to run from the battery, Clay swung his long legs off the motorcycle and stepped toward her. "Are you all right?" he repeated carefully, taking care to keep his tone nonthreatening. "Do you need help or something?"

She stirred. As Clay watched, she relaxed and unclasped her hands, extending the slim white fingers torpidly, as if she'd been squeezing them together with such force that she'd cut off the circulation. Stiffly she straightened her back, squared her narrow shoulders. Then, as Clay gawked in amazement, she raised her chin and with painful slowness rotated her head toward him, and he found himself staring into the blue gray eyes that had haunted his dreams for the past week.

"My God," he choked, "Christine."

She blinked. "Hello," she said.

Her voice was a dull, dusty whisper, and Clay wasn't altogether certain she recognized him. "Do you know who I am?" he asked.

Bloodless lips curved politely. "Of course I do. You're Clay McMurphy. We met the other day at the restaurant. It's nice to see you again."

The absurdity of the situation exasperated him. "You can forget the tea-party manners," he growled. "What's going on here? Sitting all by yourself in the middle of the night, in the middle of a downpour—"

"Downpour?" Christine echoed blankly. As Clay watched, her vision seemed to clear. She looked around, and for the first time she became truly conscious of her surroundings. Scrubbing her water-beaded hair out of her face, she stared at her wet palms and declared, "It's raining."

In a comedy sketch that ingenuous statement probably would have generated an appreciative chuckle from the audience, Clay thought grimly, but instead it only worried him. "Yes, it's raining and you're soaked," he told her. "You'd better get back inside your car before you catch your death."

Christine frowned. "Catch my death," she murmured oddly. "No, we wouldn't want that, would we?" She slid off the hood of the car and padded around to the driver's side.

When she was safely ensconced behind the steering wheel, Clay circled the Nissan and stood over her, leaning on the open door. In the feeble glow of the interior light, Christine's lovely features appeared drawn, shadowed. She shivered visibly. Clay noticed a cardigan in the passenger seat. "Put on your sweater," he said, and obediently she tugged the light wrap around her shoulders. She did not speak. On the dashboard lay her key ring, a sterling circlet with a fob shaped like a miniature frypan; she picked up the ring, but instead of starting the engine, she began toying with the keys. For several moments the only sound inside the car was the dull, metallic tinkle as they fell through her fingers.

Clay tried again. "Christine, are you in any shape to be driving? You don't look well, and you seem ... disoriented."

She exhaled raggedly. "You probably think I'm nuts," she said. "Maybe I am, a little. I got some bad news this afternoon, and I guess for a while there, I just ... lost everything." She let the key ring drop into her lap. "It was very nice of you to stop, Clay, but you don't have to worry about me anymore. I'll be okay now."

"Are you sure?" Clay persisted. "I don't like the idea of leaving you out here alone. It's not safe. There's no telling what kind of weirdos might wander by."

Christine's gaze flicked up and down the man looming over her, and just for a second she was no longer a wet, stricken waif, but the forthright, sophisticated woman who'd taken his breath the first time he saw her. "Weirdos?" she quipped. "You mean like dangerous-looking bikers with long hair and black leather jackets?"

Clay's expression was wry. "Yeah, lady, that's exactly what I mean."

She nodded. "I'll make sure to keep my eyes open, in case I see any. Thank you for the warning." She paused. When she spoke again, the teasing was absent from her voice, and her tone was sober. "Thank you for caring."

After that there seemed little to say. Clay stared down at her, reluctant to leave yet not certain why he should stay. Christine wasn't the only one liable to suffer from exposure. He could feel rain dripping through his hair, running in clammy rivulets down the back of his neck to seep beneath the collar of his jacket, chilling him. His jeans were growing increasingly stiff and ponderous as water soaked into the denim, and inside his boots his socks were beginning to squish. The last few miles to his house promised to be an extraordinarily miserable ride.

He looked across the roof of Christine's sedan toward the spot where his bike was parked, and he realized with dismay that the beam from the headlight was noticeably dimmer than it had been when he first pulled off the highway. The battery was running down. If he didn't get going soon, he wouldn't be going anywhere, period.

Taking a deep breath, he began awkwardly, "Well, if you're sure you're going to be all right, I think I'll head on—"

All at once Christine reached up to grab Clay's big, blunt hand. "Please," she begged, "don't go."

He started in surprise. The slim fingers clutching at him were trembling. Christine repeated urgently,

"Please don't go—not yet. I need somebody to talk to."

Regarding her with hooded eyes, Clay tried to ignore the stirring in his blood. God, she was beautiful. And vulnerable. And already spoken for... Sardonically he acknowledged that he was as susceptible as the next man to an appeal from a damsel in distress—but if Christine's distress was due to that tall blond guy in the designer sweater, then Clay knew he didn't want to hear about it.

"What about your boyfriend?" he inquired neutrally. "Shouldn't you be talking to him?"

"Reese is in France right now," Christine said.

"Then how about your family?"

She gestured helplessly. "They're in Germany. My stepfather's an Air Force colonel, stationed near Frankfurt." She tried to smile. "I guess I live on the wrong continent."

It was that feeble attempt at humor that destroyed Clay. "Wait a minute while I turn off my headlight," he told her. He trudged across the parking area, his boots crunching the wet gravel. When he returned to the car, Christine had closed her door and pushed open the one on the passenger's side for him.

The interior of the Nissan was as pristine as her office, and as Clay crammed himself into the tight bucket seat, he saw his boots make dirty streaks on the pale gray carpet. He chuckled mirthlessly. "I'm doing it again," he muttered. "I can't seem to get near you without tracking mud all over the place."

Christine shrugged. "It doesn't matter."

Clay shut his door, and the light flicked out, leaving the two of them closeted in shadow, cut off from the world by the rain that sluiced in sheets down the outside of the windows. Inside the car the air felt still and clammy, and Clay's wet clothes itched. Pulling off his gloves, he fished a handkerchief from his pocket to mop his forehead. A pickup truck passed by on the highway, and the beam from its headlamps skittered over them, just for an instant outlining the wan contours of Christine's face. She was gnawing her lip as if struggling for words.

The truck drove on, and darkness settled over them again. Clay suggested mildly, "Why don't you begin at the beginning and tell me anything you want to? I promise you I don't shock easily."

He heard her take a deep, harsh breath. "There's nothing very shocking to tell," she declared raspily. "It's just...upsetting. Today I went to the doctor for my annual checkup. He found a suspicious lump."

Despite Clay's promise not to be shocked, Christine's desolate words, so softly spoken, rattled him. With anguish it occurred to him that he'd been expecting her to say that her restaurant had gone bankrupt, or that her fiancé had dumped her, or even that she was pregnant. He had not entertained the possibility of anyone so young and vibrant having grave health problems.... Grateful that the gloom obscured his expression, Clay probed, "This lump—it's in your breast?"

She shook her head. "At least I've been spared that, thank God." After a moment she added drearily, "The tumor's in my side, in my armpit. I suppose it's probably some form of lymphoma."

Frowning, Clay asked, "Did the doctor tell you that?"

"No," Christine admitted. "He was very careful not to use the word 'cancer.' But he does want me to check into the hospital right away for some tests."

"Then aren't you rather jumping to conclusions?" Clay pressed. "There are probably lots of explanations for your symptoms that have nothing at all to do with cancer. The swelling could be caused by a low-grade infection, mononucleosis—"

Disgustedly Christine snapped, "Don't patronize me, Clay. I'm not a hypochondriac or an idiot, and neither is my doctor! Don't you think mono is the first thing he checked for?"

He could hear the hysteria sharpening her dull voice, and he hastened to appease her. "Please, Christine, I promise I'm not condescending to you. I realize you're worried, and, God forbid, maybe you have good reason. Most doctors have enough sense not to frighten their patients unless they're damn sure of their facts. But the point is, right now, at this moment, you simply don't know—"

"Oh, but I do know," Christine said, cutting him off. "I've seen all this before, close up, in excruciating detail. My father was the most wonderful man in the world, big and hearty and healthy, with a laugh that never stopped. He was an aircraft mechanic, and when I was fourteen, he and I won the three-legged race at his company's Labor Day picnic. The following afternoon, during a routine physical, he asked the doctor to take a look at a funny little black mole on his shoulder. The doctor packed him off to the hospital that very night—'for some tests,' he said. I never heard my father laugh again. He died on Christmas Eve."

Listening to that bleak, precise recital, Clay wished he could offer her something a little more comforting than the usual bromides. "I'm sorry," he murmured. "It must be rough, losing a parent at such an early age."

Christine turned her head to stare at him in the darkness. "I don't imagine it's easy at any age."

"No, I'm sure it isn't," Clay agreed quietly. He thought of his own father, a former real estate broker enjoying his golden years on the golf courses around Tampa. Clay's mother often griped that she'd had more leisure time before her husband retired, but the fact was that both of them were healthy and vigorous and happy. Because of the distance between Florida and California, Clay didn't see his parents very often, but at least he knew they were always there. He promised himself he'd telephone them first thing in the morning.

A false peace settled over Clay and Christine again, the silence underlined by the monotonous ruffle of raindrops on the hood of the car. Then Christine sighed dispiritedly. Clay waited. When she did not speak, he said, "Look, there's no denying you've had a blow, but the fact is, you may be worrying yourself sick over nothing. You have no proof—"

He broke off, suddenly struck by the parallels between this conversation and the one he'd had with Henry Berlinger earlier in the day. For the sake of the distraught woman, Clay hoped he was able to sound as wise and reassuring as his mentor did. In an altered tone he urged her, "Christine, you have to take things in order. You'll know soon enough whether or not your worst fears are justified. It's right this minute that should concern you now. You're stressed out and exhausted. You need to rest, you probably need to eat." He paused. "By the way," he queried acutely, "exactly when was the last time you ate anything?"

Christine considered the question. "I—I guess it must have been sometime yesterday evening," she admitted with reluctance. "I worked late, going over the receipts, and Amir had me try a new recipe that he was experimenting with, a mushroom risotto. It was very good, although I was a little iffy about the dill...." She fluttered her hands distractedly. "This morning I skipped breakfast before my checkup, and since then—well, since then, food has been the last thing on my mind."

"That's what I figured," Clay said grimly. "No wonder you're frazzled. Somebody as concerned about good nutrition as you are ought to know the risks of letting your blood-sugar become depleted. You'd better let me buy you dinner."

Christine shook her head. "Thanks for the offer, but I'm sure you'll appreciate that right now I'm just not feeling very sociable. The last thing I want to do is spend more time in a crowded restaurant."

Clay told her, "Actually I was thinking of someplace quiet. There's an all-night coffee shop just down the road in Stinson Beach—probably not up to your standards, but the omelets are passable." He hesitated. "You do eat eggs and dairy products, don't you?"

"I eat just about anything," she answered, surprising him. "The cuisine at La Courgette is vegetarian. I'm not."

Clay's brows lifted. "Sorry. I assumed you were into health food."

Christine laughed humorlessly. "Maybe I should have been."

She settled against her seat and stared glumly through the windshield at the invisible ocean. Clay gazed at her. His eyes had adjusted to the dim light, and he could make out her features clearly, her patrician profile, the generous mouth pressed into a thin, somber line. As he watched, she reached up with her fingers to loop a wing of straight, fair hair back behind her ear, revealing a surprisingly firm jawline, and a long, sloping throat, deeply hollowed. She was definitely too thin, Clay judged, allowing himself to wonder for the first time whether that fragile air about her was real, whether her mannequinlike slenderness might be due not to the dictates of fashion but to acute illness. Although he'd tried to assuage her fears, he conceded that Christine was right, the possibility had to be faced. But the very idea incensed him. It wasn't fair. Not that cancer was ever fair, but damn it, Christine was only how old—thirty, thirty-two? She was too young! Too young and too beautiful, too—too alive...

His chest felt tight. Struggling to suppress the groan of outrage that welled in him, he inhaled the air in tiny sips, forcing it soundlessly through his teeth. He became aware of the smells trapped in the tightly enclosed cab of the car, the smell of sweat and soap and gasoline, the dank, feral odor of wet leather. But the fragrance he noticed most was something more elusive, something warm and womanly and beckoning....

Trying to ignore the stirrings in his body, Clay turned away. He'd never realized before what a gentleman he was, he thought mockingly. Mom would be proud. Here he was, parked in a secluded lovers' hideaway with a woman he desired, a woman not altogether unaware of him—and he was afraid to touch her.

It was definitely time to get the hell out of there.

He massaged the wide bridge of his nose and the deep creases that felt permanently pinched between his eyes. When he trusted himself to speak without betraying the emotions that oppressed him, Clay faced Christine again. He spoke her name. She continued to stare straight ahead, but from her sudden tension he sensed that she was listening to him. "Look," he said quietly, anxious not to alarm her, "I hesitate to suggest this because I'm not sure how you'll take it, but if you really don't want to go to a restaurant, my house is just up the highway about five miles from here, and I have a steak in the freezer that's big enough to share."

When Christine did not reply, Clay pressed on. "It's only an idea, and I'm not going to feel offended if you say no. I can certainly understand why you'd be wary. After all, you don't know me."

Christine turned in her seat. In the dark her eyes were fathomless shadows, indecipherable, but her lips were parted in something that might almost have been a smile. To Clay's astonishment, she reached out and touched his cheek. "Oh, but I do know you, Clay," she breathed, stroking his weathered skin with cool, delicate fingers. "I know you're intelligent and well mannered, and you have some connection with the

Berlinger Institute, which probably means you're well educated, as well. I know you're kind and considerate and compassionate. I know you'd never hurt me.''

She paused. When she spoke again, she sounded more lighthearted than she had all evening. "You can't fool me, Clay," she told him serenely. "Even though for some reason you like to pretend you're a rough-neck, a motorcycle bum, I know for a fact that you're really very gallant."

Sweat beaded on Clay's forehead as he struggled not to grab her. "Oh, yeah, gallant," he growled, feeling feverish. He laughed edgily. "That's me, all right, Christine—a regular knight in shining leather."

He wondered how the hell he was ever going to live up to her image of him.

CHAPTER THREE

"I'M SORRY FOR THE MESS," Clay told Christine, holding open his front door for her. "If I'd realized I was going to have company, I'd have picked up a little."

As she crossed the threshold, Christine murmured politely, "Please don't apologize. Everything's just fine."

Clay watched her gaze flit around the living room of his ramshackle beach house. Books and navigational charts were piled on every horizontal surface. A tarp spread in the center of the floor held the greasy detritus from his ongoing motorcycle repairs. Clay was hardly ever aware of the disarray in which he lived, but now he tried to view it from a woman's perspective. He wondered what, if anything, Christine deduced from the long brocade sofa flanked by plastic Parsons tables, the ultra-high-tech stereo system set up on a tower of concrete blocks and pine shelving. Did the jumble of styles, expensive alongside dirt-cheap, register with her at all? Clay had always intended to get new furniture after the divorce, but buying the house exhausted his savings, and since then, whenever he had a few dollars to spare—which wasn't often, given his salary at the Institute—he tended to invest them in the Harley or scuba gear. Consequently, even after five years he still lived amid the decidedly eclectic mixture of furniture that was the inevitable result of having divided an established household. If he was honest with himself, most of the time he liked it that way.

Most of the time.

He scooped up an armload of newspapers from the couch and told Christine, "Here, make yourself at home anywhere you can find room. I'm going to have to defrost that steak before I can broil it. While we're waiting, would you care for something to drink? I don't think I have any wine, but there's some beer in the refrigerator, or I could make coffee or tea or whatever you'd like." Listening to himself babble, Clay nearly groaned aloud. He'd had women guests in his home before. Why did he sound as self-conscious as a kid on his first date?

Blessedly Christine did not seem to notice his agitation. Standing in the center of the room, she tugged her sweater more tightly around her shoulders and shivered. "If it's really not too much trouble," she said, "I'd love some hot tea, please. I'm a little chilly."

"Of course you are," Clay responded with compunction. Although the house was sealed tight against the storm, the air inside was motionless and clammy, heavy with the smell of must. He knew Christine's wet clothes must be unbearably uncomfortable. "Of course you're cold," he repeated. "This place is like a morgue." As soon as the crass analogy passed his lips, Clay winced, but Christine appeared not to hear him. Suddenly he realized that once again she was distracted, only marginally aware of his presence. While they sat together in her car at the vista point, she had seemed composed, upset but in control. Obviously her self-possession had vanished during the drive to his house. Alone in her car, while Christine had followed Clay's motorcycle along the rain-slick highway, all her fears had returned, multiplied. Now she was close to shock.

Quickly Clay ducked into the hallway and rummaged through the cluttered cupboard that he laughingly referred to as his linen closet; a moment later he returned to the living room with a thick mohair afghan crocheted in rippling stripes of green and gold. Draping the kitten-soft blanket around Christine's shoulders like a cape, he nudged her toward the sofa. "Here now," he urged gently, "you'll feel better if you sit down and stay wrapped in this. As soon as I've fixed your tea, I'll light the wood stove. I promise you'll be warm and comfortable again in just a few minutes."

"Thank you," Christine murmured vaguely. She sank onto the couch and closed her eyes, her long lashes dark against her pallor. She looked exhausted. As Clay watched, she quivered, snuggling her body luxuriously into the folds of the coverlet, an artless, almost childlike movement that he found incredibly sensual. With an effort he left her.

In the bedroom Clay slung his leather jacket over the back of a chair, then kicked his boots into a corner to dry. Padding around the wooden floor in his socks, he pulled his work-stained T-shirt away from his body and sniffed the fabric with distaste. Somehow he doubted that eau d'elephant seal would ever catch on as a men's cologne. He wished he had time for a shower, but he supposed he'd have to settle for a quick wash and a change of clothes. Stripping off his T-shirt and jeans, Clay replaced them with a baggy black sweat suit with Save The Humans stenciled across the top. He ducked into the bathroom long enough to scrub his face and hands and comb his wild dark hair back into a thick ponytail. On his way out of the bedroom he paused in the doorway, looking behind him.

In marked contrast to his otherwise dubious housekeeping skills, Clay always kept his king-size bed neatly made, partly because the habit had been deeply ingrained in him in childhood, but mostly out of respect for the heirloom-quality patchwork quilt he used as a spread. Clay's mother had made it as a wedding gift for him and Belinda, and when his wife divorced him, that quilt had been one of the few pieces of community property he'd been prepared to contend for. To Belinda's credit, she yielded it without an argument, noting that such a treasure should remain in his family. Ever since then, the quilt had graced his bed, a spot of beauty and symmetry in his relentlessly disorganized surroundings.

It was too damn bad the woman dozing in his living room would never see it.

Closing the door firmly behind him, Clay headed for the kitchen.

When Christine opened her eyes again, a mug of tea steamed on one of the plastic end tables, and Clay hunkered down beside the Buck stove, positioning logs with a poker. The sappy tang of burning wood filled the air. Closing the stove door with a loud clang, Clay stood and turned in time to see Christine taste her tea experimentally. She wrinkled her nose. Relieved to note that her expression was alert once more, Clay grinned. "I'm sorry if that's too sweet for you, but I figured you could use the sugar."

Christine tried to look grateful. "I'm sure you're right," she agreed, gulping the hot beverage down to the syrupy dregs. "Thank you," she said hoarsely. "It was really stupid of me to go so long without eating. I know better."

"Well, the steak will be ready in just a few minutes," Clay assured her. "While we're waiting, I can fix you more tea—without the sugar this time."

Quickly Christine said, "No, please don't bother. I'm fine." She sat up on the sofa and adjusted the coverlet that had fallen from her shoulders. Appreciatively she stroked the downy fabric with her fingertips and observed, "This is a beautiful afghan. Somebody invested a lot of time and care making it."

"My mother," Clay told her. "She loves to do needlework, and every few months I receive a package containing some new masterpiece. I have a closet full of handmade linens that I'm afraid to use, for fear I'll ruin them."

A fond expression played across Christine's lips. "I think most mothers would rather see the things they make for their children used and worn, or even worn out, rather than stored away like relics in a museum."

"Maybe so," Clay agreed ruefully, "but I have this nightmare that someday I'll be doing a valve job on the Harley and I'll discover that I've just wiped my filthy hands all over one of Mom's embroidered guest towels." He paused, gazing at Christine cocooned on the sofa. "However, I am sure it would make her very happy to see you bundled up like—" He broke off. "I'd better go check on dinner," he said.

Startled by his abrupt change of mood, Christine blinked. She indicated the alcove where a small dining suite was cluttered with magazines and unopened mail. "Shall I set the table?" she asked.

"I'll do it," Clay replied tersely. "You need to rest." He pivoted away and retreated to the kitchen.

When he emerged several minutes later with two laden plates in his hands, the afghan lay neatly folded on the sofa, and Christine was warming herself at the wood stove. As she flexed her chilled fingers in the radiant heat, she studied a photograph hanging on the wall, a group shot of a dozen bronzed men lounging in the stern of some small ocean-going vessel. When she heard Clay enter the room, she peered intently in his direction, then she squinted at the picture once more. Clay knew she must be trying to decide whether the lanky youth standing in the background of the photo, behind a wiry, gray-haired man with leathery skin and penetrating eyes, was really him or not. He set the plates on the table while he waited for the inevitable comment.

"That's Jacques Cousteau, isn't it?" Christine said.

As he aligned silverware with geometrical precision alongside the dinner plates, Clay answered mildly, "That's right. When I was a graduate student, I had a chance to serve briefly as a very minor crew member on one of his very minor expeditions. It's not as impressive as it sounds. I was really just a deckhand."

Christine cocked her head, her gaze narrowing. "Graduate student? I guessed you were well-educated, but what sort of degrees do you have, anyway?"

Clay looked almost sheepish. "M.A.," he admitted reluctantly. "M.S." He sighed. "Ph.D."

"Good lord," Christine whispered. She chuckled uncomfortably. "Are you telling me you're really *Dr.* McMurphy?"

He shrugged. "That's what my students at the university used to call me."

Christine choked. "You were a college professor? But—but now you're a biker!"

For some reason, her bewildered tone rankled. "Actually I'm a marine biologist," Clay said evenly. "Bikes are what I ride, not what I am."

He watched her struggle with her embarrassment. "I'm sorry," she murmured. "I didn't mean to sound like a snob. I was just surprised, that's all, although, considering where you work, I ought to have realized . . ." Her voice trailed off.

"Forget it," Clay said roughly, puzzled that he'd felt annoyed. Most of the time he rather enjoyed disconcerting people with his iconoclastic life-style. "Forget it, Christine," he repeated. "It's an honest mistake. If I'd wanted to pass for an intellectual, I never would have given up the Saab and the tweed jackets." He pulled out one of the dining chairs. "Come and sit down. Let's ignore my dreary past and concentrate on this meal I've slaved over a hot microwave to prepare. I did find some wine, after all, a *vin* that's extremely *ordinaire,* but it's bound to help a little. If you're a good girl and clean your plate, I promise that later I'll tell you anything you want to know about those long-ago days when I toiled in the groves of academe."

The steak was medium rare and reasonably tender, aromatic with garlic and pepper, but Clay suspected he could have cooked the beef till it was dry and tough as jerky, and Christine wouldn't have noticed. As he watched her sip her wine, a passable California zinfandel, and pick her way dutifully through the meat and the mushy boil-in-the-bag vegetables he'd added as an afterthought to round out the meal, he knew she was scarcely conscious of what she was eating. Which was probably just as well, he conceded wryly, considering that she was a professional gourmet and his culinary skills could only charitably be described as indifferent. Not that it really mattered, of course. At the moment the point was merely to get Christine to ingest a few nutrients. It wasn't as if he was trying to impress her.

Raindrops splattered in sheets against the picture window beside the table while they ate, the arrhythmic percussion underscoring the desultory conversation. "That's quite a storm out there," Clay observed with stunning banality. When Christine did not respond, he pressed on, determined somehow to cajole her out of her depression. "There was a storm like this the night Moonie was beached."

At last Christine looked at him. "Moonie?" she murmured politely.

"The sick elephant seal that washed ashore at Half Moon Bay about a month ago," Clay explained. "Some reporter with a feeble imagination named him. My research team at the Institute has been trying to identify his illness and track down its cause. To date we haven't had much luck, although his condition does seem to have stabilized. That's an accomplishment in itself, considering this is the first time we've ever worked with an elephant seal bigger than a yearling. It's been . . . an experience.''

Making light of the real issues involved in his job, Clay tried to amuse Christine with anecdotes about the perils of wrestling with two tons of disgruntled marine mammal, but soon he abandoned the effort. She wasn't listening—not that his words were worth listening to. Even to himself his attempts at wit sounded labored, as pretentious and phony as small talk at the faculty cocktail parties he used to attend with Belinda. He fell silent. He wondered if he ought to put on some music.

As he plowed through his meal, Clay studied Christine's delicate features, her pale, hollow cheeks, the shadowed eyes. He observed the deliberate effort required for her to lift her fork from plate to mouth, and he knew that on some level she must almost resent the fact that he was forcing her to eat. It was a funny thing about the human creature, Clay thought ironically, how in times of stress the most basic necessities were the first to be neglected. Except when caring for young, animals virtually never intentionally neglected their own needs, whereas people . . .

Clay glowered. There were a few things he could give Christine to help her cope with the blow fate had just dealt her, practical, impersonal things like nourishment and warmth—but she had other needs, as well. She needed encouragement and consolation, succor and strength. She needed a great many things that Clay had no right to offer her.

Most of all, he admitted grudgingly, right now she needed that blasted boyfriend of hers.

"I'm sorry," Christine said suddenly. "I'm not being very good company, am I?"

Her remark caught Clay off guard. "I beg your pardon?"

She tried to smile. Laying down her fork, she indicated the meal before them and repeated, "I'm sorry. You must think I'm a total ingrate. You've been very kind to me, you've gone to all this trouble, and I'm so absorbed in my own problems that I haven't even kept up my end of the conversation."

"Under the circumstances," Clay said mildly, "I think a little self-absorption is understandable."

Christine's worried expression did not change. "Are you sure? For a moment there you looked angry, almost fierce."

Clay hesitated while he backtracked in his thoughts until he realized what she was referring to. He took a large swallow of wine, hoping the astringency would clear the thickness in his throat. With care he set down the glass. Then he said, "I guess it's my turn to apologize to you, Christine. I'm certainly not angry with you. If I seemed perturbed just now, it's because, well, frankly it disturbs me a great deal that you should be enduring a situation like this on your own. Whether or not the tests establish that you have cancer, you need your friends and family with you. Your...partner, the guy I met at the restaurant, should be here."

Leaning forward, Christine insisted emphatically, "Don't blame Reese, it's not his fault. When he headed off to Europe, all he knew was that I was scheduled for my annual checkup. There was no way to predict the doctor might turn up anything out of the ordinary. Reese never would have left me alone if he'd suspected." She sat back in her chair, and her tone was wistful as she added, "Besides, he did try very hard to talk me into going to Paris with him. He wanted us to get married there."

Clay's heart lurched. He reached for his wineglass again. "I gather you told him no?"

Christine stared blindly at the rain-lashed window. "I told him the same thing I've been telling him ever since college—that we have plenty of time." She hugged her arms and sighed. "Poor Reese. He's really fed up with waiting, and I can't blame him. But now somehow I think he'll be glad I stalled him. Cancer would be a hell of a wedding gift, wouldn't it?"

Hearing the desolation in her voice, Clay said the only thing he could. "If he loves you, it won't make any difference."

She turned her gaze to him, her expression shuttered. "You know," she remarked, studying his face, "you're an unusual man and you've managed to charm and surprise me in a great many ways—but believe me, Clay, the one thing I never expected you to be is naive." She set her napkin beside her plate and pushed back her chair.

Clay frowned. "What's wrong?"

"I have to leave," Christine said. She sounded loath but determined. "You've been wonderful to me and I'm very grateful for everything you've done, but it's time for me to go home. I have a lot of work to do, calls to make."

He glanced at his watch. "I'm not sure exactly what the time difference is, but it can't be dawn yet in Europe."

She said, "I'm not planning to telephone Europe."

The statement nonplussed Clay. "You're not going to call your family? What about your boyfriend?"

Exhaling wearily, Christine explained, "No way in hell will I break news like this to my mother before I'm certain of all the facts. She'd freak out completely. As for Reese, there's nothing he can do for me six thousand miles away. He's worked hard and deserves some peace and quiet. Why should I bother him and spoil his trip?"

Good God, Clay thought, shocked by the wave of intense jealousy that swept over him. Did Reese Cagney have any idea how much Christine loved him? Did he comprehend that she was so devoted to his well-being that she was willing to suffer her most hideous personal nightmares alone in order to spare him a little distress and inconvenience? Clay would sell his soul to be loved like—

No! The thought had not yet formed in his mind before he rejected it. According to his definition, love was supposed to involve mutual support. He neither wanted nor expected abject self-sacrifice from a woman. And to be perfectly fair, from the impressions he'd gathered during that brief confrontation at the restaurant, he doubted the other man did, either.

With an effort at justice, Clay told Christine, "I think you're underestimating your boyfriend. If I were in his place, I'd certainly want to know what was going on, even at the risk of spoiling my vacation."

Christine lifted her chin resolutely. "You may well be right, Clay, but I'd still rather handle the situation my way. I figured things out while I was sitting in my car. If I can arrange for someone to take charge of the restaurant for me, I can check into the hospital right away and be out again before Reese returns from Paris. If the test results are negative, then I won't have worried him for nothing. If the news isn't good—" All at once her voice quavered. She jumped to her feet, almost stumbling over her chair. "If the news isn't good," she repeated, turning away so that Clay had to strain to hear her, "then I guess whenever Reese finds it out, it will—will be too—too soon...."

Clay stalked after her. She hovered in the middle of the floor, her head bowed, her willowy body swaying as if buffeted by the storm outside. Guessing that she did not wish to face him, Clay resisted the urge to pull her into his arms. Instead he laid his hands gently on her shoulders. Urgently he told her, "Christine, you're making a mistake. It's foolish and unnecessary to try to handle a crisis like this entirely on your own."

"I don't like to impose on people," she mumbled.

Her hair flowed in silky wings around her bent neck, leaving her nape naked except for wispy silver blond tendrils that fluttered with his breath. Clay had to steel himself not to press his lips against her bare, perfumed skin. "People who love you won't consider it an imposition if you need them," he reminded her. "You don't have to prove to them how strong you are. They're much more likely to feel hurt if you don't—"

"Oh, stop it!" Christine jerked out of Clay's grasp and rounded on him. Her eyes flashed. "Stop trying to change my mind! This isn't a game. I'm not out to prove anything. You—you don't understand how I feel."

"No, I don't," he agreed. "But I'm trying to."

Christine gestured jerkily, her usually graceful hands punctuating her distress. "Yes, well—oh, Lord, how do I explain this?'' She swallowed. ''Tell me, Clay, have you ever lost anybody you loved?''

''My grandparents all died many years ago,'' he said. ''Plus, I'm divorced, if that counts.''

Clay could tell his terse announcement surprised Christine. Momentarily distracted, her feathery brows came together, and as he watched he could almost see her thinking, mentally reevaluating what little he'd shared of his past, in light of this new information. After a few seconds her eyes cleared and she returned to the subject at hand. ''When you and your wife broke up,'' she queried, ''were you prepared for it?''

Uncertain exactly where Christine's questions were leading, Clay answered frankly, ''I don't think anybody is ever really *prepared* for divorce, but Belinda and I had both seen it coming for some time, and we'd begun making the necessary emotional adjustments long before the physical separation occurred. We coped. So, yes, I suppose in a way you could say we were ready for it.''

''You were lucky,'' Christine judged. ''Not everybody has advance warning when disaster strikes. Not everybody can cope. When my father became ill, nobody was prepared for it—least of all him. He'd always earned a pretty good salary, but the family finances were totally disorganized, his insurance coverage was inadequate, he hadn't even made a will. Then all at once he was dying and everything fell to my poor mother. She went to pieces.''

''I'm sorry to hear that,'' Clay said, his voice staunchly neutral. ''But what's your point? Right now you don't even know for a fact that you have cancer. It's a bit premature to be talking about death.''

Christine retorted bitterly, "Damn it, Clay, I haven't started designing my shroud yet! I'm not talking about death, I'm talking about emotional burdens—burdens so oppressive that they turn normally intelligent, resourceful people into blithering idiots. After Daddy died, Mom couldn't make decisions, and when she did, they were usually the wrong ones. We lost our house because she didn't know how to take steps to protect us against foreclosure while she was getting back on her feet. For a while we lived on food stamps."

"That's rough," Clay interjected when Christine paused for breath.

She waved aside the remark. "There's no need to pity me, Clay. We survived. We may have lived in cheap, grungy apartments, but at least we always had food and a roof over our heads. That's not what I'm complaining about."

"What do you mean?"

"I mean, poverty wasn't the worst part of what happened after my father died!" Christine snapped. "Poverty can be endured, even overcome. No, the worst part was that somehow while Mom and I were struggling to make order out of chaos, the parent-child roles became reversed. There I was, fourteen years old, mothering my own mother, shouldering her responsibilities, trying to ease her pain. It wasn't until after the miracle happened and Jeff Silva came along and swept Mom off her feet, that I realized I'd been so busy caring for her that I'd never even had time to grieve for my dead father."

As she spoke, Christine's breasts heaved, and her cheeks were flushed with indignation. Anger had obliterated the clouds of depression in her sparking eyes. For the first time all evening Clay thought she looked like the dauntless beauty who had captivated him on sight at La Courgette a week earlier. He felt his body stirring beneath his sweat suit. He wanted her. He wanted to sweep her off her feet the way Jeff Silva had claimed her mother. He wanted to scoop her too-slender body up behind him on his hog like the outlaw biker she'd assumed he was. With her arms wrapped around his waist, the two of them would roar off into the night so fast and so far that neither her family nor her boyfriend—or even fate—could ever catch up with them....

Squelching his fantasies with an effort, Clay asked, "Do you blame your mother for failing you when you needed her?"

Christine grimaced. "No, of course not. It'd make about as much sense to blame my father for dying. Both of them did the best they could." She took a deep breath and squared her shoulders. "But I intend to do better."

"It sounds as if you've given the matter a lot of thought."

"Since I was seventeen," Christine replied. "When this dashing Air Force officer met my mother and suddenly I was free to be a teenager again, free to be *me* again, I made a vow. From that point on, for the rest of my life, I am going to take care of myself. No matter what happens to me, whether or not I continue to be a successful businesswoman, whether or not I marry Reese, I will never be helpless, and I will never be a burden to anybody."

Clay's expression was unreadable. "I thought you told me you weren't out to prove anything."

"Only to myself," Christine said.

For endless moments the two of them stood together in the center of the room, not touching, their gazes locked. The house was silent except for the crackle of burning wood and the rattle of the rain-flailed windowpanes. At last Christine looked away. With her eyes trained on the oil-stained tarp spread on the floor next to the couch, she declared stiltedly, "Well, Clay, I know I must sound like a broken record, but I really do appreciate everything you've done for me. If you'll forgive the old-fashioned word, you're a gentleman, and I shall be forever grateful for your kindness." She paused. "But now I have to go home."

Clay scowled. "Where is home, anyway?"

"Mill Valley, of course," Christine said blankly, slightly startled by the question. "Don't you re—" She broke off. "Isn't that silly of me," she exclaimed with bemused impatience. "I keep forgetting that you and I have only just met. Somehow it feels as if we've known each other forever." She frowned suddenly, as if the thought troubled her.

"So," Clay prompted when Christine did not speak at once, "you have a place of your own in Mill Valley?"

She regarding him ironically. "I don't live with Reese, if that's what you're asking. He has a bay-front condo in Sausalito. My house is closer to the restaurant, maybe about fifteen miles from here."

Glancing dubiously through the window at the storm that continued to bluster outside, Clay muttered, "That's fifteen miles of bad road. Considering how tired and upset you are, do you really think you ought to tackle that drive at night in the middle of a squall?"

Christine followed his gaze. At the gas station visible a few hundred yards down the highway, the wind was whipping a tall light standard back and forth like a metronome. "I'll manage," she declared.

Clay came to a decision. "You don't have to manage," he told her firmly. "You can spend the night here. There's a perfectly good bed in the next room. It even has clean sheets." Out of the corner of his eye he could see her stiffen. Wondering whether he ought to feel exasperated or amused or just bloody frustrated, he added, "I'm going to sleep on the couch."

She shook her head. "A real gentleman," she repeated, her expression inscrutable. Clay started to speak again, but she waved him to silence. "I'll take the couch," she said.

Clay supposed he slept. He supposed that at some point while he sprawled athwart his tumbled bed with the patchwork quilt swathed around his naked torso, his agitated mind had withdrawn from the sensory world, briefly rendering him blind and deaf. He did not feel rested, but when he stared into the amorphous darkness he realized that for some unspecified period of time he had not seen the occasional watery smears of light that flared across his ceiling when cars passed by on the highway; his ears had not heard the whistling wind and the rhythmic boom of waves pounding the shore half a mile away.

It was the storm in the next room that he could not block out.

Christine was crying.

Her snuffled whimpers were so soft that the sound was almost subliminal, no louder than the rustle of embers cooling and contracting in the wood stove, but the din of it beat at Clay, making repose impossible. Her loneliness seemed to echo throughout the house. He found himself shaking and sweating as he tried to stifle the noise of her weeping. He could not go to her. He did not have the right. The woman who had vowed to bear her burdens in stoic silence would not appreciate his interference. She would not be grateful that he shared the secret of her weakness.

In the dark, sofa springs creaked. The wooden floor flexed beneath a soft footstep. All at once Clay heard a muffled exclamation punctuated by the jarring clatter of plastic and several faint thuds, and he knew Christine must have stumbled over one of the flimsy end tables. Bounding out of bed, he thrust his legs into his sweatpants and stalked down the hall into the living room.

At the doorway he flipped on the light switch. Transfixed by the brightness, Christine knelt on the floor, her ankles tangled in the afghan, one hand fumbling for books she'd knocked off the table. In her crouched position the oversize T-shirt she wore for a nightgown ballooned open, and Clay caught a heart-stopping glimpse of high, soft breasts and long, shapely thighs that curved into narrow hips only partly covered by sheer panties. He tried not to gawk. Christine bolted upright, and the shirt draped back into place. Her red-rimmed eyes blinked owlishly as she stared at Clay.

"Are you all right?" he asked. "I thought I heard you fall."

"I—I'm okay," she stammered, scrubbing her salt-stained cheeks with her fingertips. "I was going to get a—a drink of water, but I managed to trip myself." She scrambled to her feet. Folding the afghan, she dropped it on the couch atop the bedclothes Clay had provided for her. "I'm sorry to be so clumsy," she said. "I didn't mean to disturb you."

Clay shrugged his broad shoulders. "That's all right. I was awake, anyway."

The flexing movement seemed to make Christine aware of Clay's tanned, muscular torso, bare except for the coarse sun-bleached hair that sprinkled his chest and arrowed down beneath the elastic waist-band of the fleece pants. Averting her eyes, Christine glanced toward the window and declared huskily, "I think it must be the rain that makes it hard to sleep. We don't get many storms like this around here."

"No, not many," Clay murmured.

Christine said, "I guess that sort of makes this a night to—to remember."

"I guess." The air was clammy, and Clay could feel his chest prickle with goose bumps. Christine's nipples were clearly outlined by the soft cotton fabric of the T-shirt. "Are you cold?" he asked with an effort. "Shall I build up the fire again?"

"No, please don't bother." She grabbed her pillow and began to fluff it. "I'll be all right once I get back under the covers."

Amazed at how steady his voice sounded, Clay reminded her, "You said you were thirsty. I can make more tea."

Christine nodded jerkily. "Thank you. That would be nice."

"Just a minute, then." Pivoting away, Clay headed for the kitchen. Before he reached the doorway he heard Christine sob.

He whirled back. She had collapsed onto the sofa, hunched over the pillow. Her head was bent, and Clay could not see her expression.

"Oh, God, Christine," Clay murmured with anguish.

Slowly she looked up at him. Tendrils of tumbled hair clung to her damp cheeks, but her eyes were exposed and unblinking and utterly vulnerable. In a voice that sounded as if her throat had been seared with pain, as if she'd never spoken before, she croaked, "I'm so scared."

He was beside her on the couch instantly, pulling her slim body roughly into his arms. She burrowed against him like a wounded animal, her breasts cushioned against his naked chest, her wet face slippery in the curve of his throat. "I'm so damned scared," she whispered again, and her breath tickled his overheated skin.

Clay felt flushed. He shifted her on his lap, hoping she would not notice how her nearness was affecting him. "Hush, Christine, hush," he crooned as he rocked her, stroking her hair, patting her back. Through the thin shirt he could shape the vertebrae of her long spine. The tantalizing woman-fragrance that filled his nostrils maddened him. "Don't cry, dear, please," he murmured, the words a hoarse lullaby. "It's going to be all right, I promise."

She wailed. "Everyone who loves me is so far away. Reese is away, Mom's away, Daddy's the farthest away of all...."

"I'm here," Clay said softly.

Christine tensed, choking off her brokenhearted sobs. Slowly she eased back in his embrace to stare at him. "What did you say?" she asked uncertainly.

He wondered grimly which of the two of them was more startled by the implications of his laconic words. Did he love Christine? Heaven knew he wanted her, was almost sick with hunger for her. But how could he *love* her, by any rational definition of the word, when he and the woman he held half-nude in his arms were virtual strangers? He was not a romantic, he was a passionate but logical man with a scientist's disdain for unsupported implications. He did not believe in love at first sight. Only adolescents and fools were so quick to mistake raging hormones for something more lasting.... "I'm here," Clay repeated gruffly.

Gazing at him with an odd mixture of alarm, skepticism and hope, Christine searched his face. "Clay," she whispered, sounding dazed, "are you telling me you love me?"

Clay's lips twisted. "I don't know whether I love you or not," he admitted with blunt candor. "I only know I want to protect you. I don't want anything to hurt you."

She coughed dryly. "I don't want anything to hurt me, either—but I'm afraid it's going to."

"Not if I can help it," Clay vowed.

Christine almost smiled. "That's pretty wishful thinking for a biologist, isn't it? You probably understand cancer a lot better than I do. Do you really believe you can blast away a malignancy with sheer force of will?''

''I'll believe anything I have to, if it works,'' Clay said.

The woman perched on his lap sighed. ''I wish I could be so pragmatic.'' She relaxed and snuggled against him, artless as a child, and all Clay could see was the top of her head, the corn-silk-pale hair that shone even in disarray. For a long time neither of them spoke. The only sound was the ceaseless thrum of the rain beating at the cottage. Then Christine declared dully, ''I hate the uncertainty. Even bad news must be easier to bear than not knowing.''

''You're going to have to try to put it out of your mind until the test results are in,'' Clay said.

Christine snorted. ''Yeah, sure. Have you ever really tried *not* to think about something? It's impossible. Besides, I come from a family of chronic worriers.'' She exhaled tiredly. ''But I do wish I could stop remembering. It would be such a relief to forget, just for a little—'' Suddenly she broke off.

He felt the change in her before he saw it, the instant when lethargy became tension and purpose. Tilting her head back, the woman in his arms shook the hair out of her face and stared at him with blue gray eyes that were glazed but no longer unaware. Clay froze. She shifted her weight deliberately, rubbing provocatively against him. Delicate fingertips reached up to explore the half-healed scrape on his jaw; they traced the shape of his mouth. As Clay watched stonily, the tip of her tongue darted across her lips, dewing her skin with a pearly sheen of moisture that he thirsted for. He swallowed. The invitation was blatant and alluring, irresistible. What kind of fool was he to resist? He had wanted Christine from the first moment he saw her, wanted her with a hunger and intensity such as he hadn't felt in years, and now, miraculously, she was offering him everything he craved. Why in hell should he say no? What possible reason was there to deny himself and refuse her—apart from the daunting suspicion that at the moment she wasn't absolutely certain who he was....

"No, Christine," Clay growled, gently capturing her wrist. He guided her hand back to her own lap, but as soon as he released her, she touched him again, slim fingers splaying across his chest, tugging delicately at the tight curls, teasing his flat nipples. Clay gulped. "No, darling," he repeated with noticeably less conviction, "this isn't really what you want—"

"I want to forget," she said fervently. "You can make me forget." Nuzzling his chest, she began to retrace the course of her fingers with her mouth. "Please, love," she whispered, her warm lips moving wetly on his skin, "make me forget...."

With a guttural curse Clay laced his hands through her hair and guided her face to his.

Their mouths were still locked together when he swept her up in his arms and carried her to the bedroom. As he stalked down the dark hallway he noted absently that the noise of the storm seemed to have abated a little; the rain clattered the roof with less force, the wind no longer howled, and he could not hear the pounding of the surf against the beach. Clay prayed for the gale to resume. He wanted the wind to shriek, the waves to boom. As he gently laid Christine on his bed, on his mother's wedding quilt, he prayed for the raging sky to raise a clamor that would blot out all other sounds, all voices, make words impossible.

If she called him Reese, he didn't want to hear her.

CHAPTER FOUR

THE SUN CRESTED the peak of Mount Tamalpais and climbed high into the freshly washed sky, beaming merrily through the half-open blinds on the bedroom window. A slat of light struck Christine's face. Squinting against the brightness, she grumbled drowsily and tried to roll over onto her stomach—only to be stayed by a large, warm hand cupped possessively around her breast. She stirred, and the fingers tightened, urging her backward. Christine scooted away from the encroaching sunshine, shifting in her sleep into the haven of the potent masculine body that beckoned her. She wriggled voluptuously and relaxed spoonwise in his arms, flesh against hard, musky flesh. Her dreams had never been so delicious.

Even in her most erotic fantasies she had forgotten how it could be, the giddy response his strength and vigor could compel. Over the years they had become too accustomed to each other, habit had dampened hunger. Now suddenly, miraculously, every caress was new again, as if they were lovers for the very first time—

A truck pulling out of the gas station on the highway blared its air horn, and the raucous noise shredded Christine's silken slumber. Her eyes blinked open.

She did not know where she was.

She scowled in confusion. Jerked from sleep, her mind felt torpid and disoriented; rational thought seemed an effort. She knew she was lying on her side in a bed, her face half-burrowed in a pillow, but where? She did not recognize the room. Faded blue walls, utilitarian window blinds, a neat pine dresser that might have been assembled from a kit—nothing sparked a glimmer of recognition. Her mental blankness alarmed her. Her body felt as sluggish as her brain, oddly languid, almost as if she'd been medicated. She couldn't be in a hospital, could she? The furnishings certainly looked prosaic enough for an institution. Perhaps this was a motel? There was traffic somewhere close by. Still, the studio portrait of a pleasant-looking older couple that graced the dresser would seem to indicate this was a private home. But if so, then whose home was it? Certainly not hers or Reese's. Her own bedroom was papered with a *faux* Laura Ashley print, and Reese's condo had glass walls that opened onto a deck overlooking San Francisco Bay....

As Christine gradually grew more alert, her apprehension increased. Nothing made any sense to her. Her heart lurched with panic. Where the hell was she? What was she doing here?

And whose were those arms, proprietary and purposeful, that were wrapped around her, fondling her?

Gnawing her lip, Christine pushed herself up on her elbows. The covers fell back, revealing a big, square hand with blunt, sun-browned fingers fanned across her bare rib cage—a hand that was definitely not her fiancé's. Emerging from beneath the sheet was a sinewy wrist imprinted with the pale outline of some timepiece substantially less refined than the elegant Patek Philippe Dr. and Mrs. Cagney had given their son when he graduated from USC, but the rest of the all-too-clearly masculine figure huddled beside her was invisible beneath the heaped bedclothes. Christine averted her eyes. This couldn't be happening to her, she told herself desperately—this *wasn't* happening to her! She was still asleep, that was the only possible explanation. This had to be a dream, some nightmare fantasy brought on by indigestion, maybe an allergic reaction to Amir's mushroom risotto....

She jerked her head back and forth, trying to find some point of reference that would spur her memory. The window blinds cast ribbons of sunlight that played across the bed, glowing in jewel-toned stripes on a delicate patchwork quilt of exquisite craftsmanship. She loved fine needlework—surely she ought to at least remember the quilt? But everything in the shadowy room looked unfamiliar to her. She felt her throat constrict with frustration and fright, as if she were trapped in an episode of *The Twilight Zone*.

Then a draft of air rippled the slats on the window blind, and as Christine watched with wide, stricken eyes, a shaft of brightness lanced the gloom, striking a scarred black leather jacket draped over the back of a chair at the foot of the bed.

Memory returned with a rush, all of it, in crystalline detail. She remembered everything: the checkup—the tumor—the ocean—Clay—the rain—Clay... "Oh, no," Christine whispered.

She had done it, she had actually done it. As if the prospect of cancer wasn't enough to roil the quiet current of her life and destroy her peace of mind, after ten years of fastidious fidelity to the only man she'd ever loved, the man she fully intended to marry one day and bear children with, she had become so hysterical at her physician's bad tidings that to console herself she had hopped into bed with, literally, a passing stranger.

She must have been insane, Christine told herself, insane with shock and grief. There was no other possible explanation for actions so reckless, so out of character. Damn it, she wasn't a neurotic nymphomaniac or some low-life bimbo—she wasn't even particularly passionate sexually! She was a mature, sensible woman in love with an attractive, attentive man who fulfilled all her needs. During ten years in the restaurant business, she'd certainly had her share of passes thrown in her direction, by men of every age, shape, and social status, and never once had she been tempted by their invitations. Never once had she even considered betraying Reese. Never once had she dreamed she would ever discover herself lying naked beside another man, her body aching and sticky with the evidence of his possession. . . .

With a groan of mortification Christine collapsed back onto her pillow.

Her movements wakened Clay. Shoving aside the covers, he lifted his head and peered drowsily at her through a tangle of wild, dark hair. Paralyzed, Christine met his gaze. Clay's blue eyes glinted with recognition. His lips, shadowed with dark stubble, stretched into a crooked grin of sheer delight. "Morning, darling," he murmured.

Christine swallowed dryly. "Good—good morning," she replied with an effort. The blunt fingers

tightened around her rib cage. Slowly Clay dragged
her toward him. When he sprawled heavily over her,
holding her captive, his skin felt feverish, as feverish
as his gaze. He was very aroused. "P-please," Christine tried belatedly to protest, but the words were
crushed back into her mouth. With a grumble of
pleasure like the growl of a hungry lion, Clay kissed
her.

His bristly cheeks abraded her softness, and the
taste and scent of him made her dizzy. Breath seemed
impossible. She wriggled beneath him, hoping to shift
his weight off her, but the movements only excited
him. She felt him rigid against her thigh, and she tried
to blot out the seductive recollection of the way that
vibrant masculine strength had filled and completed
her during the night, making her something stun-
ningly alive, entirely new. Already her body was turning traitor at the memory, answering and opening to
him as his moist lips moved urgently over her skin.
They were too good together, she conceded with a reluctant sigh, that was the problem; they were better
than they had any right to be. Better than—

No! Staunchly Christine refused to let her mind
form the words of betrayal. The words were wrong,
the thought was wrong. She would not make compar-
isons. She would not try to excuse her inexcusable behavior with allusions to the faint ennui that had begun
to infect her relationship with Reese. The very least she
owed her lover was loyalty. Reese was a good man. He
had done nothing to deserve her perfidy. It wasn't his
fault that an accident of timing had sent him far away
just at the moment when she needed him most. It
wasn't his fault that for all Christine's vaunted forti-

tude, when it came to the crunch she was shamefully, humiliatingly weak and spineless and vulnerable and—and easy....

She began to cry. Big, scalding tears of despair welled in her eyes and splashed her cheeks as she averted her face from the seeking mouth of the man who held her. Clay froze. Lacing his fingers into her hair, he forced her face back toward his. He held her head immobile while he studied her expression mercilessly. "Let me guess," he said, with an ironic scorn that could have been directed at himself as much as at Christine. "You've suddenly decided that this has all been a terrible mistake. You really love your boyfriend, and you'd appreciate it very much if I'd kindly get off your body and out of your life and then go disappear somewhere, preferably in the next hemisphere."

His derisive words so accurately mirrored Christine's thoughts that she could only sniffle and nod, the faint movement tugging her hair painfully. With as much courage as she could muster she stared up at him, meeting his cruel gaze. She held her breath while she tried not to sob. Clay's hands tightened around her skull.

Then all at once he released her and flung himself away with a groan, rolling onto his back on the far side of the mattress, all desire gone. He glared at the ceiling and swore loudly. As she listened to him, Christine wondered if she imagined the anguish she heard in the crude words.

By the time Clay's bluster sputtered and died away, Christine felt emotionally battered. They lay alongside each other, exhausted, leagues apart. The room was silent except for the noise of traffic along the highway, which she noticed was appreciably louder than it had been when she first woke up. She wondered what time it was. She couldn't judge from the angle of the light rising through the blinds, and her wristwatch was in her handbag on one of the plastic Parsons tables in the living room. Whatever the hour, she was probably late for work.

Pushing herself upright, Christine flipped back the quilt and swiveled away from Clay to sit on the edge of the bed. When her bare feet touched the wooden floor, her toes encountered a small, shapeless mound of soft white cotton fabric—the undershirt Clay had lent her to use as a nightgown. Closer to the doorway she spotted her wispy silk panties. Christine presumed Clay's sweatpants were wadded on the floor somewhere on his side of the room. None of their clothes had made it to the bed. When she bent over and retrieved the scattered garments, she stared at the T-shirt, considering. She'd worn it such a short time that it seemed almost a waste to toss it in the laundry hamper. After a moment she raised her arms and donned the shirt again, slithering it down over her head, breast, belly, tugging and adjusting it around her hips as she stood up. Regardless of how their bodies had fused and merged during the night, the myriad ways they had revealed themselves to each other, in the clear light of day she was not ready to parade around naked in front of Clay.

Wincing at her stiffness, the odd disjointed ache in her lower limbs, Christine stumbled toward the door. Clay's voice stopped her. "Well, aren't you going to say it?" he demanded roughly.

She could not look at him. "Say what?" she asked dully.

His irritation seemed mixed with bewilderment as he snapped, "Isn't this the point at which you're supposed to accuse me of betraying your trust and taking advantage of you?"

Slowly Christine turned. With veiled eyes she gazed down at Clay, who was stretched out on top of the quilt, gloriously, unself-consciously nude. They had made love in the dark, and she had been too distracted by the feel of him to appreciate what a visually attractive body he had, lean and well proportioned, the muscles sculpted by years of athletic activity. Except for the pale patch his diver's watch left at his wrist and the marginally larger swatch around his loins, his skin was tan all over, dusted with dark hair sun bleached on his arms and legs. In a wry parenthesis, Christine hoped Clay was in the habit of using a good sunscreen whenever he was out of doors.

"Christine—" Clay pressed.

"You didn't take advantage of me," she informed him tonelessly.

He scowled. "Are you sure about that? Last night you were half out of your mind—"

"Only half?" Christine mused with leaden irony. Gnawing her lip, she deciphered the subtext of his peculiar questions. "What's the matter?" she probed acutely. "Now that it's the morning after, are you feeling guilty, too?"

Clay rolled onto one side, propping himself on his elbow while he gestured melodramatically with his free hand. "Guilty—*moi?* Why should I—" All at once his airy tone evaporated and he exploded. "Yes, damn it,

I do feel guilty! You were sick and scared and hysterical and I ought to have handled the situation differently. I should have exercised more self-control—" he snorted grimly "—no matter how much I wanted you."

For a moment Christine considered leaving Clay's remarks unanswered; there was definite appeal to the idea of letting him shoulder the responsibility for her rash and uncharacteristic behavior. But her innate integrity would not permit her to remain silent. Her overburdened conscience could not bear the weight of another sin, even if it was only one of omission. She could not repay Clay's many kindnesses with a lie. With resignation she confessed, "It wasn't all hysteria, you know. I wanted you, too."

Her candor seemed to startle the man on the bed. His thick, straight brows came together, and he leaned forward as if he were about to say something, but before he could speak, Christine waved him to silence. "Please, Clay, let me get this all out now," she admonished him, "because I don't know if I'll have the courage to repeat myself." He settled back, watching her warily.

Christine gulped. "What happened last night was a mistake," she announced baldly. "My mistake, not yours. You are not to blame. I'm the one with other loyalties and obligations I should have honored, obligations I... didn't honor. It would be easy—and comforting—to pretend that the only reason I cheated on the man I love is because I was so distraught that I didn't know what I was doing, but that simply isn't true. The plain fact of the matter is that I made love with you because I wanted you."

She paused. Her glance skated over him once more. He was impressively masculine even in repose, and she could feel her body quicken in involuntary response. "Are you ready for a little more honesty?" she continued quietly. "I still want you, Clay McMurphy. You're the sexiest man I've ever met, and just looking at you makes me hungry." Her soft mouth curved into a poignant, lopsided smile. "The only problem is, right now you're the very last thing I need in my life."

She turned away again and disappeared down the hall into the bathroom.

WHEN THEY STEPPED onto Clay's front porch, pools of rainwater dotted the decking, mirroring the startling blue of clean-washed sky. The air was warm and sweet and serene, but the sidewalk in front of the house was littered with ragged palm fronds ripped from the tall trees across the highway, testimony to the violence of the tempest that had passed in the night.

Long branches blocked the front steps. Christine watched Clay tread barefoot through the puddles, heaving aside the branches to clear a path for her. He was wearing only jeans and a thin shirt that he had donned hastily when she insisted she must leave, and as he worked, she tried not to notice the play of muscles across his back; it was far too easy to remember how those muscles had felt beneath her hands as she had clung to him in the darkness.

She stooped down to pick up one of the smaller limbs, gingerly avoiding the sharp serrations that edged the flat stem. "That storm certainly did make a mess," she observed lamely.

"There's always some litter after a big blow," Clay told her. "It's just one of the hazards of living beside the ocean. It's worse when it happens in the summertime, because then all the trash tourists have left beside the road winds up in my front yard. I've picked up everything from old paper cups to foil condom wrappers." He grimaced with distaste. "I don't know why it annoys me so much. After all these years you'd think I'd be used to the sheer delight people seem to take in polluting their environment."

Christine could think of little to say. Shifting her purse strap onto her shoulder, she commented, "Well, it does appear that it's going to be a beautiful day. The view from the restaurant should be spectacular. After a good rain, the hills always look so fresh and green."

Clay regarded her levelly. "So you're still absolutely determined to go into work today?"

"I have to. I'm the boss," Christine reminded him.

He scowled. "Are you sure you're going to be all right?"

"I don't see why not," Christine insisted. "Even though I'm late, my staff all know what they're supposed to do. When I telephoned to tell them I'd be delayed, Tish checked the reservation list for me. There's nothing special on the agenda except for a small anniversary party this evening—"

"Christine," Clay interrupted her sternly, "I wasn't talking about your restaurant. Are *you* going to be all right?"

She shrugged. "I expect so. While I'm in the hospital, there will be staff to take care of me, and if I schedule it right, Reese should return from Europe about the same time I'm discharged." She hesitated, looking worried. "Poor Reese. That's going to be some homecoming surprise."

Clay kicked at the pile of debris beside the walk. Shoving his hands into his jeans pockets, he muttered, "Don't do it that way, Christine. Don't wait until after the fact to tell him what's going on."

She gestured helplessly. "But I've already explained to you—"

"And you're wrong," Clay countered, biting out the words. The planes of his face looked sallow and taut with strain, and his eyes burned. When he spoke, the sounds seemed ripped from his throat. "If you love this man," he told her harshly, "then you'll call him before you check into the hospital. You may think you can shelter him from pain by keeping him in the dark, but in fact you're only being selfish and unfair. Don't shut Reese out. You owe him the right to decide for himself whether or not he wants to be there with you."

For several moments Christine mulled over Clay's statement. Then she asked, "I suppose you think it's selfish of me not to want to tell my mother, either?"

Clay shrugged stiffly. "I don't know. I don't know your mother. But I do know how hurt my own parents would be if I ever tried to hide news like yours from them."

Christine looked away. It really was a beautiful morning, she thought idly. The salt-perfumed breeze that danced inland from the ocean was mild and balmy, and the cloudless canopy overhead was a blue of such astonishing clarity that it almost seemed that if she squinted hard enough, she could glimpse the face of the Creator smiling back from the other side.

Christine couldn't recall having seen a sky quite so perfect since she was a girl, since the Labor Day picnic when she had won the three-legged race with her father....

She turned to Clay again and nodded in resignation. "Very well," she said quietly. "I promise that as soon as I go home to change, I'll telephone my mother. It won't be easy to break the news to her, but of course you're right—she'd want to know. However, I'll have to wait until later in the day and call Reese from the restaurant, because he's so busy with convention activities that he probably won't be back in his hotel room before late evening, Paris time."

Clay pulled his hands from his pockets and laid them gently on Christine's shoulders. "You're doing the right thing, I promise you," he assured her gravely.

"God, I hope so," she muttered. Her expression was as skeptical and disgruntled as her tone.

Clay gazed at her with hooded eyes. "Christine," he probed huskily, pressing his fingers through her thin shirt into her soft flesh, stroking the slim column of her throat with his thumbs, "when you do finally speak to Reese, are you planning to tell him about you and me?"

Her mouth felt very dry. Licking her parched lips, she swallowed and admitted hoarsely, "I don't know what I'm going to tell Reese—or when. I've had about all the emotional trauma I can handle for right now. I owe him a confession, or at least some sort of explanation, but for the love of me, I don't know how I'm supposed to explain what happened last night when I honestly don't understand it my—"

She broke off as a disturbing premonition suddenly occurred to her. Regarding Clay with apprehension, she ventured carefully, "You—you weren't thinking of telling Reese about us, were you?"

His eyes flashed. Dropping his hands from her shoulders, he smiled with mordant cynicism as he growled, "Lady, even bikers have *some* standards."

Christine felt her face sting with embarrassment. "I—I'm sorry," she stammered. "I didn't mean to—to—"

"Forget it," Clay said roughly, glancing past her. In tight-lipped silence he stared out toward the highway, as if fascinated by the parade of traffic that trundled by. Through his shadowy beard Christine could see a white line of strain edging his jaw.

"Please, Clay," she apologized awkwardly, "I didn't mean to insult you. You don't understand—"

"Oh, but I do," he countered, turning to face her once more. He relaxed visibly, and his expression softened. "I do understand, Christine," he repeated. "I probably understand better than you do." His tone was sympathetic, almost kindly. "I understand that with all the things you have to worry about right now, something has to go—and that something is me. I understand that you have prior commitments and loyalties you still intend to honor, regardless of what happened between the two of us last night. I understand that no matter how good we are together, all I really am to you, all I can ever be, is just a minor glitch, an aberration in your well-ordered life."

He paused. Christine saw his hand lift as if he were about to touch her again; it fell back to his side. Clay

said gruffly, "I wish you well, Christine Dryden.
Please don't kiss me goodbye."

He whirled away and stalked up the front steps,
slamming the door behind him.

"EXCUSE ME, ma'am, do you mind if I turn on the
television? I don't want to bother you, but it's almost
time for my favorite soap."

The tentative voice that pierced Christine's daze was
female and young, too young to be one of the nurses,
and it definitely did not belong to Dr. Patricia Fong,
Christine's oncologist. Groggily she opened her eyes,
half expecting to see a candy striper who'd sneaked
into the room for an unauthorized break. Instead she
registered with mild surprise that the second bed in her
semiprivate hospital room, empty ever since she'd
checked in three days earlier, now appeared to be oc-
cupied. The curtain separating the two beds was partly
drawn, blocking Christine's view of the other patient,
but she spotted a frilly bathrobe draped across the foot
of the other bed. Strewn over the robe was what
looked like an eclectic collection of comic books, romance novels, and teen magazines. Christine's eye-
lids drooped shut.

"Ma'am, the TV?" the girlish voice prompted
plaintively.

Forcing her lashes up once more, Christine struggled to shake off the lingering effects of her most recent dose of tranquilizers. She hated being sedated,
hated the oppressive, smothering blankness that settled over her mind whenever she was on medication,
but at least she'd been able to get some rest since
checking into the hospital. She had drowsed, only

marginally aware of the passage of time, almost able to forget the purpose of the battery of uncomfortable, sometimes humiliating, tests to which her body was being subjected.

One incident alone was clear in her memory. Prior to undergoing a CAT scan, Christine had been given an ultrasound exam, a routine precaution to make sure she wasn't pregnant. Because she'd always been very responsible about birth control, Christine knew perfectly well she wasn't pregnant, would have been shocked to learn otherwise, but when the radiologist announced that the results of her test were negative, something had twisted agonizingly inside her. Despite her resolve to endure the indignities forced upon her with stoic indifference, suddenly Christine had burst into tears, spilling out with blubbery sobs her fear that now she would never be able to have a baby....

The other patient spoke a third time, and Christine tried to sit up. The effort proved too much for her. Collapsing back against her pillow, she mumbled woozily, "The TV won't bother me. Go ahead and watch whatever you want."

"Thank you," her new roommate chirped, and Christine dozed again, lulled by swelling organ music and an announcer's sonorous baritone that spoke of sands through an hourglass. When at last she awakened completely, the curtain dividing the room had been pushed back against the wall. A birdlike girl in a nightshirt and oversize Oakland A's cap sat crosslegged on the other bed. An IV drip was attached to her wrist, and she was thumbing through a comic book.

"Hi there," the girl greeted brightly, laying aside her magazine. She gazed at Christine with huge, unearthly looking brown eyes. "It's about time you woke up. I was beginning to think you were going to sleep all day."

Christine blinked in confusion. "Uh—hi. I'm sorry if my sleeping so much bothered you. Was I snoring or something?"

"Oh, no," the girl said, shaking her head, causing the cap to ride down almost to her nose. "You sleep very nicely. It's just that it's so quiet in here, not like in Pediatrics. This is my first time to stay in an adult ward. I'm not sure I like it very much. I really ought to be with people my own age, but that wing has been swamped with a measles epidemic or something, so they had to put me over here. I hope you don't mind having a kid for a roomie."

"No, of course not," Christine murmured, studying her young companion thoughtfully. The girl's exact age was difficult to judge, but from the adolescent softness of her not-quite-defined features—and the cartoon character on her nightshirt—Christine guessed she couldn't be more than about fourteen. When she pushed up the bill of her baseball cap, Christine realized that the odd cast of those enormous dark eyes was due to the fact that they had no lashes. Christine also realized that the reason the hat sat so low on the girl's head was that she was bald.

Trying not to gawk, Christine quickly reiterated, "Of course I don't mind having you here. I'll enjoy the company."

The teenager grinned wryly. "Well, I'm afraid I won't be much company once they start my chemo in the morning, but until then I'll try not to be a pain. My name's Samantha Harris, by the way."

"I'm Christine Dryden." Struggling to suppress her instinctive shudder when she realized that this smiling child was a cancer patient undergoing the rigors of chemotherapy, Christine added hastily, "I'm sure we'll get along just fine," and automatically she stretched out her hand. An arrow of pain shot through her body. "Oh, damn," she gasped.

Samantha looked alarmed. "What's wrong?"

Christine sighed. Through the thickness of her hospital gown, she touched the bulky dressing padding her armpit, the adhesive tapes that impeded the motion of her shoulder. "Every time I try to move my arm, I'm forcibly reminded that I had a biopsy performed yesterday," she explained. "I guess I must be an idiot. Even though I've never been in a hospital before, I should have known better, but after the way people kept assuring me it was only minor surgery, it never occurred to me that it was going to *hurt*."

Wrinkling her nose, Samantha observed wisely, "Yeah, the first couple of days are always kind of rough. But don't worry, you'll probably be heaps better by tomorrow."

Her sympathy made Christine feel like a wimp. When she considered what Samantha would soon be undergoing—and obviously not for the first time—she knew she had no right to complain just because her stitches were raw. Praying she was able to match the girl's insouciant tone, Christine agreed lightly, "I'm sure you're right, or at least I hope you are. I'm supposed to be discharged tomorrow. Just picking up my overnight bag is going to be a struggle. Heaven help me when I try to drive!''

To Christine's amazement, her casual quip appeared to genuinely shock the teenager. Samantha exclaimed in dismay, ''Good grief, you mean you're going to have to go home *alone?* Don't you have anybody to help you?''

''I'm afraid not,'' Christine murmured, unaccountably abashed. She found herself making excuses for absent loved ones. ''Lots of people wanted to be here with me,'' she insisted, preferring not to explain that they'd stayed away at her insistence. When Christine broke the news to her mother on the telephone, Meg had become almost hysterical, and it was only by imploring Jeff, her stepfather, to reason with his wife that Christine had been able to prevent the woman from hopping on the next jet out of Frankfurt. Reese had been just as distressed as Christine's mother, but he reacted with a little more composure, and in the end he agreed to complete his tour of France according to the original timetable, if that was what Christine truly wanted him to do.

Christine repeated, ''Lots of people wanted to be here with me while I'm in the hospital, but my family lives in Europe, and my fiancé's off on a business trip, and there's really very little they could do for me, anyway.'' She indicated the several lavish bouquets that flanked her bed, gifts from Reese, her family, Reese's family in Beverly Hills, and the staff of La Courgette. ''Everybody sent flowers,'' she added lamely.

Dubiously Samantha eyed the elaborate sprays of roses, carnations and gladioli. ''Very pretty,'' she muttered. "When my mom and dad get back here from taking my little brother over to Grandma's, they'll probably bring me balloons, or maybe a new video cartridge." She picked up her comic book and immersed herself once more.

Aware that she had failed somehow in the opinion of her young roommate, Christine sighed and pressed the control switch that raised the head of her bed. As she tried to make herself comfortable, she glanced again at the gorgeous blooms that surrounded her. The flowers *were* very pretty, their lush colors breathtaking, their combined perfumes a heady counterpoint to the sterile hospital air. Unfortunately the wire-service arrangements also struck Christine as stiff, impersonal, and just the teeniest bit funereal. She wondered why it never occurred to anybody to send her balloons or a fun, fast-moving video game.

Settling back on her pillows, Christine shook her head remorsefully. If she was feeling lonesome and neglected at the moment, she had no one to blame but herself. The only reason those flowers had been selected from florists' order books, with tender, encouraging notes penned by strange hands, was that she had made it impossible for her loved ones to do otherwise. She couldn't have it both ways. She couldn't deliberately keep the people she cared about at arm's length and then complain because they weren't closer. And it was definitely time to let them get closer. Regardless of the ultimate results of the tests that were being performed on her, the stay in the hospital had convinced Christine of one thing: it was time for her to forget her lingering qualms and make everybody happy by regularizing her relationship with Reese.

They should have married years ago. They belonged together. And once they were together, everything would fall into place, finally make sense—including that bewildering, uncharacteristic fling with Clay.

WATCHING SAMANTHA chatter happily with her parents made Christine feel like an intruder, so she shifted her gaze back to the dinner tray in front of her and picked through a dog-eared copy of *Sunset* magazine that one of the hospital volunteers had dug up when Christine realized she'd forgotten to pack any reading material in her overnight bag. Skimming the recipe section with professional interest, she mentally noted a couple of clever garnishing ideas that she might suggest to Amir once she returned to La Courgette, but unfortunately, thinking of the restaurant only made her conscious of the vast gulf between the meal on her tray and the standard of cuisine she was accustomed to.

"Is the food in this place as gruesome as it looks?" a deep voice with a peculiar roughness queried softly, and Christine jerked up her head to gape at Clay. She felt herself beaming with surprise and delight as the burden of her self-imposed isolation lifted.

Dressed in his usual uniform of jeans, leather jacket and motorcycle boots, Clay looked vibrant and alive against the antiseptic background of the hospital room. Samantha's father, noticing the newcomer, rose from his chair and drew the curtain between the beds to give them some privacy.

"Oh, Clay, it's good to see you," Christine exclaimed, too happy to dissemble. "I never expected—

I thought—how did you know where to find me, anyway?"

Clay shrugged. "I stopped by your restaurant," he said laconically. "One of the waitresses told me where you were."

Something about his clipped words unsettled Christine. Her animation faded slightly when she recalled the terms on which they'd parted. Dropping her lashes, she made a show of replacing the covers on her dinner tray and pushing the bed table aside. As she closed her magazine and laid it on the nightstand, she confessed tonelessly, "I didn't think you'd want to see me again."

"Neither did I," Clay said. He loomed over her, his hands shoved into the pockets of his zippered jacket, which seemed bulkier than usual. He was vibrantly sexy, incredibly dear, and Christine couldn't begin to imagine what he was thinking. With narrowed eyes he scanned the flowers that banked her bed. "If you prefer me not to stay, I'll understand," he said tightly. "I don't want to make things awkward for you."

Christine felt her heart lurch. He couldn't go, not yet. No matter how crazy the idea was, especially now that she'd finally made up her mind to marry Reese, she needed Clay to be with her for just a little while. "Please stay," she urged. "I've been so lonesome."

Clay scowled. "No visitors?"

"I called everybody just the way I promised you I would," Christine insisted. "Reese and my mother both agreed that there was no need for them to dash back to California to be with me."

"You mean they stayed away because you told them that was what you wanted them to do," Clay countered acutely.

Christine felt her cheeks grow warm. "I guess they did, at that," she conceded in a tiny voice. "It seemed like a good idea at the time."

She patted the edge of her bed. Clay perched beside her, his muscular leg only inches from her hip. The mattress shifted beneath his weight, and Christine slid closer, until she could feel his radiant warmth through her thin blanket. For a moment she could think of nothing to say to him. "How's work?" she ventured feebly.

Shrugging, Clay said, "It's okay. Denny and I took the boat out yesterday, but when we reached the quadrant where we'd planned to dive, the water was still so turbid from all the sediment stirred up by that storm last week, that we ended up returning to port without ever even putting on our wet suits."

"Oh. That's too bad," Christine murmured. She fell silent, trying not to remember all the other things that had been stirred up by the storm....

Clay regarded her somberly. "What about you? Is the staff here treating you all right? I notice you didn't eat much."

"I'm sort of out of the habit. Until this morning I was being fed intravenously." Spreading her hands to reveal the purple blotches dotting the soft skin on the inside of both forearms, Christine explained lightly, "They kept dribbling nutrients into one arm and drawing blood out of the other. I told my doctor I thought it'd be a lot easier for everybody if they just eliminated me from the loop and went directly from one tube to the other, but she—''

Christine broke off, aware that Clay was staring at the marks on her arms. Self-consciously she tugged up the top sheet to cover the contusions, while she forced a chuckle and declared nonchalantly, "It's not as bad as it appears, Clay. This fair skin of mine has always tended to bruise dramatically at the least little bump. During my tomboy days I usually looked as if someone had laid into me with a two-by-four. I'm all right, really."

His gaze bored into hers, and suddenly she knew the time for teasing had passed. "*Are* you all right, Christine?" he probed. "Are you, really?"

She took a deep, ragged breath. "I don't know," she admitted frankly. "I won't know until all the test results are in, several days from now."

"What are you going to do in the meantime?"

Christine considered the question at length. Twining the hem of her sheet around her fingers, she said, "For starters, as soon as I'm sprung from this joint tomorrow, I'm going to head home, where I intend to give myself a shampoo and a manicure and scarf down an entire Chicago-style pizza. Then, the next day, assuming I'm feeling a lot less sore than I do now, I'm going to the restaurant to find out whether that manager I hired to fill in for me deserves the hefty salary he demanded." She paused. Lifting her head to meet Clay's eyes squarely, she added, "Then, on the day after that, I'm going to pick up Reese at the airport and tell him I've finally decided it's time for us to get married."

Clay did not flinch, but Christine could have sworn that the lines on his weathered face were suddenly deeper and more pronounced. "I see," he murmured, his tone carefully neutral. "I'm sure you're making the decision that's best for you." He rose to his feet. "Well, I can tell you're tired, so I won't bother you any longer. I just wanted to see how you were doing."

Knowing she could not stop him this time, Christine said simply, "Your visit means a lot to me, Clay. Thank you for coming."

"Always glad to oblige," he muttered. Despite his announced intention to leave, he seemed reluctant to walk away. Rocking on the thick heels of his boots, he lingered at her bedside, his deep blue gaze darting restlessly. He stared at the long-stemmed red roses that, perhaps too predictably, Reese had dispatched from Paris. "Sorry I didn't get you any flowers," Clay said distantly. "I meant to, but I wasn't sure how to carry them on the back of the bike."

"That's all right—" Christine began automatically, but suddenly Clay interrupted her.

"Oh, hell," he declared impatiently, "I almost forgot. I don't know where my mind has been the past few days." He jerked down the zipper tab of his jacket and reached inside. "I did bring you something, after all. I hope you like it. I've been carrying the silly thing around with me since this morning." With a flourish he produced a small purple plush walrus and dropped it into Christine's lap.

With its gaudy nylon fur, plastic tusks, and the slightly loopy grin stitched beneath its button nose, the doll was ridiculous and utterly adorable. Christine felt her eyes sting. While she gaped in confusion and delight at the unexpected gift, Clay explained huskily, "I didn't know how you'd feel about stuffed animals, but I thought this one was kind of cute. I looked all over for an elephant seal, but apparently nobody makes them. I hope you'll settle for a walrus. If it matters, at least they're in the same suborder, Pinnipedia..."

Squeezing her lashes tight against the tears that threatened, Christine picked up the doll and stroked it luxuriously against her cheek. She could smell the musky scent of Clay's body in the soft plush fur. "Oh, darling, it's perfectly wonderful," she murmured, opening her eyes again to smile up at him.

He was gone.

CHAPTER FIVE

CHRISTINE SPOTTED Reese's flaxen hair gleaming like a beacon above the heads of the other passengers swarming up the jet way—a beacon that promised sanctuary, comfortable domesticity, all the things she'd deluded herself into believing she was too independent to really need. Aching with longing, she wormed her way through the milling crowd to greet him. They met at the top of the ramp. Reese was so weighed down with carry-on luggage and purchases from the duty-free shop in the Paris airport that when Christine raised on tiptoe to kiss him, he could only bend his head and gently graze his lips across her mouth. She settled back on her feet, almost colliding with a very pregnant woman who dashed past, squealing shrilly, and flung herself into the outstretched arms of a gawky young man in a khaki uniform.

"Hey, lover," Christine murmured provocatively, trying to take the garment bag Reese carried slung over his shoulder, "why don't you let me relieve you of some of this load so you can kiss me properly?"

Reese scanned the throng that swirled around them, and his grip tightened on the handles. "I think I'd better hang on to my own stuff for the moment," he told Christine. "Anything I set down in this mob is liable to get trampled or else disappear."

Christine felt rebuffed. "But it's been so long..."

At her disgruntled expression, Reese grinned. "I know, sweetheart, I know. If you'll just be patient, there'll be lots of time for kissing later—but in the meantime, I really think we'll get out of this madhouse faster if I do the carrying. Besides—" his hazel eyes narrowed, and he studied her slender figure comprehensively "—you look tired."

"You sure don't," Christine rejoined, choosing to ignore the unspoken question in his words. There would be ample opportunity later to discuss her health. With deliberate brightness she declared, "You look so rested and relaxed that it's downright disgusting. After spending sixteen hours on a plane, at the very least you ought to be a little rumpled."

"Sorry about that," Reese quipped. He scanned the crowd and scowled. Hoisting the garment bag higher on his shoulder, he suggested, "I suppose we'd better get a move on. It's going to take forever to clear Customs, but the sooner we start, the sooner we'll be out of this place—"

"And stuck in a traffic jam on the freeway," Christine finished with a pout. "The congestion is really miserable today, near gridlock."

Reese laughed. "So what else is new? Poor Chris, no wonder you look down. Tell you what—just to prove how much I love you, I'll drive us home. After you've seen my imitation of a French taxi driver, I guarantee you'll be too scared to think about being tired!"

In Christine's Nissan, deep in the bowels of the parking garage, they kissed as ardently as two people in bucket seats separated by a gearshift could manage, but their embrace was interrupted by the approach of a large family with several boisterous youngsters. Chattering excitedly in some foreign tongue, the people piled into a van parked in the slot directly alongside Christine's. As the children loitered, a couple of small faces turned to stare curiously through the windows of the car. Reese and Christine pulled apart. "Cute kids," Reese muttered, settling back behind the steering wheel.

Christine nodded and adjusted her seat belt. She wondered why she had the suspicion that Reese had almost welcomed the intrusion.

Despite Reese's promise to entertain Christine with anecdotes about his trip, he was unusually quiet during the endless drive north from the airport, through the city of San Francisco. Christine noticed that whenever she prompted him with queries about Paris, his answers tended to die out half-spoken. By the time they crossed the Golden Gate Bridge into Marin County, he hadn't uttered a dozen complete sentences. Studying Reese's somber expression, Christine decided that his journey had tired him more than he was willing to admit; the poor guy was probably suffering from a major case of jet lag. She reached over to squeeze his leg sympathetically. Conversation could be postponed. For now it was enough just to have the man she loved at her side once more, it was enough for them to be together.

In the entryway of his condominium, Reese dropped his bags in the center of the lush kilim rug and announced with a grunt of relief, "Lord, it's good to be home! As much as I love Europe, these conventions do have a way of wearing one down. The past two weeks have been rough."

"The past two weeks haven't exactly been a picnic for anyone," Christine murmured.

Reese winced. "Oh, hell, Chris, I'm sorry," he said with compunction. "After all you've been through, I must sound like a real jerk, selfish and insensitive." He held out his hands to her, and she went to him, nuzzling her face in the lapels of his jacket. His lips brushed her hair. "Poor baby," Reese crooned. "Has it been so very awful?"

"Pretty awful," Christine admitted, closing her eyes to savor the familiar heat and texture of his body. "I never knew I had so many nooks and crannies, until people started poking around in them."

"Well, I'm certain everything they did was for your own good," Reese assured her stoutly.

Christine sighed. "Of course, I don't know what right I have to complain. I was only in the hospital for a few tests. The night before they discharged me, a girl was moved into my room, a leukemia patient. Her name was Samantha, and she seemed like a bright, sweet kid, but it broke my heart to look at her. Fourteen years old, as thin as a rail, and chemotherapy has caused her to lose all her hair. Dear God, when you think of what she's been through already in her short life—"

Reese's arms clamped convulsively around Christine. "Don't think about it!" he growled. "There's nothing you can do for that girl, so don't upset yourself more by worrying about her. You're through with the hospital, and I want you to put the entire experience out of your mind. *It's all over now.*"

Christine grew very still. Lifting her head away from the jacket, she stared up into her fiancé's face and said quietly, "We don't know that, Reese. The test results aren't in yet. Until my doctor tells me differently, for all we know I may be as sick as Samantha."

She watched in astonishment as Reese's cool patrician features twisted with fierce emotion, anger and disbelief and denial. She could feel his body shake. *"No!"* he almost shouted. "You're not sick! I refuse to believe it. It's all been a stupid, hateful mistake. You know how doctors are these days, the way they go overboard with tests to protect themselves from malpractice suits. Why, even my dad—"

"Reese, darling, please calm down!" Christine cried out in anguish. Covering his mouth with her fingers to still his tirade, she repeated more gently, "Darling, please. God knows I hope you're right. More than anything in the world, I want this to all be a mistake—yet we must face the possibility that it isn't. There's nothing to be gained by hiding from the truth."

He captured her hand and pressed his lips urgently into her palm. Against her skin he muttered, "What is the truth? The truth is that you're a beautiful, perfectly healthy woman—anyone can see that by just looking at you."

"But sometimes looks can be deceiving," Christine reminded him.

Reese flinched. As Christine gazed up at him, he seemed to contract, draw into himself. Releasing her hand, he squinted as if in intense pain; when he looked at her again, his expression was shuttered. Stretching his arms until the joints creaked, Reese rolled his head around his shoulders and began massaging the back of his neck with his knuckles. With a windy yawn he told Christine, "Listen, sweetheart, I know this isn't the way either one of us envisioned my homecoming, but will you be terribly offended if I don't invite you to spend the night tonight? I'm worn-out, and as much as I want you, I'm afraid I'd be a real dud."

"We don't have to make love," Christine said, realizing with amazement that she felt relieved. If she was honest with herself, she had to admit that she was no more in the mood for sex than Reese appeared to be. Still, she'd been certain that once they were together again, she'd finally be able to make sense of the bewildering events of the past few days—*all* the events. In a tiny voice she suggested hopefully, "We could just hold each other and talk."

Reese smiled ironically. "Yeah, sure. Do you really think I could hold you without trying to make love to you?"

"Then how about just talking?" Christine asked. "We have an awful lot to discuss."

"That's a lovely idea," Reese concurred in a voice suddenly balmy with charm, "but not for tonight." Gently he drew her back against him and framed her face with his hands. "I'm sorry, darling, but please do as I ask. You're too much of a distraction, and I—I need some time to think."

Christine's throat felt tight with hurt. "Okay, if that's what you want," she said softly.

Reese pressed his lips delicately against hers, kissing her as if she were made of porcelain, as if she were too fragile to touch. As if he were afraid of her.

He whispered, "Thank you for being so understanding, Christine. I love you."

"I love you, too," she said. The words stuck in her throat.

She stepped back away from him and glanced around for her handbag. "Now what did I do with my purse?" she muttered distractedly. "If you're going to get some rest, I guess I'd better be taking off now. I'll see you at the restaurant tomorrow. There's nothing we need to talk about that can't wait till then."

No, there's nothing that can't wait, she repeated to herself as she slid behind the wheel of her Nissan and began the solitary drive away from the waterfront to her own house in the hills. *Nothing at all.* Suddenly she knew she would never tell Reese she was ready to marry him.

"OH, HI, Clay," Liberty Abrams greeted him with a start, glancing up in surprise from her computer terminal when Clay ambled into the Institute's main office. He was dressed for the water, in cutoffs and deck shoes, and his thick mane hung damp and dark around his face. Lib said, "I didn't realize you and Denny were back already. I didn't hear the pickup. How'd the dive go? Any finds today?"

Clay grimaced. "You mean apart from the usual soda cans and other garbage we always spot on the ocean floor? I'm afraid not, hon. Denny took the water samples to the lab, but there's no reason to think anything new will show up when we analyze them."

"That's too bad," Lib said, tossing back the grizzled brown hair that fell straight to her waist. The jerky movement of her head caused the Turkish coins on her long earrings to jingle. She continued, "I didn't expect you two to be onshore again before dark. Some woman has telephoned for you several times in the past hour. I could have forwarded the call to the marina, if I'd realized you were already back. Instead, I guess you'd better check your voice-mail."

Clay grinned at his friend. Lib was Dr. Berlinger's secretary and the Institute's office manager, and despite the fact that her taste in clothing and music remained unchanged from when she'd been a student at Berkeley in the mid-sixties, on the job she was completely at ease with current technology. With a laugh Clay told her, "You can blame your husband for our premature return. I was all set to keep diving for another hour, but he insisted we quit early. He mentioned something about having to go shop for paper plates. I didn't understand that at all. I thought you were morally opposed to disposables."

Lib made a glum face. "We are—but in a case like this, disposable dishes are preferable to the alternative. Denny's mother is flying in from New Jersey on Sunday, which means he and I have two days to make our place pass muster as a kosher household."

Clay looked interested. "Is that really a problem? Since you guys are vegetarians—"

"Oh, it's more than just the food," Lib said. "Believe me, where my mother-in-law is concerned, the easiest way out is just to buy paper plates."

Nodding sympathetically, Clay said, "Well, good luck, dear. At least paper's recyclable." He paused.

"Did this person who kept calling for me tell you what she wanted?"

Resuming her professional attitude at the change of subject, Lib shook her head. "She wouldn't give me her name. All she said was that it was important she speak to you. Eventually I gave her your extension number and suggested she leave a message on your machine. I don't know whether she did or not."

"I guess I'd better go check," Clay muttered. "Thanks, Lib."

"Anytime," she replied. When Clay turned and headed for the cubbyhole that served as his personal work space, Lib called after him, "By the way, that report you wanted from the University of California is on your desk. I had them fax it to me."

In his tiny, cluttered office, Clay saw that the light on his answering machine was not blinking. The woman who'd telephoned repeatedly had left no message. Clay scowled. He wondered who she was. The first answer that leaped to mind, he rejected instantly. He refused to torment himself with wishful thinking. Christine wasn't going to call him. She'd turned to him only because he happened to be on hand during a moment of crisis, and now the crisis was over—or, at least, his part in it was. Whatever happened to Christine now, whether or not her worst fears were confirmed, she had Reese to help her. She'd made her choice, and even Clay had to admit that Christine's decision had been the only rational one....

Settling behind his desk, Clay picked up the report Lib had obtained for him, a study on lead contamination in sea otters, and he began to thumb through it. As he had for days, he hoped to sublimate his per-

sonal anxiety with hard work. If he concentrated his
frustration and rage on battling the government
shortsightedness and corporate indifference that
threatened the animals he loved, then maybe he could
forget that a woman he loved was being threatened by
forces he was helpless to combat.

He read until Lib knocked and poked her head into
his office. "Clay, are you planning on hanging around
here much longer?" she asked. "It's getting late.
Denny finished up in the lab, and he and I are about
ready to take off. The volunteers have fed the animals
and departed, and Dr. Berlinger left hours ago. That
leaves just you."

Stretching stiffly, Clay told his friend, "Oh, I
thought I might stay here and wade through the rest of
the report. It's really fascinating. They've taken otter
teeth dug up in archaeological excavations and compared them to modern—"

Lib interrupted him sternly. "Clay McMurphy, it's
Friday night. You've been pushing yourself like crazy
lately. It's time for a little rest and recreation."

Clay tried to parry the motherly reprimand. "Liberty, darlin', I just spent a whole day on a boat. Most
people would consider that R and R."

"Most people wouldn't use that day searching for
toxic waste dumps," Lib countered with a sniff.
Brushing back a wing of long graying hair, she admonished candidly, "Please, Clay, the only reason I'm
saying this is that Denny and I both love you like a
brother, but I want you to pay attention. It's been five
years since your divorce. Don't you think it's high time
you started dating again? I'm not talking about a casual fling with some chick you meet at a bike rally—I

mean dating seriously. There is more to life than motorcycles and marine mammals. You need to find yourself a good woman.''

With great care Clay marked his place in the report he'd been reading and centered the folder on his desk. Staring at it, he told Lib hoarsely, ''I couldn't agree with you more. I agree with you so much that I actually did go out and find myself that good woman I need.'' When he looked up at his friend again, the despondent expression in his blue eyes did not match the mocking twist of his lips. ''There's just one problem. She doesn't need me.''

After changing into his riding gear and locking up the office, Clay took a final stroll through the compound, something he customarily did whenever he was the last person to leave the Institute. Twice before dawn a private patrol car would swing past on its rounds, but Clay always rested better after assuring himself to his own satisfaction that the creatures he cared for were safely bedded down for the night. Slowly he made his way among the pens, stepping cautiously to prevent his steel-toed boots from clattering on the concrete and disturbing the sleeping animals. The stark shadows cast by the mercury-vapor lamps ringing the area sometimes made it difficult for Clay to see the inhabitants of the individual enclosures, but he knew them all well: a pregnant harbour seal recovering from a close encounter with a boat propeller; a California sea lion that had been found stranded near San Luis Obispo, suffering *grand mal* seizures; Moonie, the elephant seal... Clay gazed down at the drowsing beast, a huge, shapeless mass in the unnatural light. After more than six weeks in cap-

tivity, the elephant seal's condition had not improved—but at least it had not deteriorated, either.
That was something to be grateful for, Clay supposed
humbly, considering the precious little that biologists
like himself actually knew about marine mammals. In
their ignorance of basic information such as how the
animals' immune systems worked, it was probably a
miracle that any of the creatures survived their cap-
tors' bungling attempts to help.

Clay shivered. It was still happening, he realized
grimly. Despite his mentor's stern warning weeks ago
and Lib's counsel now, Clay was still letting his job get
to him, courting burnout. He definitely needed a
change of scenery. He needed to go somewhere, do
something that had no connection with his work. Clay
thought about his friends frantically preparing for the
arrival of Denny's mother, and he recalled suddenly
that Hester and Frank McMurphy's thirty-seventh
wedding anniversary was coming up before too long.
Clay wondered what Dr. Berlinger would say if he
asked for a week's vacation. There was just about
enough room left on his credit card to finance a trip to
Florida.

Feeling his spirits lift in anticipation of his parents'
reaction to a surprise visit from their long-lost son,
Clay left the animal pens and headed toward the main
entrance of the compound. One of the bushy cy-
presses that flanked the gate had been so severely
damaged by the storm a couple of weeks earlier that
Dr. Berlinger had reluctantly decided to have the tree
cut down; limbs and brush awaiting removal now were
stacked high on the sidewalk in an aromatic heap that
obscured the view of the parking lot. After Clay made

certain the gate was locked securely behind him, he dodged the woodpile, suddenly grateful for his leather jacket; away from the makeshift windbreak, the salty night breeze was nippy. He started to lope across the vacant asphalt to the spot where he'd parked his Harley at the base of one of the lamp standards. He froze in midstride. His motorcycle was not the only vehicle in the lot. Beside it in the pool of light stood a silver gray Nissan sedan. In the sedan, her head bent over the steering wheel, was Christine.

Clay groaned. He did not have to see her face to know why she was there.

He started to run. The ringing of his boots on the pavement caught Christine's attention. Lifting her head, she spotted him, and then the door of her car was flung open and she ran, too, stumbling in her haste. When they collided, Clay wrapped his arms around her too-slender body and half lifted her off the ground to cushion the impact. "You're here, you're here!" she sobbed, burying her face against his shoulder. "Thank God! Your secretary said—I was so afraid—I need—no one else to talk to—" Muffled by Clay's jacket, the broken phrases were little more than incoherent whimpers—all except for one word that was all too chillingly clear.

He held her welded in his arms until she calmed, and then he set her down with care. "When did you find out?" he asked.

"This—this afternoon," Christine stammered, "sometime after four, maybe four-thirty. Usually I'm not even home by then, but I had to go into work at five this morning to supervise the installation of a new stove. I'd only just stepped through my front door when—when Dr. Fong telephoned.''

Despite Christine's pallor and the quaver in her voice, Clay thought she appeared fairly steady on her feet, and he allowed himself to relax a little. He probed, "This Dr. Fong—he called you personally?"

"*She*—Patricia Fong," Christine corrected Clay tonelessly. "She's one of the finest oncologists in northern California and, yes, she gave me the news herself, so there's no point in hoping the message got garbled by a subordinate. Dr. Fong is sending my records to another physician, in case I want a second opinion, but she told me the test results look conclusive. I have cancer."

Clay's oath was succinct and obscene. Christine said, "Yeah. That's the way I feel, too."

Even in the harsh, unflattering light she was still beautiful, Clay thought as he studied her shadowed features—a little pale, a trifle too thin, yet there was nothing about her appearance that couldn't be dismissed as a whim of fashion, nothing at all to hint to the casual onlooker that Christine was gravely ill. With dread Clay wondered how long it would be before, inevitably, the disease began to show.

He exhaled raggedly and asked, "So what happens now?"

Christine flashed a ghastly smile. "The usual, I suppose—radiation, chemotherapy." Her fingers strayed to her sleek, fair hair. "Maybe—maybe I'll go bald...."

"Not every chemo patient loses his hair," Clay asserted.

"I know," Christine admitted drearily, "and I guess it's a stupid, vain thing to worry about, considering the alternative.... In any case, I'm supposed to see Dr. Fong Monday to work out the gory details. She did say that it appears we've caught it early."

Clay nodded. "You're lucky. Early detection is certainly a point in your favor."

She could not keep the bitterness out of her voice. "Oh, yes, I'm very lucky, aren't I? Just think of all the fun I'm going to have these next few months—the same fun my poor father went through—"

"That was nearly twenty years ago," Clay cut in sharply, recognizing the very real fear that fueled Christine's uncharacteristic sarcasm. "Things have changed since then. Heaven knows cancer is still scary, but nowadays lots of people are able to beat it."

She looked at him miserably, abandoning her brittle mockery. "Oh, Clay, I'm only thirty-two years old!"

"Christine, you're going to be all right," Clay declared staunchly. "You've got everything going for you. You're young and strong, the disease has been detected early, you've got a good doctor and a loving, supportive family to help you pull through. Of course you're going to be all right." He paused. "You don't have to take my word for it. Surely your fiancé must have said the same thing when you told him."

Christine said, "I haven't told Reese yet."

In his astonishment, Clay gave up all attempts to dissemble. *"What?"* he gasped.

The bad light could not disguise the hot color flooding Christine's wan cheeks. Biting her lip, she repeated, "I haven't told Reese yet. I haven't told anyone—except you."

For several moments Clay did not trust himself to speak. When he was able to choke out the words, his voice sounded unnaturally low, gravelly. "Why?" he demanded. "Why the hell have you come to me now instead of Reese?"

His obvious bitterness startled Christine. Gazing up at him with round pleading eyes, she floundered, "I— I can't explain it. I—I guess it's because—because you're so easy to talk to—"

Clay erupted. "Goddammit, Christine, I am not a bartender! I am also not your personal confessor or some kind of trained eunuch—as you have excellent reason to know—so don't make the mistake of thinking you can treat me like one! You cannot simply waltz into my life and dump your problems on me because I'm easy to talk to!"

Bewildered by his fulminating anger, she recoiled. "But—"

Her retreat only infuriated Clay further. Seizing her shoulders and hauling her back against him, he barked, "And don't cringe like some damned shrinking violet! You're gutsier than that—" All at once he broke off, suddenly aware that he was yelling into her ashen face only inches from his, that his punishing grip was bruising her soft skin. He jerked away, swearing at himself. "Oh, Lord, I'm sorry, Christine," he exclaimed contritely. "I didn't mean to hurt you."

She watched him warily as she crossed her arms over her chest and rubbed her aching shoulders. "Nobody—ever means—to hurt anybody," she said, the words coming out in raspy puffs, "but they do, anyway."

Her tone troubled Clay. "Has Reese hurt you?" he asked deliberately, knowing the wrong answer would send him gunning for the tall blond restaurateur.

"Reese hasn't touched me," Christine said.

Clay's eyes narrowed. "What do you mean?"

She sighed forlornly. "I mean he hasn't touched me, not since he returned from his trip. He acts as if he's afraid I might be contagious or something. If I didn't know better, I'd almost think he's waiting for my doctor to issue me a clean bill of health before he makes love to me again." Gesturing helplessly, she added, "Can you imagine how he's going to react when, instead, I tell him I actually am sick?"

Clay knew he ought to be ashamed of the relief that flooded through him at Christine's artless announcement. He knew that in a moment of crisis, a man with the gentlemanly instincts she'd always credited to him would put aside all petty jealousy. The only problem was, Clay was no gentleman and there was nothing the least bit petty about the jealousy he felt where Christine was concerned. From that moment in the restaurant when he'd had to stand back and watch Reese Cagney smile his smarmy smile and put his lily-white hands on her, Clay had experienced a rivalry, a sense of outraged possessiveness, that was fiercely primitive. Clay wanted Christine. He'd had her. He was going to have her again—and this time he was going to keep her.

Aloud he said gruffly, "Listen, lady, if you're trying to ask me how to get Reese back into your bed, please don't."

Startled by his blunt words, Christine blushed. "I don't want Reese in my bed," she mumbled uncomfortably. "It's over between us."

"What do you mean, over?" Clay demanded. "Less than a week ago, you told me you were going to marry him."

She shook her head. "I was wrong. When Reese came home from France, I fully intended to tell him that I was finally ready to set the day for the wedding. I think that in the back of my mind I thought that if I was a good girl and did what everybody wanted me to, I'd be rewarded and the cancer scare would turn out to be a bad dream or something. But when it came time to say the words, I just couldn't. I don't know why."

"Don't you?"

She stared breathlessly at Clay. "No, I..." she began, only to have her voice trail away. As Clay watched, a subtle change came over her face, a wonder, a dawning revelation, and it occurred to him with deflating irony that despite everything that had passed between the two of them since they met at La Courgette, only now was Christine truly seeing him for the first time. She blinked.

"I should have known," she murmured hollowly. A faint line appeared between her eyes as she remembered. "The night we—that night at your place, you told me you loved me, but I didn't pay any attention to you. I'm sorry."

"Don't worry about it. You had other things on your mind," Clay pointed out dryly. It was easy to sound magnanimous now that he was sure he'd won. He cupped his hand around her cheek, and his heart lurched when, almost instinctively, she closed her eyes and nuzzled her face into his palm. Her skin was warm and velvety in the cool night air. As his fingertips shaped the graceful, fragile line of her jaw, he added gently, "Besides, Christine, are you really so sure you didn't listen to what I said? I think maybe a part of you heard what your mind wasn't yet ready to accept."

When she lifted her lashes again, her expression was unguarded, her tone a little wistful. "I don't believe in love at first sight," she admitted candidly, "but I suppose maybe I must be falling in love with you, too. It doesn't make a whole lot of sense. You and I scarcely know each other. Reese and I have been together for more than ten years. I expected to be with him forever."

Clay let his hand drop away from her face. "When I married Belinda, I expected it to last forever," he noted. "Sometimes, even with the best intentions in the world, relationships simply run out of steam."

Christine fell silent again, and Clay stood patiently. He knew the grudging confession she had just made confused and frightened her; despite the attraction she felt, she was still skittish around him. And regardless of how deliciously easy it might be for Clay to yank her into his arms again and vanquish her insecurities with sheer physical passion, he resisted the temptation. He wanted Christine's love, not her submission.

Wrinkling her nose, she muttered, "Our timing really is the pits, you know."

"I know," Clay agreed gravely. "The last thing you need to worry about right now is a new love affair."

Christine regarded him askance. "Is that what you want, an affair?"

Clay shook his head. "No."

She looked baffled. "What, then?"

His expression was enigmatic. "Well," he said slowly, "I suppose I could say I want to be part of your life. I could say I want to take you to bed and bury myself in you so deep that both of us forget we were ever two separate people—but I won't. What I want isn't very important right now. The only thing that matters is getting you well again. So, for the moment, at least, I'll settle for whatever you're willing to give me. I won't make any demands."

Christine laughed skeptically. "I'll bet."

Encouraged by the only spark of humor she'd evinced all evening, Clay amended, "All right, I admit that there is one demand I'm going to make of you...."

Her amusement faded. "What is it?"

With care Clay laced his fingers into the sleek, fair hair at her temples. He studied her features intently. Taking a deep breath, he said, "I'm a jealous man, Christine. I want you to make a clean break from Reese."

He watched her eyes widen, and he realized with dismay that Christine was just now beginning to consider the wider implications of terminating her engagement. Perhaps his victory wasn't quite as assured as he'd presumed. She said, "But Reese and I work together."

"I don't give a damn about you working together," Clay dismissed, trying to sound undaunted. "Your professional involvement is none of my concern. It's your emotional involvement that I'm worried about.''

"What makes you think the two can be separated?" Christine asked bluntly. "He and I were lovers before we became business partners."

Clay's mouth tightened. "I can't answer that question for you. I only know that the future for you and me already looks murky enough without lies clouding it, as well."

Christine did not respond at once. As Clay waited, it occurred to him that one of the most pivotal and intensely personal dialogues of his life, the sort of tête-à-tête traditionally conducted against a background of violins and roses, was being played out in the center of a dark cheerless parking lot, while he and the woman he was courting shivered in the night air. He wished he could find the situation funny.

At last Christine spoke. "You're right, Clay, of course you are. I have to speak to Reese. After so many years, it's not going to be easy, but I must do it."

Clay exhaled painfully. He hadn't realized he'd been holding his breath. He bent his head to hers and kissed her with gentle restraint. The time for passion would come later, after old bonds had been severed. Clay ventured, "When you talk to Reese, do you want me to be there with you?"

Christine lowered her lashes. "No, Clay," she said somberly. "Thank you, but no. Considering how much I've wronged him already, the very least I owe him is the courtesy of breaking up in private. But first I have to tell him about the cancer."

REESE SET DOWN his wineglass precisely on the lace tablecloth. The flames from the tapers in the floral centerpiece danced with mocking merriment on the facets of the crystal flute. "Why you?" he asked stonily.

Christine gazed at her plate. The sole *amandine* that she'd labored over all afternoon was untouched. She couldn't remember now why she'd decided to go to the effort in the first place; she ought to have guessed neither one of them would feel much like eating. Laying aside her fork, she murmured, "Why not me? Nobody's immune, you know."

Perplexed, Reese persisted, "But you don't smoke, you don't work with hazardous chemicals, you hardly ever even eat red meat! You've always been downright finicky about your health—"

"And my doctor says all those precautions will weigh in my favor when we start treatment," Christine told him. "Please, dear, there's no point in tormenting ourselves with unanswerable questions. My condition is a fact. I have cancer."

Reese shuddered. In the wavering light, his patrician features looked gaunt. Drumming his fingertips on the table, he mused dejectedly, "When you invited me over here tonight and I saw the candles and the flowers, I felt so happy. I was sure this was your way of telling me you're all right, that we could..." His voice trailed away.

Christine regarded him tensely. "I *thought* you were afraid to touch me," she declared with frosty emphasis. "You really have been waiting for me to get a clean bill of health, haven't you?"

Bristling, Reese countered, "I was only thinking of you, Chris. I didn't want to impose on you when you were sick."

She shook her head. "Don't try to con me, Reese—I know you too well. There's more to your attitude than a simple concern for my welfare."

His tone grew coaxing. "Christine, darling," he began, reaching for her hand.

She jerked away. "And don't try to charm me, either," she snapped, "because it's not going to work this time. I am not a fussy diner or a restaurant reviewer."

The lambent warmth in Reese's hazel eyes dimmed. With trepidation Christine noticed a pulse throbbing in his set jaw; she experienced an appalling premonition that for the first time in more than a decade, her fiancé was about to be absolutely frank with her. She watched him take a deep breath. All at once he blurted, "All right, Chris, I admit it. I hate myself for feeling the way I do, but the fact is that the very idea of disease has always given me the creeps. I can't stand being around sick people. Why the hell do you think I didn't become a doctor like my father?"

Considering the circumstances, considering that she'd been on the verge of breaking their engagement in any case, Christine knew she ought not to be hurt by Reese's lack of compassion. But she was. His rejection stung her. She ached to realize that she'd never known him quite as well as she'd thought, that for so many years she'd been blinded by evasion and self-deception. How much time they'd both wasted...

With resignation she murmured, "Well, thank you for being honest with me, at least. I guess it's a good

thing we never got married, isn't it? Otherwise you'd
have had to keep your fingers crossed when the minister came to the 'in sickness and in health' part.''

Reese flushed. "I'm not that much of a wimp,
Chris. I promise I'd have been there for you. In case
you've forgotten, I did offer to cut my trip short so
that I could get home before you went into the hospital, but you told me you didn't need me.'' He grimaced. ''That's the great thing about you, of course.
You're so strong you never need anybody.''

''That's not true,'' Christine cried, wondering how
he could make strength sound like a fault. "I've never
been more frightened in my life than I was when I was
in the hospital. I needed someone then, I need someone now. If it hadn't been for Clay—'' She broke off,
but too late.

''Who's Clay?'' Reese asked.

Christine felt queasy. The conversation was not going as she'd intended. She'd planned to break the news
to Reese in easy, tactful stages; she'd thought to convince him it was time to terminate their engagement
without ever bringing up Clay's name at all. Now that
hope was dashed.

''Who's Clay?'' Reese repeated, an edge to his
voice.

Biting her lip, Christine answered, ''Clay's a friend.
He visited me in the hospital.''

''I thought I knew all your friends,'' Reese said. He
scowled as he ruminated on the name. ''Clay—Clay—
where have I heard—'' he mumbled. Suddenly his
brows shot up. ''Good Lord, Chris, you're not talking about that motorcycle bum who tracked up the
restaurant the day before I left for France, are you?''

"Clay isn't a motorcycle bum," Christine asserted quietly. "He's a marine biologist. He used to teach college. He's worked with Jacques Cousteau."

Reese stared at her. "How interesting. I had no idea." His eyes narrowed as he observed, "It sounds as if you two must have struck up quite an acquaintance."

Christine felt her cheeks prickle with heat. "I guess we did," she agreed.

His tone remained cool, chatty. "That's remarkable, considering what different kinds of people you and your new friend appear to be—and considering that I was only gone for a couple of weeks. However, I guess it does explain why you weren't eager to have me come home any sooner than I did."

"Reese, please," Christine murmured.

He pounced, demanding acidly, "I don't suppose you'd mind telling me exactly how close this new acquaintance has become in that brief time, would you?"

His toying sickened her, but Christine refused to quail. "Don't play games with me," she told him evenly. "What happened, happened."

"You bitch," Reese said.

Struggling to maintain her composure, Christine noted, "For what it's worth, I didn't plan this. I never meant to hurt you."

Her outward calm infuriated Reese. He exploded. "Hurt me?" he shouted, banging his fist on the lace-covered tabletop, making the cutlery rattle. "*Hurt me?* Damn it, Christine, what do you know about hurt? Hurt is finding out that the woman I've loved faithfully for ten years has made a prize fool of me! Hurt is feeling guilty as hell for not being more supportive about your illness, and then discovering that you've been cheating on me with some—some—" He sputtered, choking on his rage. "I can't believe you'd do this to me, to us! We deserve better. After all we've been through together—"

Christine bowed her head and endured the cruel lashing in passive silence, unable and unwilling to defend herself. There was no defense. Her new-sprung feelings for Clay seemed puny and selfish, compared to the justice of Reese's accusations. He was right. Whatever their differences, after all the two of them had been through together, they deserved better.

The diatribe seemed endless, but eventually Reese sank back into his chair, all emotion spent. His handsome face looked slack, enervated. He gazed bleakly at Christine.

She sighed. "Well, Reese, I believe we've reached the point where, traditionally, I'm supposed to hand back your engagement ring. Too bad I never let you give me one."

He gestured dismissively. "Maybe now I finally understand why."

"What do you mean by that?" Christine asked.

Reese shrugged. "Oh, nothing very profound—but it occurs to me that the two of us ought to have guessed years ago that there must be something fundamentally unsound about a relationship that drags on inconclusively for so long. If we'd been better together, I'm sure you wouldn't have been vulnerable to that...biker. I suppose in a way we've both had a lucky escape." He craned his neck, twisting it stiffly. "I do apologize for yelling at you, though," he added, almost as an afterthought. "Whatever—whatever the provocation, I ought to have remembered that you're sick. Your health is more important than my wounded pride."

"That's very generous of you," Christine muttered. She watched Reese uncertainly, mistrustful of his conciliatory tone. Despite his polished manners, her erstwhile fiancé was a possessive man with all the usual male vanity, and she and Clay had hurt him. She could not imagine Reese simply letting the matter drop.

She asked, "So what happens now? You and I work together. We've invested our whole working lives in La Courgette. We can't just divide our record collection and go our separate ways."

Reese's mouth twisted. "We're both mature, civilized adults," he reminded her calmly, picking up his wineglass and draining it to the dregs. "I don't see why we can't continue to conduct our business as usual, in a professional manner, regardless of whether or not we're still engaged."

Christine wished she found his words more reassuring.

CHAPTER SIX

"HI, CLAY," Christine said with a gulp, unaccountably bashful as she greeted the man who waited at her front door. "It's—it's nice to see you. Thank you for coming."

The yellow porch light gilded his dark hair and the smile playing across his lips. "It's nice to see you, too," he responded formally. "Thank you for inviting me."

She stepped back, and he followed her into the house. His shoes were noiseless on the ceramic tile in the passageway. Christine peeked down at his feet, shod in trim loafers. "What happened to the boots?" she asked curiously.

"I left them by the bike, along with my jacket. It's parked right next to the house, so there shouldn't be any problem. I thought I'd surprise you and dress up for a change."

Christine's gaze slid over him. His long locks were neatly combed, if not controlled, and he was wearing casual slacks, creased razor-sharp, and an oversize rugby shirt that failed to disguise the breadth of his muscular shoulders. Somewhere behind her breastbone her body began to tingle. "You look...very good," she said throatily.

"So do you," Clay judged, returning the comprehensive inspection. Christine was dressed with elegant simplicity. A row of tiny pearl buttons fastened the collar of her creamy silk blouse high under her chin, but the clinging fabric draped softly over her breasts, while her long hostess skirt flared over her narrow hips and fell to the floor in graceful folds that swayed with every movement of her slender frame. The ensemble was demure, almost staid—and somehow so provocative that Clay ached to rip it off her.

They fell silent. Clay glanced around. From the entry, Christine's home appeared to be small but well arranged, and it had been furnished with imagination and taste—the sort of taste he could appreciate, even if he lacked the patience to exercise it in his own life. He said, "I like your house, Christine."

"Thank you," she responded brightly. "Did you have any trouble finding the address?"

Clay shook his head. "You give very clear directions."

Conversation lagged awkwardly. Christine found herself staring down at the tile, studying the cracks. She felt clumsy and inarticulate, unable to speak. The atmosphere grew more strained by the second.

Clay asked gently, "Why so shy, love?"

"I don't know," she admitted, fidgeting with the folds of her skirt. "This is—this is silly. I can't imagine what's wrong with me. All of a sudden I feel as self-conscious as I did in eighth grade, when I went to my first dance."

She could hear a rumble of laughter deep in Clay's chest. He reached over and captured her nervous fingers in his warm grasp. His big thumb began to explore her palm, tracing the lines, caressing the soft mounds. "This isn't junior high, Christine," he said conversationally.

"I know," she squeaked.

Quietly he reminded her, "This isn't our first date, either."

She lifted her drooping chin to meet his gaze squarely. Despite the soothing, almost tender note in his voice, his eyes were ardent and intent, hot with unmistakable purpose. Swallowing thickly, she said, "I know that, too, Clay."

His cheek twitched. "Then maybe you'd better come here," he growled. Tugging her hand, he pulled her close against him.

There was nothing shy about the kiss. In Clay's arms Christine's trepidations evaporated, burned away by the heat of his mouth on hers, the searing imprint of his body. He was startlingly new, deliciously familiar, as heady as young wine. Lips and teeth and tongues collided, hands caressed and explored, until at last, reluctantly, the two lovers were forced to pull apart, panting and aching for more.

Christine slumped weakly against Clay. Bright flags of color painted her cheekbones as she rested her head on his chest. Beneath her ear she could hear the erratic throb of his heart. "Oh, my," she declared inadequately, not sure her wobbly knees would support her.

Clay's arms clamped around her waist. "Oh, my, indeed," he mocked, sliding a hand down her spine to cup her bottom through her long skirt and urge her against him. In spite of their clothes she could feel that he was explicitly, magnificently aroused. He rasped,

"For a genteel innkeeper, you pack quite a wallop, lady. You see the effect you have on me?"

She tittered. "I-I'm impressed. Maybe we'd better do something about that."

To her amazement, Clay shook his head. "Not yet, love," he said, nuzzling his face in her hair. "Let's take things slowly. There's no hurry—not this time."

They held each other tightly, not speaking, basking in their mutual warmth, savoring each other's particular essence, until at last Clay inhaled deeply and observed, "Something certainly smells good."

Christine smiled dreamily. "Must be my new perfume," she breathed, her mouth curving against the cotton knit of his shirt. "Do you like it? It's a little heavier than I usually wear."

Clay wrinkled his nose and sniffed. The fragrance she was wearing was some exotic floral spice mixture, probably outrageously expensive but not nearly as appealing to him as the more subtle scent she'd favored in the past. "Well, the perfume's okay," he decided dubiously, "but at the risk of sounding prosaic, I think the aroma I noticed a second ago smelled more like chicken."

Christine's eyes flew open. "Oh, no, I almost forgot dinner!" she gasped. She wrenched away from him and dashed toward the back of the house. Clay ambled after her. By the time he reached her spotless kitchen, she was arranging luscious-looking delicacies with artistic precision on a pair of pink Spode plates.

When Clay entered the room, she glanced up from her task, regarding him through her lashes. "Don't you dare refer to my creation as just 'chicken,'" she chided him. "I'll have you know that tonight we're dining on chicken breasts stuffed with leeks and truffles, *céleri rémoulade,* raspberry soufflé—"

Clay looked suitably overwhelmed. "Good Lord, you really are a gourmet cook, aren't you?"

"I'm not bad if I have the time—which I hardly ever do, anymore," Christine admitted with a buoyant shrug. "When we first opened the restaurant I did most of the cooking, and even now I still have to fill in on those rare days when Amir and his cousin are both away. Reese has always said that if it weren't for me..." Her voice trailed off, and she sobered at the mention of her former fiancé.

Clay did not miss her sudden frown. He asked, "Have you spoken to him yet?"

"Yup," Christine muttered.

Clay pressed, "And you were able to resolve the situation?"

"Everything's just peachy." Abruptly Christine picked up the plates and shoved them in Clay's direction. "Here, you'd better set these on the table," she told him tightly. "We ought to eat before everything gets cold."

Despite Christine's tension at the start of the meal, she found herself unwinding as dinner progressed. Clay proved a witty and companionable guest, and by the time he finished his second helping of the raspberry soufflé, Christine felt very relaxed, mellowed by the felicitous combination of good food, good wine, and good company. She poured coffee for both of them and settled back to relish her own, poignantly aware that such a moment of simple, perfect pleasure was as evanescent as the steam rising from the dark brew in her cup.

Clay declared, "That was wonderful, Christine. I enjoyed every bite."

"Thank you," she said. "I enjoyed it, too—not just the eating but the preparation. I like cooking for people."

"It shows. You obviously put a tremendous amount of attention and work into preparing this meal."

The remark amused Christine. "I appreciate the kind words, but you mustn't get the idea that suppertime is a continual feast around here," she told Clay mildly. "When the stars are all in the right positions, cooking becomes almost a form of meditation for me, but frankly, it's usually just a chore, like doing laundry. I'm perfectly capable of tossing something frozen into the microwave and calling it dinner." She paused. "The thing is, tonight was sort of my swan song. After all, who knows how long it will be before I have another opportunity to cook like this again...."

Her offhand words jarred him. He gazed at her and asked with spurious calm, "Have you been to the doctor again?"

Grimacing, Christine told him, "Actually I saw two of them this morning. First I had an early appointment with an oncologist, who reviewed my test results over the weekend, and once he confirmed Dr. Fong's diagnosis, I went back to her office."

"It was wise of you to get a second opinion," Clay said.

"Patricia—Dr. Fong—insisted." Christine watched Clay closely. She could tell he was determined not to let his reaction to her news upset her, and she was touched by his efforts; she wondered exactly what that outwardly sanguine composure was costing him. After a moment she added, "Patricia wants me to be absolutely certain I understand what's at stake before we begin treatment."

Clay observed, "She sounds like a very good doctor."

"One of the best," Christine agreed. "Actually they're both good doctors, and they both agree that my prognosis is very hopeful. We seem to have caught the disease early, and if it hasn't meta—" she stumbled over the unfamiliar word "—if it hasn't metastasized, spread to other parts of my body, then they say there's a better than even chance I can be cured."

"I could have used odds like that the time I went to Las Vegas," Clay bantered.

Christine smiled at the feeble jest, but then her look became fearful. She slid her hand into his, and his fingers wrapped compellingly around hers, as if he was trying to transfuse his strength into her through his fierce grasp.

When Clay finally released Christine, the outline of his fingers was imprinted in her soft skin. Absently she massaged the back of her hand, smoothing away the marks, while she reflected, "Do you have any idea how unreal all this seems to me? My life-style has always been pretty hectic, but now suddenly I have a million extra things to do. Before I can even begin treatment, I have to arrange for someone to fill in for me at the restaurant, I have to update my insurance, I have to write my will.... In just a few days my entire world has been turned completely upside down, and the hell of it is that I feel fine. I don't even have a cold.'' She raised her eyes to gaze at the man seated opposite her. ''You're a scientist, Clay, so maybe you can explain it to me. How can I have a life-threatening illness and still feel perfectly normal?''

He could only shrug. ''I can't explain it. I wish I could, but the patients I work with don't talk a lot. All I can tell you is that every creature, human or otherwise, is an individual, and there's no way to predict how they—we—will react to disease or any of the other challenges thrown at us. If you're lucky, you may find that you're able to weather your illness with few symptoms and surprisingly little discomfort.''

Christine shook her head ironically. ''I guess it's kind of perverse to complain because I *don't* have any pain. Talk about sounding ungrateful...''

Clay said, ''You don't sound ungrateful, just confused.''

Christine nodded. ''You got that one right. I am very confused—and for someone who's always prided herself on being levelheaded and in control, that's an unsettling sensation.'' She glanced at the table and made a face. Sternly she declared, ''However, being confused and unsettled is no excuse for being a poor hostess. Give me a second to clear up here, and we'll go into the living room. Shall I put on another pot of coffee, or would you prefer a liqueur? I have Grand Marnier and Amaretto.''

Recognizing Christine's need to change the subject, Clay told her, ''Grand Marnier sounds delicious. Shall I help you with the dishes?''

''I'm just going to dump them into the sink to soak,'' Christine said, pushing back her chair. ''Everything else is already cleared away.''

Clay laughed. "Good heavens, you're not only a great cook, but you're neat, too. I'm not sure I'm going to be able to live up to your standards. Is there anything you can't do?"

As Christine methodically stacked plates and silverware to carry into the kitchen, she noted lightly, "For starters, I can't ride a motorcycle. As a matter of fact, I'm terrified of the things. Watching you on that Harley gives me the willies."

"Oh, really? How come?" Clay muttered, looking interested.

Pursing her lips, Christine said, "I'm not sure, really. I've just always been afraid of motorcycles. I suppose it was something to do with the fact that when I was a girl, I saw a boy on a moped get run over by a pickup. It was a very uneven confrontation, and not an easy sight to forget."

Clay scowled. "I'm sure it wasn't. In my opinion, mopeds and little scooters have no business being out in traffic with automobiles. But at least with a bike the size of mine—" He was interrupted when all at once the telephone on the sideboard rang.

Christine shot a surprised glance at Clay. "I wonder who that can be. Would you excuse me for a moment? It might have something to do with work."

"Go right ahead," Clay said. He removed the soiled plates from Christine's hands and headed toward the kitchen. "I'll take care of these for you."

Sinking back into her chair, Christine picked up the handset just as the telephone jangled a second time. When she pressed the receiver to her ear and heard the hollow crackle of static that indicated a very long distance connection, she was suddenly glad to be sitting down. She'd been dreading this conversation and would have been happy to postpone it indefinitely.

"H-hello, Mom?" Christine stammered, gulping painfully. "What on earth are you doing calling at this hour? It must be the middle of the night in Germany."

From half a world away, Meg Silva's gentle, loving voice was husky with concern, and the sound of it made her daughter's heart ache. "It's just now sunrise, dear," Meg told Christine. "Jeff and your brother are still in bed, but I—well, I had a bad dream, so I decided to go ahead and get up."

Christine tried not to imagine the content of her mother's nightmare. She said, "I'm sorry you couldn't sleep, Mom. I was planning to call you a little later in the day. I promised last week that I'd get back to you just as soon as I knew something definite."

"I do remember you saying that," Meg agreed gravely, "but I couldn't wait any longer." She paused. When Christine did not speak, Meg prompted, "Well, did you see your doctor again?"

"Yes, Mom," Christine answered. She tried to say more, but the words stuck in her throat. Across two continents the silence thickened.

Meg sighed. "Since you're not bubbling over with good news, I assume the miracle didn't happen, did it? The diagnosis hasn't changed?"

"I'm afraid not. A second doctor confirmed everything."

"I see," Meg muttered, and from the strained, unnatural pitch of her voice, Christine could tell that her mother was struggling not to cry.

Christine chewed her lip. "Please, Mom, I know it's a blow, but both doctors say my chances of recovery are good. With prompt treatment—"

Meg interrupted, and suddenly her voice was firmer. "When do you check into the hospital again?" After Christine told her, her mother said, "Good. That gives me a few days to make sure Jeff and Adam are all taken care of before I catch my flight."

"What flight?" Christine asked blankly.

"I intend to be there with you when you start chemotherapy," Meg announced.

"But, Mom, it's not necessary—"

"Of course it is," Meg countered severely, her tone a mixture of hurt and exasperation. "Don't try to shut me out, Christine. I need to be there. *You* need me to be there. I'm sure you don't remember what it was like with your father, but I do, and believe me, you'll need me. You'll need both of us, me and Reese—"

Christine's heart sank. Here was another topic she was not eager to pursue. When Meg paused for breath, Christine ventured, "Uh, Mom, there's something you ought to know...."

"What, dear?"

Taking a deep breath, Christine declared baldly, "Reese and I have split up."

"*What?*" Her mother's flabbergasted exclamation was so loud that Christine hoped it didn't wake the rest of her family still sleeping in Germany. Meg cried, "My God, Christine, what happened? *When* did it happen! Less than a month ago Reese called us from Paris, and he acted as if everything was fine between the two of you."

"It was—then," Christine said, suddenly acutely aware of the man rinsing dishes in her kitchen. Clay was being as discreet and unobtrusive as possible, but Christine knew he could not avoid overhearing every word she said. Urgently she amended, "No, it wasn't fine, Mom. Reese and I have been drifting apart for a long time, but neither one of us wanted to admit it. Finally everything just came to a head after he returned home from Europe."

Meg considered for a moment before counseling sagely, "I'm sure you mean what you say, Christine, but I do hope you're not letting the shock of your illness make you act rashly. At times like this stress can cause people to do a lot of crazy things they regret later. Believe me, I know. As much as your father and I loved each other—"

"It's more than just the illness," Christine cut in quickly, unwilling to listen to intimate confessions about her parents' marriage. "Please, Mom, take my word for it. Reese and I are through. There's—there's someone else."

Meg snorted in patent disbelief. "That's impossible. I knew you must be imagining things. Reese adores you, he always has. He'd never leave you for another woman."

Christine inhaled raggedly, struggling for the words. Suddenly a big, warm hand squeezed her shoulder. She glanced up. Clay loomed over her, his expression full of sympathy and encouragement. Christine rubbed her cheek against the back of his hand. His skin was damp and smelled of dish soap. He smiled bracingly. Christine's eyes locked with his as she spoke into the telephone. "But, Mother, you don't understand the situation," she corrected Meg gently. "Reese didn't leave me. *I've* found someone else."

The line was so silent that for a moment Christine was afraid her mother had hung up on her. When Meg did speak, she sounded bewildered and despondent. "Oh, Christine, what have you done?"

Christine continued to gaze up at the man beside her as she answered candidly, "I've gotten cancer and I've fallen in love, Mom—not necessarily the greatest combination of events, I'll grant you, but I guess that's life."

Meg sighed again. "Well, dear, I really don't know what to say."

"Say you're happy for me?" Christine suggested wistfully. "Please, Mom, don't be upset. Clay's a wonderful man. You'll understand when you meet him."

"Oh, Christine, I—" Meg broke off once more, and Christine could almost see her mother squaring her shoulders. Meg said, "We'll talk later, dear. I'll call you again as soon as I know exactly what my travel plans are going to be. In the meantime, you take care of yourself. We love you."

"I love you, too, Mom," Christine whispered. "Kiss Jeff and Adam for me." When she heard the dial tone, she carefully replaced the receiver in its cradle and stared at the keypad on the telephone until she felt Clay's fingers stroking her hair.

"That must have been tough," he commiserated, and Christine knew he wasn't referring to her telling Meg about the cancer.

Christine nodded. "It wasn't fun—but then, I never expected it to be. You have to remember, when Reese and I first started dating, my little brother wasn't even old enough to walk yet. My mother regards Reese as part of the family. For that matter, Reese's parents have always indicated that they think of me as their daughter-in-law...." She lifted her chin and smiled bleakly at Clay. "See what a mess you started when you stumbled into my restaurant that day?"

"Are you sorry?" he asked her.

Christine didn't have to think. She stood, and her mood began to lighten. "No, Clay, I'm not sorry," she said firmly as she faced him. "I'm sorry the breakup with Reese has to hurt innocent people, but I'm not sorry I met you. I'll never be sorry for that."

"I'm glad to hear it," he murmured as he drew her into his arms. Framing her face with his hands, he said, "I don't ever want you to regret anything that happens between us."

"Never," Christine promised, and when Clay pressed his lips against hers, she knew they were sealing a vow.

In the living room, as Clay lounged against the thick cushions of the sofa, he tasted the orange-flavored liqueur Christine had served in thimble-size crystal glasses and he asked lightly, "So when do I get to meet your mother?"

Christine, curled up next to Clay with her long skirt tucked beneath her, frowned. "Oh, dear, I guess I have committed you to meeting Mom, haven't I? Do you mind?"

"Of course not," Clay drawled, "assuming, that is, that you're able to reassure her I'm not really the vile seducer and home wrecker she probably thinks I am."

"She's going to love you, I guarantee," Christine teased. "When Mom was a young teenager, she fell madly in love with Marlon Brando in *The Wild One.*"

Glancing askance at Christine, Clay muttered, "I certainly hope you're only drawing that comparison because of the motorcycle."

"Naturally, dear," she replied demurely, allowing her eyes to drift downward in a languid examination of his long, lean body. "I'm well aware that you don't look anything like Marlon Brando."

Clay continued to study her with suspicion. "But I do look like an overage delinquent? Gee, thanks."

Christine laughed. "Don't worry, darling, if my mother gets the wrong idea about you, I promise I'll try my best to convince her that you're a fine, up-standing, productive member of the community—not that I'm sure I'll be able to convince her of anything, at the moment. You heard how much luck I had try-ing to change her mind about flying here from Ger-many."

"But don't you want your mother to be with you when you go into the hospital?" Clay asked curi-ously.

Christine sipped her drink and pondered the ques-tion. "I guess I do," she conceded after a moment. "Whenever I let myself think honestly about what I'm going to be facing during the next few weeks and months, there's a real urge to run home to Mommy and start bawling.... On the other hand, when I re-member how shattered she was by my father's illness, I can't help feeling that having Mom around would only add to my problems." Christine paused. "Still, I have to admit that I was very surprised by how strong-minded she sounded on the telephone just now. It may be a callous thing to say, but the fact is that when Daddy got sick, Mom showed about as much backbone as a jellyfish.''

"She's older now, maybe she's stronger, too," Clay reminded Christine. "Besides, most mothers have a remarkable ability to come through for their children even when they don't seem capable of taking care of themselves.''

"I suppose," Christine agreed. "Whatever the answer is, I expect we'll find it out soon enough. Mom is bound and determined to be here.''

Clay responded, "And I'm looking forward to meeting her—and the rest of your family. I hope that before too long I'll be able to introduce you to my parents, as well.''

Christine smiled winsomely. "That's a lovely thing to say, you know. I didn't realize you were ready to make that kind of—"

At the last moment she broke off, hesitant to utter the word, but Clay heard. Faint lines grooved his forehead. Carefully he removed Christine's liqueur glass from her fingers and placed it alongside his on the cocktail table, then he shifted on the couch so that he faced her directly. Their bodies were only a touch apart as he amplified conversationally, "You didn't think I was ready to do what, Christine, make a commitment? If that's true, then I owe you an apology. I'd assumed it was already very clear to you that I intend to be around for a long, long time.''

Biting her lip, Christine said, "Sometimes we want things so badly that it's hard to believe when they actually come true.''

"I know what you mean." Clay reached up to stroke her features with wonder, shaping the delicate slope of her jaw, the high cheekbones. The rough pads of his fingers skittered over her skin, as if her face was some holy relic almost too precious to touch, but his blue eyes were luminous with naked hunger. Christine could see his chest lift as he inhaled raspily, painfully. "You know what I find hard to believe in?" he breathed. "It's you. You're so damn beautiful. When I look at you, I can hardly believe that I've already held you—or that I ever thought I could let you go."

Christine lowered her lashes. "But you did let me go. When I close my eyes, I can still picture your expression that morning, just before you turned away from me and slammed back into your house."

"One of the few noble moments in my life," Clay acknowledged ironically. "Just don't expect me to make a habit out of being self-sacrificing." He paused. After a moment, with forced lightness, he probed, "Out of curiosity—and even though I realize that the answer probably isn't going to do my ego any good at all—exactly how much do you actually remember about what happened between us that night at my place?"

"Not a whole lot," Christine confessed. "After the doctor discovered the lump in my side, I was in such a state that most of the twenty-four hours following my checkup is a blank." Her mouth curved in a dreamy arc. "But I do recall that you were very sweet to me."

Clay's brows arched. "Sweet?" he echoed gruffly. "We were great together, but somehow *sweet* isn't exactly the word I'd use to describe it."

Christine splayed her hands on Clay's chest. "I wish I could remember," she murmured, leaning forward to nuzzle her face against the base of his bronzed throat. His skin was warm and musky, and stray tendrils of crisp hair tickled her through the open neck of his shirt. As her tongue darted moistly, tasting him, she could feel his heart thud beneath her palms. Suddenly she pulled away from him and leaped lithely to her feet.

The abrupt movement startled Clay and he scowled, but Christine smiled encouragingly and held out her hand in invitation. "Please, Clay," she whispered, "I want to remember, too. Won't you help me make a memory we can share?"

Clay groaned. Reaching up, he laced his fingers through Christine's. Despite her apparent aplomb, he could feel her tremble. Slowly Clay stood. In a gesture as reassuring as it was courtly, he bent his head and brushed his lips across her knuckles. "Oh, lady, I love you," he said, and Christine, shivering, heard herself whimper with anticipation as she guided him out of the living room.

Christine's bedroom was much like Christine herself, Clay thought abstractedly, quickly scanning the chamber before returning his attention to the woman in his arms. The charming English-country-garden decor was understated and traditional, gracefully feminine without being frilly. From the Monet print over the dresser to the cherrywood four-poster with its hand-woven coverlet, everything in the room was harmonious and tasteful; nothing jarred—except the purple plush walrus perched atop the stacked pillows.

Ogling the gaudy nylon toy with its plastic tusks and button nose, Clay laughed. "I can't believe you still have that silly thing."

Christine looked affronted. "Of course I still have him. He's slept with me every night since you gave him to me."

Clay sucked in his breath. "Lucky walrus," he quipped. He gazed down at Christine, and his eyes grew hooded and intense. "Lucky me," he said thickly, slipping his hands around her throat. Gently his thumbs nudged her chin upward, and he began to fumble with the tiny pearl buttons on the high collar of her blouse.

Tilting her head back, Christine lowered her lashes and smiled dreamily as the silky fabric fell away, exposing her throat and chest. The air was deliciously cool on her overheated skin, but not as delicious as the glide of Clay's mouth, following the progress of his hands. When the last button was unfastened, he peeled back the blouse to reveal a wispy bra, fastened with a single front closure. Just for a second Clay hesitated. Instinctively Christine arched against him, pressing into his hands. The two halves of the clasp separated, and with awe Clay unveiled her naked torso to his greedy gaze.

"From the beginning I've wanted to see you," he declared artlessly, a hard flush of color streaking his cheekbones as he stared at her small, high breasts. "It was dark the other night, but I knew you were beautiful. You had to be. Nobody could feel as good as you do and be anything less." Worshipfully he cupped her alabaster softness in his big brown hands. When he brushed his thumbs across the hypersensitive nipples,

Christine gasped, and almost magically the areolas crinkled into twin rosebuds. Clay sighed in satisfaction. "I'm glad I can see you now. It excites me to watch your body respond to my touch."

Hoarsely Christine declared, "I want to see you, too. I want to see all of you." She caught the hem of his shirt and stretched on tiptoe, swaying against him as she tried to tug the bright cotton over his head. The sun-bleached hair on his chest tickled her. When the rugby shirt settled in a colorful heap at their feet, Christine smiled in wonder at the plates of smooth, hard muscle clearly delineated beneath Clay's weather-darkened skin. She murmured, "You have great pecs."

"Yours aren't bad, either," Clay told her deeply.

Christine giggled. "It's not the same thing at all."

"Thank heaven for that," Clay drawled.

Tracing his sculpted chest with the tip of a fingernail, she asked, "Do you work out?"

"Not in a gym. I do lots of swimming. I've probably spent half my life in the ocean. It's great exercise, but—" he grimaced "—it also happens to be the reason my hide is as tough as an old boot."

The flippant remark distracted Christine. Lifting her head, she studied Clay's face, noting the telltale signs of premature aging, the character lines fanning from the corners of his eyes—not unattractive, but far too deep for a man only in his mid-thirties. "You ought to use a sunscreen," she muttered worriedly.

"Too late, love," Clay countered with a shrug. "After all these years, the damage has already—" He broke off, recalling why even offhand references to skin cancer would be less than tactful. Stoutly he declared, "You're right, Christine. I do need to start using sunscreen. You'll have to remind me."

"I will," she said, mollified. Relaxing again, she wound her arms around Clay's waist and leaned her cheek against his chest. She murmured, "I like your skin. I like touching it."

"I'm glad," Clay agreed solemnly. "I like you touching me, too. Want to do some more?"

Christine glowed. "Oh, yes," she breathed. Her slim fingers trembled slightly as she reached for his belt.

They lay naked together on the bed, cocooned in the soft flannel sheets. Despite their eagerness, there was no haste now. Both moved slowly, deliberately, savoring each moment between anticipation and ecstasy. Propped on one elbow, Clay loomed over Christine, studying her with avid gentleness, and his hair fell heavily into his face. She reached up to brush back a thick strand that dangled over his forehead, obscuring his eyes. Looping the dark lock back behind his ear, she inquired idly, "Did you have long hair when you taught college?"

Clay shook his head. "Not until the last year. I quit going to the barber about the same time I traded the Saab in on a motorcycle. I should have realized then that I was never going to meet the approval of the tenure committee."

"I'll bet the kids loved you," Christine reflected. "I'll bet every female student on campus had a crush on Dr. McMurphy."

The remark amused Clay. "Oh, a few, maybe," he agreed airily, "but the infatuations rarely seemed to last beyond the first pop quiz." He chuckled. "What about you? Do many of the diners at your restaurant assume you're listed under *Dessert?*''

"Of course not," Christine rejoined with a grin. "Everyone knows we don't serve flesh at La Courgette.''

Clay's eyes grew murky. "I could do with a serving of your flesh," he rasped. He rolled heavily onto her, pushing her legs apart. Surging against her, he made her aware of his need, blatant and tantalizing. "Feel how hungry I am for you," he muttered. Christine wriggled with pleasure beneath him. Breathlessly she began her own exploration of his rangy body, stroking his long spine, his taut buttocks, using her lips and her clever, inventive fingers to drive him maddeningly close to the edge, until he captured her wrists and stretched them back over her head—and Christine winced.

Clay grew still. "What's the matter?"

"N-nothing," she stammered, shaking her head. "It's nothing, really, just a twinge."

Gripping her hands so that she could not squirm away from him, Clay lifted his body away from hers just enough so that he could quickly glance over her. At once he spotted the livid weal of half-healed skin deep in her armpit. "What's that?" he asked sharply.

In a tiny voice Christine told him, "It's the incision from my biopsy. If I move in just the wrong way, it's still a little sore."

Clay grew pale. Instantly he released her wrists and unwound his legs from hers. He slid his weight off of her, leaving her cold and bereft. "You should have warned me," he said darkly. "I would have been more careful.''

Christine tried to smile. "I forgot." She searched his face worriedly. "Darling, don't be upset," she soothed. "You didn't hurt me. I'm hardly aware of the stupid scar now, anyway."

With her fingertips Christine sketched the deep grooves of strain bracketing his mouth. "Please, Clay," she invited, "the only way you can hurt me is if you don't go on making love to me."

He gazed at her intently. Then he bent over her again, and with a rumble of fierce tenderness he pressed his lips against the blemish on her side.

The time for leisurely exploration was past. Clay's mouth moved on Christine, and she began to moan, a high, keening cry of yearning and delight that quavered and dipped as he tasted her breasts, her navel, her scented, secret softness. The sensations he aroused in her were so shattering that she tried to escape him, flailing and arching, fighting—yet beckoning. By the time he hovered over her, poised to claim her, Christine's skin felt hot and taut, so sensitive that the whisper of his breath was almost painful. "Please, Clay," she gasped when he waited, "don't tease me. I need you."

His lips stretched back in a snarl of passion. "But do you love me?" he demanded. "I know you need me. Do you love me, too?"

She stared up at him with eyes glazed and wild. "Yes, I love you," she panted, clutching at him restlessly. "Oh, yes, yes, *yes!*"

Clay's smile was feral. Lifting his head like a triumphant lion, he growled, "Good—that's what *I* need." Then he clamped his mouth over hers and plunged into the burning heart of her, where need and love were one, inseparable and forever inescapable.

"THIS IS TERRIBLY decadent, you know," Christine giggled, "eating raspberries in bed. French aristocrats were probably guillotined for a lot less."

Clay watched with hooded eyes as Christine dipped her spoon into a crystal bowl of berries and thick cream left over from the soufflé. Juice from the luscious fruit had tinted the cream a pale pink, not much lighter than Christine's naked shoulders emerging from her nest of snowy sheets. "You're the one who said you were hungry," he reminded her.

"Well, I am," she insisted blithely. "For some reason I seem to have worked up quite an appetite." She scooped up the remaining few raspberries. "Are you certain you don't want some? There's one good bite left."

Clay nodded. "Sure, I'll take it."

Obligingly he opened his mouth, and Christine fed him the last of the fruit by hand. Snuggling together in bed made the motion awkward, and when she withdrew the spoon from between his strong teeth, a droplet of cream and juice dribbled over his lip. Leaning close, Christine licked up the rich fluid greedily, bathing his chin with quick, soft strokes like a kitten. The cream was sweet, and through her darting tongue she could feel the rasp of whiskers just below the surface of his skin. When she lifted her head again, she looked replete, sated. "You taste good," she murmured as she set the empty fruit bowl on her nightstand.

"So do you, lady," Clay said thickly, dragging her against him. They burrowed beneath the covers, and for a long time neither of them spoke.

When Christine emerged again to the cool night air, she stretched luxuriously and declared, "I feel so wonderful. I am going to cherish the memory of this evening forever."

A faint frown line appeared between Clay's heavy brows. "Why do you say that as if tonight were the end of something?" he probed darkly. "I was under the impression that the two of us were going to be together for a long time to come."

Christine said, "I hope we are—but under the circumstances, I'm afraid that just being together, having any privacy, is going to be a major accomplishment. In case you've forgotten, my mother has invited herself to stay with me while I start my treatments." She heaved a sheepish shrug. "Mom is a wonderful woman, and quite broadminded, but there's just no way she's going to conveniently disappear so that you and I can make love."

"No, that would probably be asking a bit too much of most mothers," Clay agreed drolly.

Christine continued, "I don't know exactly how long she expects to stay here, but it can't be for long. After all, she has a husband and son in Germany who need her as much as I do. But even after Mom does head home, I expect privacy is still going to be a little hard to come by."

"How so?" Clay asked.

Gesturing helplessly, Christine explained, "Well, it will probably all depend on how I weather the chemotherapy, but the more I think about it, the more I

realize that I'm going to be forced to hire someone, a
housekeeper or a maid or a private-duty nurse, somebody who can keep an eye on me when I'm not feeling strong enough to care for myself.'' She grimaced
with distaste. ''Lord, I hate the very idea of a stranger
taking over my house, but I guess I don't have much
choice.''

''You could stay with me,'' Clay suggested.

Startled, Christine eyed him warily. ''That's a very
kind offer, Clay, but I can't ask you to make a sacrifice like that. You're a busy man.''

''You're a busy woman,'' he shot back, ''but you're
going to need help for a while. Considering how I feel
about you, it wouldn't be much of a sacrifice to give
you that help.''

Christine remained hesitant. ''But I've lived alone
my whole adult life, ever since I moved out of my college dorm.''

''I know that,'' Clay said. ''Why do you think I
suggested you stay with me, even though your house
is a lot more comfortable than mine is? Apart from the
fact that I don't know whether I could cope with
flowered wallpaper for an extended period of time,
I'm sure you'd feel less threatened if you didn't think
I was invading your space.''

Christine nodded reluctantly. ''That's very generous—and very perceptive—of you.''

Clay's cheek twitched. ''Oh, that's me, perceptive
to a fault.'' With a blunt fingertip he outlined a rosy
abrasion his teeth had left on the naked slope of
Christine's breast, while he noted idly, ''Of course, it
doesn't take much perception to realize that even
though I think we belong together twenty-four hours

a day, you're not ready yet to consider the idea. But I also realize that the last thing you need right now is some jerk pressuring you to make a radical change in your life-style. So I leave the choice up to you. If you prefer to hire a nurse to take care of you while you're recuperating, then fine, that's what you should do. But if you're willing to move in with me—without obligation, knowing you're free to return here anytime you want to—then I would be happy and honored to share my home with you."

Christine bit her lip. She was silent for so long that Clay began to wonder if he'd somehow offended her. But before he could speak, she looked at him with wide, anxious eyes and pleaded, "You know, don't you, that we'd probably turn out to be the odd couple? I'm compulsively neat, and you're so much more . . . laid back."

"You mean I'm a slob?" he mocked dryly.

Bristling, Christine contradicted him. "I didn't say that! I mean I love you too much to risk damaging our relationship bickering about petty details like—" she grimaced "—like housekeeping."

Clay relaxed, heartened by the matter-of-fact way in which Christine had admitted she loved him. As long as the two of them remained steadfast in their feelings toward each other, all their superficial differences could be resolved. Framing her face with his hands, he told her, "Calm down, darling. I promise you we won't damage our relationship bickering about housekeeping. We're also not going to bicker about our careers, your mother, or the state of the world economy. We're both too intelligent." He paused to gaze tenderly at her. Then, nudging her back against

the pillows, he breathed, ''On the other hand, sweetheart, if, in a fit of temporary insanity, you and I
should ever be stupid enough to start squabbling about
anything, just think what fun we'll have making up
afterward....''

CHAPTER SEVEN

THE HAND THAT REACHED through the rails of the hospital bed to stroke Christine's cheek was soft and warm in the chilly, sterile-smelling air. With an effort Christine opened her eyes and gazed up blearily at her mother. Meg Silva's fair, pretty features seemed to shift in and out of focus. "Hi, Mom," Christine mumbled. "You're here early." The words sounded fuzzy.

Meg smiled gently. "I told you I'd come back before they started your treatment." Her light eyes, grayer than her daughter's, narrowed. "Are you comfortable, darling?" she asked bracingly. "The nurses said you've already been given a tranquilizer."

Christine tried to nod. "They woke me for it. I was sound asleep, and they woke me up to make me relax."

"That's hospital routine for you," her mother commented. The two women fell silent. Meg began to fidget with Christine's bedclothes, and as she tucked the sheet around her daughter's shoulders, she uncovered a gaudy stuffed animal half-burrowed beneath the pillow. Picking it up, she regarded it curiously. "This is cute. I've never seen a purple walrus before."

Drowsily Christine beamed at the bright plush toy. "Clay gave him to me," she murmured.

Meg looked troubled. Carefully she returned the walrus to Christine's side. She hesitated for a moment, then she told her, "After I went back to your house last night, I telephoned Reese. We had a long chat."

Shifting restlessly, Christine said, "I wish you hadn't done that."

"Don't be silly, darling," Meg chided. "You can't expect me to come all the way to California and not talk to Reese—he's almost as dear to me as Adam is. What's more, he seemed delighted to hear from me. He made me promise we'd have lunch together before I fly home."

Christine sighed. Despite her drug-induced lassitude, she could not suppress a twinge of resentment at the idea of her mother and her former fiancé arranging a rendezvous behind her back, but at the moment she felt incapable of protest. "That's good, Mom. I hope you have a nice visit," she mumbled sleepily, praying Meg would drop the subject.

Her mother persisted. "Reese is very worried about you. He's afraid your illness is making you... irrational."

"I'm perfectly sane," Christine declared, but even to her own ears the words lacked conviction.

Shaking her head, Meg countered, "I'm not so sure about that. Reese is such a dear boy, and from what he tells me about this person you're involved with—"

Christine wished she had the energy to sound indignant. "Reese doesn't know Clay. Neither do you."

"I know he didn't care enough to be here with you today," Meg said accusingly.

With limp fingers Christine fumbled for the stuffed walrus. "Clay wanted to come this morning, but I asked him to wait until tonight," she told her mother. "There was no point in him missing work. You're with me now, and I'm going to be asleep all day anyway...." Hugging the toy childishly, Christine turned her face away and demanded with dull petulance, "Where's the nurse? I want to get this over with."

At last Meg seemed to realize that she was hounding her daughter. Flashing a wan smile, she patted Christine's shoulder and crooned, "The nurse will be back in a minute, darling. Everything's going to be fine." Christine, lulled by the soothing whisper of her mother's voice, dozed.

Soon—or perhaps it was hours later, Christine conceded afterward; the drugs made her lose all sense of time—the nurse reappeared, and with her was Patricia Fong, Christine's oncologist. Dr. Fong greeted her patient and then introduced herself to Meg. Patricia said, "Mrs. Silva, I don't know whether or not Christine has told you exactly what we plan to do here, but as her next of kin, it's important for you to understand the procedure. Shall I explain it to you?"

Meg looked ashen, but her voice was surprisingly strong. "That won't be necessary, Doctor," she said staunchly. "I've seen it all before, years ago when Christine's father—" glancing down at her daughter, she caught herself "—when her father was ill."

Patricia nodded gravely. "I understand. It's probably just as well that you have some idea of what to expect. However, I do want you to remember that the technology is being improved and refined all the time. Chemotherapy is never easy, but if Christine weathers this initial bout reasonably well, then her future sessions can probably be handled on an outpatient basis.''

"I hope so," Christine muttered from the bed. "I hate hospitals."

Glancing down at her, the doctor chuckled lightly. "So do I." Patricia gave her patient a quick but comprehensive inspection. As she checked her pulse, she queried, "Well, do you think you're ready for this?"

"I guess so," Christine said dubiously.

"That's good. I promise we'll try to make it as painless as possible." Picking up a tiny paper cup from the tray the nurse carried, the doctor said, "Here, Christine, we'll begin by having you take these sleeping pills. There's also some antinausea medication. Once you've got the pills down, we'll follow them with a shot of steroids to suppress your body's reaction to the cytotoxins, and then, after you're asleep..."

Dr. Fong's abstruse words continued, but Christine did not hear them. She stared with dread at the rainbow-colored pills in the bottom of the paper cup. They looked like candy—but Christine knew that as soon as she swallowed them, everything was going to change. Words like "nausea" and "toxin" were not nearly as frightening to her as the realization that she was about to surrender control of her body, her very life, to strangers.

At her side, Meg urged quietly, "It's time to take your medicine, Christine." Her voice was tender and compassionate, and suddenly Christine remembered being tiny and feverish with chicken pox, when nothing but her mother's lullabies could comfort her.

She shivered. "Mom, I'm afraid," she whispered hoarsely.

Meg nodded. "I know, darling, I know." Her grayish eyes glistened as she stroked a strand of fair hair back from her daughter's face. "Take your medicine, Christine," she repeated softly, "and I promise that when you wake up, the worst will be over."

"You'll be here?" Christine pleaded.

"I'll be here," Meg vowed.

Christine heard her own voice rise. "Clay, too?"

Her mother hesitated fractionally before echoing, "Yes, dear, Clay will be here, too."

Christine relaxed. "Thank you, Mommy," she murmured politely, and she gulped down the pills from the paper cup.

"WHERE'S Christine Dryden?" Clay barked, startling the nurse seated behind the counter. The young woman jerked up her head with alarm and gaped at him as if he were a madman. He looked like one, Clay admitted grimly. He'd caught a glimpse of his reflection in the glass doors as he stalked through the entrance of the hospital. His eyes were red, he was grimy and sweaty, and the wind had whipped his hair into dreadlocks during the wild ride from the Institute. It was a wonder the burly security guard by the admitting desk had allowed him inside—fortunate, too, because Clay knew that in his present state of mind it would have taken armed force to prevent him from seeing Christine.

All day long he'd been going insane with worry, wondering every second exactly what the woman he loved was enduring, cursing himself for being stupid enough to give in to her seemingly plausible request that he wait until evening to visit her. He'd been worthless at work; worse than worthless, he'd been careless, and because of his distraction, one of the student volunteers had almost been hurt. Clay and the youth had been wrestling with a sea lion, trying to immobilize the infuriated creature while Henry Berlinger took a blood sample, and at a crucial instant Clay had let his attention wander. Instead of concentrating all his energy on keeping the snapping, thrashing animal's neck pinned to the ground with a plywood collar, Clay had thought about Christine—and the sea lion had lunged. The wooden shield flew out of Clay's hands, exposing the hapless college kid to the animal's big, sharp teeth, and only Dr. Berlinger's swift response had prevented him from being bitten viciously. With strength and dexterity astonishing in a person of his age, Dr. Berlinger had grabbed the student bodily and flung him out of harm's way; then all three men had vaulted over the low wall enclosing the pen. As soon as Dr. Berlinger was sure they were safe, he turned on Clay and ripped into him. The sea lion quit bellowing long before Henry Berlinger did.

Struggling to appear halfway civilized despite his agitation, Clay flashed a winsome smile at the nurse and murmured, "Forgive me, I didn't mean to shout. Can you please tell me which room Christine Dryden is in?"

The smile seemed to do the trick. Relaxing, the nurse consulted her computer screen and instructed Clay, "Left at the end of the hall, then three doors down. Ms. Dryden is allowed visitors, but she's been heavily sedated all day, and I don't know whether she's awake yet."

"I promise I won't disturb her," Clay assured the young woman as he turned in the direction she'd indicated. He strode quickly, forcing himself not to break into a run. When he approached Christine's room, he was greeted by the unpleasant sound of someone being violently ill.

He paused in the doorway. Christine's bed was immediately to his right. A blond, middle-aged woman, slightly faded but still attractive, clucked soothingly while she stroked Christine's hair.

Clay must have made some noise, because the woman glanced up suddenly. At the sight of him, her light eyes widened, and her lips pressed together into a thin, disapproving line. Her penetrating gaze studied him. Clay stood still, enduring the inspection with a stoic silence, knowing he was failing miserably. He looked like a bum—worse, even—and the woman was obviously taking him as presented. With rare compunction Clay regretted the unruly image he'd cultivated with such relish since leaving the university. It was going to take more than facile charm to correct the incredibly bad first impression he was making on Christine's mother.

He said, "You must be Mrs. Silva. I'm Clay McMurphy."

"I know who you are," Meg replied tersely. Christine choked, and instantly Meg returned her attention to her daughter.

Clay stepped forward, reaching out instinctively to touch Christine, but Meg tensed as if he threatened her. Clay let his hand drop. He gazed on helplessly. When the retching stopped, Christine flopped back against her pillow, her chest heaving, her smudged eyes closed. Clay stared at the gray face, the dull hair that only a few days before had fanned like living sunlight across his pillow, and he winced. "What in the name of heaven are they doing to her?"

"They're trying to save her life," Christine's mother snapped. "If you expected it to be pretty, you'd better think again."

Clay bristled at Meg's rudeness, but instead of spitting out the bitter retort that quivered on his tongue, he forced himself to remain calm. Considering the stress Christine's mother was under, the woman could hardly be expected to concern herself about his feelings. All that mattered at the moment was the welfare of her child. It was up to Clay to overcome her prejudices and convince her that Christine's well-being was all that mattered to him, too.

He watched Meg sponge Christine's slack features with a damp cloth. "Mrs. Silva," he began guardedly, "I realize we're strangers, but you must believe that I have every intention of taking good care of your daughter. I've already begun getting my house ready so that she'll be comfortable while she's staying with me."

Meg's hand stilled. Lifting her head, she regarded him with distaste. "You're expecting Christine to move into your house, to—to *live* with you?"

"For at least as long as she's convalescing, yes," Clay answered matter-of-factly. "The plans have already been made."

"Well, the plans can be unmade," Meg shot back. "After my daughter leaves the hospital, as soon as she's strong enough to travel, I'm taking her home to Germany with me."

Suddenly Clay felt a great, booming hollow where his gut had been. Gulping sourly, he asked, "Have you discussed this with Christine?"

Meg shrugged. "Not yet, but I expect her to see reason. She's a sensible girl—about most things, at any rate—and I'm sure she'll realize that under the circumstances, she belongs with her family, whatever happens."

Clay stared at the woman. "You say that as if you expect her to die."

"Her father did," Meg told him stonily. She took a deep breath, and when she spoke again, Clay could tell that by her own standards, at least, she was making an effort to be fair. "Look, Mr. McMurphy—"

He corrected her coldly, "It's *Dr.* McMurphy, but what the hell, you can call me Clay." As soon as the spiteful retort passed his lips, he regretted it. Stiltedly he apologized. "I'm sorry, but it makes me a little crazy to hear you talking as if I have no rights where Christine is concerned. I happen to love her. I've loved her since the first moment I saw her."

Meg's expression was frankly skeptical. "And when was that—a month ago, six weeks?" she reminded him. "I've been in the business of loving Christine for over thirty-two years. I think that gives my feelings a little more weight than yours, don't you?" She paused. "Very well . . . Clay . . . I'm willing to give you the benefit of the doubt and accept that when you tell me you intend to take care of Christine, you really mean what you say. But I am absolutely sure that you have no idea what taking care of a cancer patient entails. The work is grueling, and it's physically and emotionally draining. It's a tremendous obligation— and frankly, you don't strike me as somebody who's very good at living up to your obligations."

"You don't know anything about me," Clay said.

"I know what I see," Meg countered with a sniff. She started to say more, but Christine coughed thickly and whispered her mother's name.

Clay said, "Let me hold her."

Meg stiffened and shook her head. "No," she declared tightly. "She's my child, my responsibility."

Scowling, Clay watched grimly. He could see that Christine was completely unaware of his presence, conscious of nothing but the sweet voice and cool hands that assisted her in her weakness. When the attack passed and she drowsed, Clay shifted his gaze to Meg's face, studying her drawn features with concern. Her eyes were fierce, faintly wild, and her pallor was almost as pronounced as her daughter's. He wondered how long it had been since she'd had a decent night's sleep. He urged gently, "Mrs. Silva, you're exhausted, you need to rest. Let me take care of Christine for a while—please."

Meg wavered. "I don't want to leave her," she insisted, her tone less emphatic. "I promised I'd be here when she wakes up."

"You will be here," Clay assured her. "I'll ask the nurse for a cot for you, and you can stretch out right here next to Christine and still be within arm's reach if she calls for you." Without waiting for Meg's reply, Clay hurried out of the room. Moments later an orderly was setting up a narrow roll-away bed in a space out of the lane of traffic, next to the wall.

Meg eyed the cot with wary longing, then glanced back at Clay. Biting her lip, she asked him, "You'll wake me up if Christine needs me?"

"Of course," he murmured. "The instant she stirs."

Slipping off her shoes, Meg settled herself on the portable bed, collapsing the last few inches as if she was suddenly too weary to hold herself upright anymore. She was asleep before her head touched the pillow.

At once Clay forgot about Christine's mother. He turned to where the woman he loved lay sleeping, watching her—aching for her. He stroked her slack white cheek and stared around him with distaste at the soulless medical apparatus that assaulted as it sought to protect. Clay was a scientist, he believed in technology—but there was something perverse, even obscene, in the idea that a smiling, vibrant woman in apparently perfect health had to be rendered senseless and stripped of vitality and dignity in order to be "cured" of an invisible disease....

He heard a footstep and glanced up. Patricia Fong was standing at the foot of Christine's bed. Clay gazed at the oncologist and declared with bitter outrage that he made no effort to conceal, "There has *got* to be a better way!"

The doctor nodded somberly. "I'm sure there is," she agreed with quiet humility. "The trouble is, nobody's discovered it yet."

Clay sank bank in his chair, ashamed of his outburst. It wasn't Patricia Fong's fault that Christine was ill. The woman was a wise and diligent physician always doing the very best she could for her patients—and always humbly aware that her best efforts were compromised by blind human ignorance. Considering the parallels between her situation and the pitiful progress Clay had been making in his own work with the elephant seal, he knew that he of all people ought to be able to sympathize with the doctor's dilemma.

Despite his anxiety, he forced himself to remain silent while Patricia examined her patient. The oncologist's manner was smooth and professional, her face a mask of detached concern that revealed nothing. Finally, when she stepped back and began making notes on Christine's chart, Clay took a deep breath and inquired apprehensively, "How is she doing?"

For the first time, Dr. Fong allowed herself the indulgence of a faint smile. "I know that under the circumstances it's probably hard for you to believe, but Christine is doing very well. Her vital signs are strong, her body appears to be functioning normally. Apart from feeling as sick as a dog, I think she's going to be okay."

"What about the cancer?" Clay asked bluntly.

Patricia said, "Hopefully we've made a start at killing the malignant cells. Only time will tell." She paused, glancing past Clay to the cot where Meg slept as if comatose. "I'm glad Mrs. Silva is having some rest," Patricia said sympathetically. "Because of the past history of her family, this whole experience has been doubly difficult for her. I wish I could convince her that things have changed since Christine's father died. I wish I could make her understand that nowadays people *do* get cured of cancer."

Clay said, "I guess you'll just have to prove it to her by curing her daughter."

"I'm doing my damnedest," Patricia said, and after jotting the last of her notes on Christine's chart, she nodded to Clay and left.

Clay sat motionless, trying not to think. Sounds of activity penetrated from other parts of the hospital—footsteps in the corridor, the creak of gurney wheels, bouncy theme music and canned laughter from a television in another room—but at Christine's bedside all was still. The preternatural silence boomed in his ears.

His gaze wandered. It occurred to him that there were no flowers adorning Christine's stark cubicle. He recalled the lavish bouquets that had surrounded her bed during her previous hospital stay, gifts from Reese and his family. Assuming there was no policy forbidding flowers to a chemotherapy patient, Clay promised himself he'd bring some the next time he visited. Maybe she'd like something to read. He observed that there were already a couple of library books on the nightstand. Curiously Clay picked them up—and found himself staring at Cousteau's *World Without Sun* and a popular field guide to marine mammals.

Clay swallowed, overwhelmed by the realization that in the midst of her personal trauma Christine was trying to learn more about *his* interests.... His hands shook as he replaced the books on the nightstand.

Suddenly she was fully awake. Clay was stroking her cheek with a fingertip, noting with dismay how transparent and waxy-looking her skin was, when all at once her lashes fluttered and flew up. She blinked and gazed at Clay with startled blue gray eyes. Her bloodless lips moved mutely, followed half a beat later by her voice, like a movie with its sound track out of sync. "Hi, there," she whispered hoarsely.

Clay slumped with relief; shooting pains in the muscles knotted at the back of his neck and shoulders made him realize how rigid he'd been holding himself, waiting for this moment. He gulped and murmured, "Hi, yourself. How are you feeling?"

She considered the question. Her fair brows came together in a moue of confusion as she said, "My—my throat is raw, and I feel—I feel hot and prickly all over, like there's electric current in my veins."

"Considering the stuff they've been pumping into you, that's not surprising."

Christine nodded. "Have you been here long?"

"About an hour. I would have preferred to come sooner, but I did what you wanted and put in a full day at work."

She frowned. "A full day? What time is it?" When Clay told her, she gnawed at the corner of her mouth and muttered blankly, "But I don't remember any of it. A whole day's gone, and I don't remember anything after this morning, when Mom—" She broke off, looking worried. "Where's my mother? She promised she'd stay with me."

Clay shifted sideways so that Christine could see Meg stretched out on the cot behind him. "She hasn't left your side," he said.

Struggling to raise herself on her elbows, Christine lifted her head just enough to peek through the bedrails, then she fell back limply against her pillow. "Poor Mom, she must be worn out," she declared with a sigh. "She was here at dawn, and I don't think she got much sleep the night before."

"Who did?" Clay quipped. He paused. "You're a lucky woman. Your mother loves you very much."

"I love her, too," Christine said. Her troubled gaze shifted to Clay's face, drained and shadowed in the cold fluorescent light. "You look awful."

Clay shrugged. "I don't think any of us is exactly at his best right now."

"No, probably not," Christine conceded. She tried to shift position in the bed, but her movements were sluggish, as if her body was still half-asleep. She moaned. "I feel so rotten."

"Shall I get the nurse?" Clay asked.

She shook her head listlessly. "Not yet. She'll only start poking at me, and I'm not ready for that. But if—if I could have a drink of water—there's this vile taste in my mouth...."

Clay glanced around. There was a plastic bottle of ice water on Christine's nightstand next to the books; he presumed it wouldn't have been left there if she'd been forbidden fluids. Holding the tip of the straw to her dry lips, he urged, "Here, darling, take it slowly, just a little sip at a time."

But even a little sip proved too much for Christine's offended stomach to tolerate. As soon as she swallowed the water, her eyes grew round and she groaned, "Oh, no!" and then the nausea engulfed her. With patience and efficiency Clay tended to her needs, but when at last the convulsions stopped and Christine half swooned, her ashen face wet with tears of shame and weakness, he realized that he was crying, too.

MEG FLUFFED Christine's pillow and urged her, "C'mon, dear, you have to try to eat something, even if it's only a little soup. It's important for you to get your strength back."

"I know that, Mom." Christine stared without enthusiasm at her lunch tray. Even though the worst of her nausea seemed to have passed with the night, it was impossible to look at food without experiencing a certain amount of trepidation. "I know I have to eat," she said grudgingly, picking up a packet of crackers that accompanied her bowl of clear broth. Her fingers felt shaky and strangely numb as she struggled to tear open the plastic wrapper. Gingerly nibbling a corner of a cracker, she observed, "The problem with eating is that everything tastes so weird."

Meg reminded her patiently, "Your doctor told you the chemicals were liable to affect your sense of taste for a few days."

Christine wrinkled her nose. "I remember. But I'm a professional gourmet. How am I supposed to enjoy my food when it's all the flavor of cardboard?"

"Forget about enjoying it and just get it down," Meg said sternly.

"Yes, ma'am," Christine murmured. Dutifully she chewed the rest of the cracker. She noted with surprise that the salt, at least, seemed to register normally on her palate. Maybe she could live on pretzels and potato chips until the aftereffects of the chemotherapy wore off.

Meg continued, "You really must try to put on some weight, darling. When you met me at the airport, I was shocked by how thin you've become. You're skinnier now than you were as a teenager."

"Only by one size," Christine told her mother defensively. "Being sick does that to people, you know." Reaching for her spoon, she dipped it into the broth while she added, "But don't worry, I've promised Dr. Fong that I'll make a concerted effort to fatten myself up. I guess I'll have to start ladling on the gravy and cream."

Meg said, "In that case, you'd love German cooking. Everything's served *mit Schlag*—sinfully delicious, but murder on the waistline. I put on twenty pounds the first year I lived in Frankfurt."

"If I remember correctly, you were pregnant with Adam most of the first year you lived in Frankfurt," Christine countered, "and besides, Jeff adores every blessed ounce of you."

"He claims he does," Meg agreed with a secret smile. After fifteen years of marriage, Meg and her husband remained passionately devoted to each other, and Christine never ceased to thank God for the miracle that had brought Jeff Silva and Meg Dryden together. Still, she stiffened when her mother ventured hesitantly, "Christine, dear, your stepfather and I have been talking."

Suddenly uneasy, Christine laid down her soup spoon again. "Yes?"

Meg told her, "As soon as your doctor says you're strong enough to travel, we want you to come stay with us."

Christine didn't pretend to misunderstand. "You mean stay with you indefinitely, don't you, Mom?"

"We both think it would be for the best," Meg asserted brightly, oblivious to the sudden edge in Christine's voice. "We've always hated you being far away, and if you hadn't seemed so settled here, we would have invited you to come live with us years ago. Now that the situation has changed, well, I can't be away from my husband and son forever, and you're going to need someone to take care of you."

"I have someone to take care of me," Christine said.

Her mother grimaced. "Yes, your...friend...told me last night that you intend to move into his place, wherever that is."

"Clay has a little house in Stinson Beach," Christine explained patiently. "It's close enough to his job that on those days when I need somebody to keep an eye on me, he can commute back and forth during his lunch hour to check up on me."

"And you have no problem with the idea of living with this man?" Meg pressed.

Christine said, "I regret the imposition, of course, but since the arrangement's only going to be temporary and Clay swears he doesn't mind the inconvenience, then no, I don't have any problem with living with him."

Meg's lips quivered. Suddenly she blurted, "For heaven's sake, Christine, I don't understand any of this! Who is this man? What's he doing in your life?

You've been with Reese since college—doesn't that mean anything to you? How can you suddenly just decide to fall in love with somebody else?"

Because Christine could hear the anguish and confusion in her mother's voice, she answered with forbearance. "I didn't 'decide' anything, Mom, it just happened. You ought to understand that. After Daddy died, you swore you'd never love again, but Jeff managed to sweep you right off your feet."

"It's not the same thing," Meg maintained primly.

"It's more the same thing than you realize," Christine said.

The two women fell silent for a moment, then Meg pleaded, "Darling, we have wonderful doctors in Germany, and there shouldn't be any problem continuing your treatment. If it's finances you're worried about—and nobody knows better than I do how expensive cancer can be—you know Jeff and I will take care of everything. He says that for insurance purposes he might even be able to get you listed as his dependent—"

"Mother," Christine cut in with crisp emphasis, no longer able to tolerate Meg's importuning, "I am not anybody's dependent. It's very sweet of Jeff to offer, but I have my own medical insurance. For that matter, I also have a home and a career, and I intend to go back to both of them just as soon as I'm better."

"But what if you're never—" Meg swallowed the tail of her sentence, but Christine supplied it for her.

"What if I'm never better, what if I'm dying? Well, Mom, if that's true, then I don't suppose that in the long run it will make a whole lot of difference to me whether I go back to Germany with you or stay here in California, will it?''

Christine watched the blood leach from her mother's face, leaving her pretty features livid and lined, scarred with the memory of unbearable pain that even a happy second marriage could never quite eradicate. When Meg opened her bruised-looking eyes, there were teardrops on her lashes. In a trembling voice she implored, ''Christine, please let me take care of you. I *need* to take care of you. I—I need to do a better job than I did when you were a little girl.''

Suddenly Christine could not bear to see her mother abase herself. ''Mom, you don't have to say this,'' she told her, but Meg continued urgently.

''Don't you think it's bothered me over the years, remembering how when you father died, I was so absorbed in my own grief that I didn't even notice you were grieving, too? I've always regretted that. I can't begin to tell you how much I've regretted that. You were a child, and you needed me, and I was too selfish to—''

''Mom!'' The force in Christine's sharp cry startled even her. Meg gawked at her, and Christine repeated more gently, ''Mom, there's no need for you to feel guilty or to think that you have to make up for failing me in the past. Whatever happened when Daddy died, you did the best you could, and that's all that matters.''

''I only want to do what's best for you now,'' Meg persisted.

Christine nodded. ''I know that. But you have to remember that I'm not a child anymore. I'm the one who has to determine what's best for me.'' She paused.

When she spoke again, her tone was soft but resolute as she warned, "I love you very much, Mom, but if you force me to choose between you and Clay, you may not be happy with my decision."

Meg blanched. "For heaven's sake, Christine—" She broke off her anguished entreaty when a small, birdlike figure in a brightly colored sweatshirt materialized at the foot of the bed.

Glancing up in surprise, Christine's scowl dissolved into a grin of genuine pleasure as she recognized the girl with the knit cap pulled low over her dark eyes. "Samantha, it's great to see you! I didn't know you were here. What's a nice kid like you doing in a place like this?"

The teenager shrugged and giggled. "Oh, it's time for The Treatment again—" she spoke the words as if they were capitalized "—and Dr. Fong told me you were a patient here, too, and she said it was okay for me to hop over for a minute to say hi. I hope you don't mind."

"Mind? I would have been deeply hurt if you hadn't," Christine declared. Out of the corner of her eye she noticed her mother trying hard not to stare at Samantha's thin, ravaged face and bald head. Quickly Christine made introductions. "Mom, this is my friend and former roomie, Samantha Harris. Samantha, this is my mother, Meg Silva." Recalling how shocked the girl had been that none of Christine's family had visited her during her earlier hospital stay, she added, "Mom just flew in from Germany a couple of days ago."

Samantha extended her hand formally to Meg, then she asked Christine, "Well, what do you think of chemo?"

"Not much," Christine admitted. "All things considered, I prefer Disneyland."

Samantha rolled her eyes dramatically. "Don't we all! Have you been sick much?" When Christine nodded, Samantha told her sympathetically, "That's too bad—but if it's any consolation, after a while you get sort of used to it."

"I hope so," Christine murmured weakly.

Samantha said, "Even better, after a while it ends. This is my last treatment." She paused for emphasis before announcing proudly, "Dr. Fong says I'm going into remission."

An enormous lump of emotion formed in Christine's throat. "Oh, Samantha, thank God," she breathed. "That's wonderful news. I'm so very happy for you."

The girl shifted restlessly, a shy, hopeful smile transforming her thin face. "I'm pretty happy for me, too. I'm going to get to start high school in the fall with the rest of my friends, after all. I know that's still months away, but it means I'll have all summer for my hair to grow back." Nervously she touched the cap covering her bare skull. "I've worried about that, you know. There's this...guy...who sort of likes me, and I sort of like him, and I've wondered what I'd do if he asked me to the Homecoming Dance, and I still didn't have any..."

As Samantha's voice trailed off, Christine tried to imagine what it must be like for her, a teenager already plagued by the usual adolescent doubts about self-image and sexuality, and then at the same time to be confronted with disfiguring and life-threatening illness. Christine didn't see how the girl could cope. Gently she murmured, "You're going to be beautiful, dear."

"That's what my parents keep telling me," Samantha admitted with a sigh. Suddenly, with a lightning-swift change of mood, she laughed and said, "It's going to be really interesting to see what my hair looks like when it grows back. Sometimes after chemo it comes back in a different color. My hair has always been sort of mousy brown—wouldn't it be *wild* if this time I turned out to be a flaming redhead?"

"Wild, indeed," Christine agreed. "But I want you to promise you'll come show off your new hair to me, whatever color it is."

Samantha nodded enthusiastically. "Sure thing. I'd love to keep in touch." She paused, glancing at her neon-pink wristwatch. "Oops," she declared, "I'd better scoot, or Dr. Fong is going to send out a search party for me. You take care of yourself, Christine, okay?"

"Okay, Samantha. You take care of yourself, too." Christine watched the girl duck out of the room. As soon as she'd vanished into the corridor, Christine glanced at her mother and noted, "You know, it's very humbling being around someone like Samantha. When I think of what that child has endured already in her short life, I wonder what right I have to complain."

Meg said darkly, "You've only just begun your own treatment. You have no idea what you're going to be called to endure. That's why I find it so disturbing that you refuse to listen to my—'' Again she broke off when a visitor entered the room.

At first glance Christine almost didn't recognize him. When the man in the sport coat and slacks strolled through the door, carrying a basket of carnations, she assumed he was calling on another patient. Then he stopped beside her bed, and Christine stared.

His dark hair was still long, but skilled professional hands had obviously been at work, trimming and taming the wild curl. Christine had to admit that the results were striking, especially the way the new style opened up his face, reinforcing the strong line of his jaw and emphasizing his deep blue eyes. The Harris tweed jacket with leather patches on the elbows was somewhat less of a success; the coat appeared to be of excellent quality, but it fit awkwardly, too snug across the shoulders, too loose at the waist. Everything else he wore—white dress shirt, dark tie, trim wool slacks, and the loafers she'd seen once before—was classic and conservative, and as Christine finished her comprehensive inspection, the corner of her mouth twitched.

"Oh, my Lord, it's Professor McMurphy," she breathed.

Clay set down the flowers and greeted both women, kissing Christine, nodding solemnly to her mother. Meg seemed perplexed by his altered appearance, and Christine was struggling with some fierce emotion. "What's the matter, darling?" Clay asked innocently, "aren't you feeling good? You're looking much better than you did last night."

"I wish I could say the same thing about you," Christine shot back.

Feigning bewilderment, Clay asked, "You mean you don't approve of my new—old—image?"

Biting her quivering lip, Christine admitted, "Well, I do like the haircut very much, but the jacket doesn't fit right."

"I haven't worn it in a long time," Clay explained. "I get more exercise now than I used to back in my teaching days. You should be grateful I was able to air out the mothball smell."

At Christine's side, Meg was looking at Clay in confusion. He smiled broadly at her, then returned his attention to Christine, who was snickering helplessly. "Oh, come on, sweetheart, I can't look all *that* funny. You've seen men in suits before."

She sputtered between gasps for air. "I'm not trying to be rude, the outfit is very nice, really. But—but this is all a gag, isn't it? The change isn't permanent? I mean, you're not going to tell me that you've traded in your Harley for a Saab, are you?"

"Would it bother you if I did?" Clay queried. "I thought you hated motorcycles."

"I don't hate them, I just find them sort of overwhelming," Christine insisted. "Almost as overwhelming as this sudden change in you. You look— you look so *clean-cut* all of a sudden, like a mass-murderer who's been dressed up by his attorney to make a good impression on the court—"

"I think your mother here is tougher than any judge," Clay drawled, glancing at Meg, inviting her to join in the joke. Without waiting for her response, he turned again to Christine and announced gravely, "You don't have to worry, darling, I couldn't find a Saab dealer who'd take my bike for a trade-in—so I had to settle for borrowing Dr. Berlinger's Volvo instead."

Christine dissolved into a gale of giggles, throwing back her head so that for an instant her hair caught the light, losing its drabness, and her pale face grew rosy with mirth. Clay watched her tenderly, wondering if it was true what they said about the healing power of laughter. He looked across the bed at Meg, gazing down at her daughter with concern. He could see the emotions tearing at her, and he knew it would take time for the woman to learn to trust him with her child's welfare, to realize that he and she were not rivals for Christine's affection but two different people made allies by their mutual love for a third. Meanwhile it was enough to listen to Christine laugh—and pray that there would be more opportunity for laughter in the trying days to come.

CHAPTER EIGHT

FROM THE DOORWAY Clay watched worriedly as Christine peered into the mirror over the sink and dabbed extra blusher on her wan cheeks. She was wearing an old bathrobe of his, vastly too big for her, and the bulky fabric enveloping her thin body only emphasized her fragility. "Are you sure you're feeling up to this?" he probed.

"Yes, I'm sure," Christine replied. She returned her blusher to the small travel case sitting next to Clay's shaving gear. Retrieving a tube of mascara, she continued with her makeup while she talked. "I told you before, I have to go to work, at least for a while. Everyone's expecting me."

He persisted. "I wish you hadn't said you'd be there today. I don't like the idea of your driving, not so soon after—not yet."

Christine glanced at him, frowning her puzzlement. "But I've driven already."

"That was a quick dash to the supermarket three blocks away," Clay reminded her. "It's nearly ten miles from here to La Courgette—not to mention the fact that when you drive across the peninsula, you're liable to get caught in commuter traffic."

Carefully Christine replaced her makeup in the travel case. When she picked up a brush to smooth her hair, Clay pretended not to notice the way she inspected the bristles afterward to assure herself that no extra tendrils had been left behind. Christine's doctor had told her that hair loss was not an inevitable side effect of the drugs being used in her particular treatment, but Clay knew it was going to take time for Christine to accept that she had been spared.

With a sigh she turned to him and admitted, "Sweetheart, I realize you're worried about me, and I promise I'll be extra careful whenever I'm behind the wheel. But the fact is that I don't have much choice about getting back into harness today. My job isn't the kind that I can handle via telephone. Besides, even if the people at the restaurant weren't expecting me, I'd go out in any case. I need to swing by my house to pick up my mail and grab a few things."

"I could do that for you," he offered.

"You wouldn't know what I need. I have to get some more cosmetics, moisturizers—" She glanced at her reflection in the mirror over the sink, and just for an instant her unguarded expression revealed how perplexed and distressed she was by what she saw. Biting her lip, she muttered, "My skin—my skin is so dry."

Carefully Clay stepped between Christine and the mirror. Slipping his arms around her waist, which felt as if he could span it with his fingertips, he drew her close and kissed her cheek. "Dry or not, it's very nice skin, darling," he reassured her. "I'm just trying to take good care of it."

"I know," she said. She laid her head against his chest, and for a long moment they simply held each other, savoring each other's nearness. Clay felt his body stir, and with rigorous self-control he squelched the response. Since Christine had moved into his house, they'd shared a bed but they had not made love. As the oncologist had warned might happen, chemotherapy had temporarily dampened Christine's appetite for sex, and Clay had not pressed her. No matter how much he wanted her, for the moment he forced himself to be content with the cuddling and caresses that she still seemed to welcome, while he waited for her fatigue and distractedness to pass so that the two of them could be together again completely.

Christine begged, "Please don't worry. I'll be okay, and you have much more important things to do than fuss over me." She sniffed. "I get enough of that from my mom."

"Well, I did promise Meg I'd look after you," Clay reminded Christine wryly, thinking of the uneasy truce he and the older woman had arrived at before she flew back to Germany. Clay knew that Christine's mother still did not really approve of him, but once her daughter had made it absolutely clear that she had no intention of leaving either California or Clay, Meg had surrendered to the inevitable. After extracting a vow from Clay that he would keep her informed of Christine's progress, Meg had headed back to Frankfurt and her husband and son. So far she'd telephoned at least three times a week, and Clay found himself hoping a colonel's pay would be sufficient to cover the long-distance charges.

Clay said, "Your mother only wants what's best for you. That's all any of us want."

"I know," Christine said again, disentangling herself from his embrace, "and right now I think the best thing for me will be to get dressed and go face the world for a while. I refuse to let myself be held hostage by this illness. I've moped here in the house too long."

"Good for you," Clay cheered, "but I do hope that after all the time I spent sprucing up this joint for you, you're not implying that my home is depressing." During Christine's hospital stay, while Clay was half-crazy with worry and frustration, he had managed to work off a small amount of his nervous energy by giving his little beach cottage the most thorough cleaning it had received since he bought it. He'd even slapped a fresh coat of paint on the bathroom walls and bought some new towels. Now, although he knew no amount of effort would ever make his house compare to Christine's tasteful, attractive suburban bungalow, at least his books were all shelved and dusted, and the living-room floor was no longer littered with motorcycle parts.

Hastily Christine rejoined, "The house looks just fine, Clay. I've been meaning to tell you how sweet it was of you to fix it up for me." She reached up to stroke his hair, the hair he was keeping neatly barbered because she preferred it that way, and her eyes sparked with a light Clay had not seen there in weeks. "You've been so sweet to me about everything," Christine murmured.

"Nothing could be easier," Clay said. He bent his head to kiss her, but she pulled away.

"I have to go to work," she reminded him reluctantly. "You're running a little late yourself."

Clay checked his watch. "I'm supposed to meet Denny at the marina in about half an hour. We're diving again today."

"Lucky you." Christine glanced at the crystal blue sky visible through the open window. The curtains fluttered. "It looks like it's going to be a gorgeous day," she observed. "When I'm at my desk, I'll think of you guys out on the ocean, swimming and sailing."

"It's a dirty job but somebody's got to do it," Clay quipped.

Christine smiled wistfully. "I wish I could go with you."

Looking surprised, Clay asked, "Would you like to? It could be arranged. Denny's wife, Lib, tags along occasionally. She even dives a little."

"I suspect scuba diving is probably a bit beyond me at the moment," Christine drawled. "Still, I'm sure that on a nice warm day like today, just being in the fresh air would perk me up. While you're underwater, I could watch for whales or something."

Clay laughed. "Sorry, darling, it's too late in the year for whale watching. By now most Pacific species are summering near the Arctic circle. But around the Farallon Islands, there's a phenomenal variety of marine life to observe. You wouldn't have to swim, you wouldn't even have to leave the boat. All you'd need is a pair of binoculars."

"I'd love that," Christine said eagerly. "I've been trying to read some of your books on marine mammals, but most of them are too technical for me. Maybe actually seeing some of the animals in the wild would make the subject clearer to me." After a second her smile dimmed. "Of course, I'll have to check with Patricia first. I'm supposed to be careful about getting too much sunlight."

"Of course," Clay said. "But if she gives you permission, then one of these days we'll pack a picnic lunch and go for a sail. If you like, maybe we could invite Denny and Lib to join us."

Christine told him, "I can hardly wait. I want to meet your friends, and I'd love to watch you work." Peeking up at him through her lashes, she smiled provocatively. "I'll bet you look very sexy in a wet suit."

Clay caught his breath. "Consider it a date," he responded. "After all, what man can resist a chance to show off for his lady?" This time when he kissed Christine, she did not pull away.

When Christine arrived at La Courgette, the restaurant had not yet opened for lunch, but she could hear the chef and his cousin banging pots back in the kitchen, and the air was already redolent with the wonderful aromas of Amir's spicy, simmering sauces and freshly baked bread. As Christine stepped into the pastel entryway, she inhaled hungrily, her appetite stirring for the first time in what seemed like ages. She hadn't realized how much she'd missed her restaurant while she'd been away, the familiar scents and sounds, the people she worked with. She'd invested a decade of her life in this business, and from now on she intended to treasure every moment she spent here.

The first person to spot her was Tish. The young waitress stood at the front desk, speaking on the telephone while she jotted notes in the reservation log, and Christine observed at once that instead of the simple white blouse and black skirt customary for the female staff members, the girl was wearing a stylish beige frock not unlike the dresses Christine wore whenever she was on duty as hostess. It was obvious the teenager was trying to appear older and more sophisticated, but the instant she hung up the telephone and noticed Christine, her soignée air dissolved.

"You're back!" Tish squealed, dashing across the terrazzo to Christine. Just as she reached her, Tish stopped short, hesitating, and Christine could almost hear the girl asking herself whether her effusive greeting was the proper way to welcome her employer. Awkwardly Tish said, "It's—it's so good to see you again, Ms. Dryden. I—we—everybody's missed you."

Christine smiled reassuringly. "I've missed you, too, Tish," she told her, and she held out her arms for a hug.

Suddenly from every corner of the building people appeared, servers, busboys, the cooks, calling Christine's name, embracing her with affection and almost unbearable gentleness—studying her face, then glancing away, troubled. When the usually stolid souschef wrapped his burly arms around Christine, she spotted tears in the man's dark eyes. She wished she could convince herself that they were tears of happiness.

Then Reese stepped out of the office, and the crowd clustered around Christine evaporated. Everybody scattered with such haste that she almost laughed. Reese was far too discreet to broadcast his personal problems, but it was obvious that the employees had somehow already guessed that the two business partners' relationship had altered in some fundamental way. Christine realized the staff were probably worried about what the ramifications would be concerning their own jobs, and for the moment, no one was taking a chance on being nearby when Reese and Christine met again. With a sigh she turned to face the man she'd once thought she'd love forever.

He lounged in the doorway, casually but effectively barring Christine's entrance to her own office. With his fists jammed in his pockets, he surveyed her with narrowed hazel eyes. They had last seen each other shortly before she entered the hospital for her first chemotherapy treatment, and she knew he must be studying her for signs of change, for marks left by her illness. She lifted her chin. "Hello, Reese," she said.

"Hello, Christine," he replied stiffly. His speculative gaze lingered on her hair. She wondered if he thought she was wearing a wig. "How are you feeling?" he asked.

Christine shrugged. "So-so. A little shaky, but determined to start work again."

Reese said, "After I received your message, I tried to contact you to let you know that there was no need for you to come in just yet. Even though your stand-in has headed back to Berkeley, I've been managing okay." He paused. "I telephoned your house several times. Nobody answered."

"I haven't been at my house lately," Christine told him.

He frowned. "You've been in the hospital all this time?"

"I've been staying with Clay," she said.

Watching Reese's mouth tighten, suddenly Christine recalled with compunction the numerous occasions when she had declined his invitation to move in with him. She explained, "I'm not really living with Clay, you know. The arrangement's only temporary, until we're sure I'm strong enough to stay on my own again."

Reese's lean, handsome face grew taut. "You don't have to justify yourself to me," he asserted in a clipped tone.

Christine blinked, feeling rebuffed. "You're right, I don't," she said stiltedly. Taking a deep breath, she marched toward him. For a moment she wondered whether he intended to block her entrance bodily, but at the last instant Reese stepped out of her way, allowing Christine to glide past him into the office. He did not touch her. When she was safely inside, he closed the door behind them.

She saw at once that the items on her oak desk had been rearranged in her absence. The Laurel Burch mug of pens and pencils had been shifted to the opposite side of the telephone, and the magazine cover in the silver frame was buried facedown beneath a pile of printers' proofs. Christine seated herself and began sifting through the litter. Retrieving the photo, she set it upright again, biting her lip at the sight of the happy couple wreathed in golden radiance. Brightly she exclaimed, "Well, it's obvious someone's been busy while I was gone. Apart from promoting Tish to hostess, what other changes have you made?"

Reese indicated the proofs on her desk. "Not much. I went ahead and ordered the new menus."

Christine picked up one of the pages and scrutinized it carefully. She and Reese had worked together on early drafts of the revised menu before his trip to Paris, but several of the food descriptions were unfamiliar to her. "What's this?" she asked, pointing to one of the new entrées.

"That's a Caribbean-style ragout the chef suggested," Reese told her lightly. "Black beans, peppers, lots of spices. Fruit garnish. Amir wants to expand his repertoire, cut back on some of the pasta, serve more regional dishes. I let him try out some of his ideas as daily specials. The customers seemed to like that one in particular. The tortellini hasn't been moving lately, so we pulled it and replaced it with the beans."

Christine stared. "Are you saying you authorized a change in the menu without consulting me?"

Reese's tone hardened. "You weren't available, remember? That manager you hired was reasonably competent to handle the day-to-day running of this place, but when it came to making executive decisions, I was on my own."

Flabbergasted, Christine gestured weakly. "I can't believe you'd change the *food* without even talking to me first," she declared.

Reese snapped coldly, "And just what the hell did you expect me to do—carry covered dishes to the hospital?" As soon as the words were uttered, Reese looked contrite. "I'm sorry, Christine, truly I am. I have no right to take out my anger on you. God knows you didn't ask to get sick. It's just that—well, sometimes I think this whole bizarre situation is making me crazy."

Christine answered hoarsely, "It's—it's not just you, Reese. This is a very difficult situation for—for everyone. We're all under a lot of strain."

"Strain—yeah, I guess you could call it that," Reese griped, his mouth twisting sardonically. "I haven't been sleeping worth a damn since this mess started. Most nights I just stare at the ceiling and listen to the foghorns. But if I do manage to catch a little rest, it's even worse, because when I first wake up in the morning, for a moment or two I think it's all been a bad dream. I imagine that it's still early spring, before I went to France, and that if I try hard enough, I'll be able to talk you into going with me, so that we can finally get married."

Glancing at the magazine cover, Christine shook her head. "Reese, don't do that to yourself. No matter how hard we try, we can't turn back the clock."

"I know," he said stonily. "And that's why we need to talk."

Christine tensed. "What about?"

Reese shook his head. "It can wait. It's not fair to hit you with something like this the instant you return to work."

"Whatever it is, I'm sure I can handle it," Christine snapped. "So go ahead and tell me what's on your mind."

Her former fiancé regarded her intently. "Very well, if you insist." He took a deep breath. "I think it's time for you and me to discuss dissolving our partnership. I want to buy out your half of La Courgette."

Christine gasped as if she'd been blindsided. For some reason, Reese's announcement was the one development she hadn't foreseen. Leaning forward, she began earnestly, "Look, if you're worried about me not doing my share of the work, I promise you that's not going to be a problem. I'm arranging my schedule so that it'll cause the least inconvenience for everyone. I know how disruptive it must have been to bring in a stranger to take my place, but things are going to be different in the future. From now on my chemotherapy will be handled on an outpatient basis. It's only going to be once a month. We're closed here on Mondays, so I figure that if I have chemo on a Monday morning and then take Tuesday as my regular day off—''

Holding up his hand, Reese halted her babbling. ''Chris, please, it's not just your health. There's also a personal aspect to this situation that has to be considered.''

She subsided in her chair. ''You mean you don't feel you can keep on working with me now that we're not engaged anymore.''

Reese tilted his head. ''That's a succinct way of putting it,'' he admitted. ''I've been doing a lot of thinking while you've been away. You and I built this business together with the expectation that we were building a life together as well, and now that the situation has changed, I have to confess that I find it painful and almost insulting that you blithely assume we can continue as before.''

Christine looked bewildered. ''But you told me yourself that you thought we could behave as two professionals.''

''Behaving professionally is not the same as being a masochist,'' Reese snapped. ''Damn it, Chris, you hurt me! I'm willing to make allowances because of your health, but I don't see why I should be expected to sit back passively while you flaunt your relationship with another man.''

"I'm sorry, Reese," Christine murmured. "I'm not trying to flaunt anything. I don't want to hurt you. I've never wanted to hurt you."

Reese grimaced. "I know that—but I don't think it matters anymore. Your decision has been made. You've dumped me, and now we have to deal with the consequences."

Christine asked quietly, "So what do you want to do?"

His expression was ironic. "Fortunately the attorneys who drew up our partnership agreement were foresighted—or cynical—enough to prepare for the possibility that our love might prove less than eternal. In order for one of us to buy out the other, basically all we have to do is reach mutually agreeable terms."

Christine protested, "But, Reese, I love La Courgette. I don't want to give it up."

"Then you buy out my half," he suggested.

"Oh, sure," she scoffed dryly. "You know I can't afford to do that. Considering what the business is worth these days, I'm surprised you can afford it, either."

Reese said, "Dad has offered to put up the money."

Christine's eyes widened in blank surprise. Although over the years Dr. Cagney had developed a grudging respect for his son's success, he'd never made any secret of his disappointment that Reese had not followed him into medicine. "Why should your father do a thing like that?" she asked. "He has no interest in the restaurant business, and he's never invested in anything riskier than government bonds."

"I think he regards this as an investment in his family," Reese offered mildly. "My father wants grandchildren. He told me that since you're not going to provide them, it would be better for me to get you out of my life entirely, so that I can find someone who will."

Christine felt the last tint of color fade from her already-pale cheeks. Wincing with pain, she bowed her head. "I'm sorry your parents hate me," she murmured.

She heard Reese sigh. "Nobody hates you, Chris. A lot of people are disappointed in the way you've been behaving lately, but, well, we're trying to understand. Sometimes serious illness can cause radical personality changes. The only important thing is for you to get better." He stepped toward her, and out of the corner of her eye, Christine could see Reese reach out as if he wanted to touch her; instead he let his hand drop. Crossing his arms, he observed briskly, "You know, it seems to me that you'd probably recover more quickly if you didn't have to worry about this place. There's a lot of stress in the day-to-day running of a busy restaurant, and it can't be good for your health. Think what a relief it would be just to kick back for a while. You could live a long time on what your share of La Courgette is worth." When she did not respond at once, he added, "Naturally I would insist that any agreement we make includes the very best insurance coverage for you...."

"Naturally," Christine muttered. Slowly she lifted her head, her gaze focused on Reese's face. "I don't know what to say about your proposition," she stated with precision. "I'll have to think it over. But I do love this business, and I have no wish to give it up."

Reese said smoothly, "If you really love this business, then maybe the best thing you can do for it *is* give it up. Even if you were miraculously able to raise the money to buy me out, do you think that in your current condition you're the proper person to run—"

"Why?" Christine interrupted bitterly. "Are you afraid I don't fit the restaurant's 'healthy' image anymore?"

Reese shivered with distaste. "My God, Chris, what kind of man do you think I am?" he rasped. "If you truly believe I'm capable of such contemptible behavior, then I *know* I don't want us working together anymore!" He glared at her. "What I was trying to say, before you butted in, was that after all the years of effort and the money you and I have staked in this business, it would be a terrible waste for it to fail at this late date because you lack the stamina to operate it single-handedly."

With mortification Christine recognized the justice of Reese's words. She thought of the ten years of grueling effort the two of them had invested in La Courgette, years of cooking and cleaning and waiting on customers, years of training staff and bargaining with produce vendors and repairing recalcitrant kitchen equipment. Christine had even picked out the linens and suggested the design for the logo on the menu covers. Reese worked hard, too—he was great with numbers and he always kept his cool, even with the most persnickety health department inspectors. They'd progressed a long way since that time a decade earlier when Reese had had an inheritance and an Arts degree from USC and a vague notion that it might be fun for him and his girlfriend to start a restaurant "somewhere up north." It would be a shame to let it all fail now.

Turning away, Christine automatically started trying to create order out of the clutter that had accumulated on her desk during her absence. While her slim hands sorted through the jumble of bills and flyers and printouts, she conceded quietly, "Reese, there's a lot of justice in what you're saying, but I'll need to think over your proposal before I can give you any sort of answer. I don't want to make a snap decision I might regret later. I do hope you'll be patient for a while. In the meantime, if you'll excuse me, I'm busy. We can talk later, but right now I have a lot of catching up to do."

As soon as Clay entered his back door that evening, he sensed something was wrong. Although Christine's Nissan was parked in the garage, indicating that she'd returned from Mill Valley, there was no sign of her in the house. The kitchen was dark and empty, the only odor in the air the faint chlorine tang of scouring powder. When Christine moved in with Clay, she had taken over the cooking almost as once. Clay's protests had been minimal, even when she brought in her own utensils, copper-bottomed skillets and carbon-steel knives, and relegated his motley collection of cheap, chipped pans to the back of a closet. Christine enjoyed the light work, and as long as she promised not to overtire herself, it had seemed foolish for Clay to insist on subjecting the two of them to his own indifferent culinary skills. He had to admit it was extraordinarily easy to become accustomed to finding Christine waiting for him at the end of a long day with another of her gourmet creations simmering on the stove....

But tonight the range was cold, the counter empty. When he stepped out of the kitchen, the dim light illuminating the bare dinner table came from the direction of the living room.

He found Christine curled on the couch, swathed in a velour dressing gown and his mother's green-and-gold mohair afghan. She did not appear to notice his arrival. By the light of a single small lamp she was studying a sheaf of papers on her lap, papers of various sizes and colors that he recognized as the muddy pastels of carbonless invoices. With a dazed expression she read each sheet slowly, then folded it neatly and inserted it into its window envelope; she arranged the envelopes in a tidy stack on the cushion beside her. As the stack grew higher, her face grew chalkier.

Clay called her name. She did not hear him. He stripped off his jacket and tossed it across the back of one of the dining chairs. Stepping out of his riding boots, he deliberately dropped them on the plank floor with a thud. Christine jumped. Clay murmured soothingly, "Sorry about that, love. I didn't mean to startle you."

Her stricken expression changed to a smile of welcome and relief. "I didn't hear you come in," she said. She glanced at her wristwatch. "I seem to have lost all track of time." Hastily she laid aside the last of the mail and dropped the afghan atop it. Leaping to her bare feet, she padded across the room to greet Clay.

When his arms wrapped around her slender body, she melted against him, clinging. "I'm so glad to see you," she whispered as they kissed. When the embrace ended, she settled back on her heels and asked, "So how did the dive go today? Do you and Denny think you're any closer to finding what you're looking for?"

"We didn't stumble across any leaking barrels conveniently labeled Toxic Waste, if that's what you mean," Clay replied, his insouciant tone masking his concern. He could not forget the look he'd spotted on her face when he first stepped into the house. "The dive itself was pleasant, but the real work will be done in the lab, when we analyze the samples we've collected."

Christine nodded thoughtfully. "That's the way it is with most jobs," she agreed. "The tedious, unglamorous tasks are the ones that produce the results. Do you do the analysis yourself, or is there someone else at the Institute who handles the lab work?"

"I do what I can, but actually Denny's the one with the degree in chemistry," Clay explained as they sat together on the sofa. With Christine's encouragement, he outlined the duties of the various staff members.

"Sounds fascinating," she told him with what sounded like genuine enthusiasm. "I wish there was some way I could help out. Unfortunately I'm not sure what good I'd be as a volunteer, unless you need somebody to ensure that the animals' feed troughs are tastefully garnished." When Clay chuckled, Christine exclaimed, "Oh, dear. Speaking of food, I'm running way behind schedule. I need to start cooking dinner." She tried to stand, but Clay's grip prevented her.

"Forget about cooking. We'll order pizza," he dismissed. "I'm more interested in hearing about your day." He paused, giving Christine an opening, waiting for her to mention the correspondence she'd obviously found so distressing. She said nothing. He pressed, "So how did things go for you this afternoon? Did you enjoy being back to work?"

"It was nice to see all the people at the restaurant again," Christine said. "It made me realize how much I've missed everyone. But I didn't stay there very long. Since I had other errands to run, I thought I'd better do them before I wore myself out completely."

Clay's eyes darkened. He fingered the robe she was wearing. "I can see you must have dropped by your house to pick up more clothes. Did the driving overtire you? You haven't felt nauseous again, have you?"

"Oh, no, nothing like that," she responded. "Just a little sleepy. When I came back here, I changed because I meant to take a nap, but somehow I got...sidetracked."

Frustrated by her reluctance to open up to him, Clay persisted, "When I walked in you seemed engrossed in your mail. What was so interesting?"

Christine smiled poignantly. "There was a note from my little brother. Bless his heart, it can't be much fun for a twelve-year-old to write to a grown-up sister he scarcely knows, but I do love him for making the effort. Other than Adam's letter, there was a card from my old college roommate. That's about all...." The lie died on her lips as slowly Clay began to shake his head back and forth.

"No, that's not all, Christine," he said seriously. "I don't know why you're trying to hide things from me.

I spotted that stack of bills in your lap the instant I walked into the room."

He felt her bristle, then all at once she slumped against him. "I didn't want to bother you," she told him. "It's not your problem."

"Anything that concerns you is my problem," Clay said.

With his arm wrapped around her, gently he massaged her side through the thickness of the plush robe while he thumbed through the heap of forms and statements from various doctors, hospitals, and labs. Words like *copayment* and *deductible* appeared with depressing regularity, and he tried not to wince as he added numbers in his head.

When he finished glancing over the last of the bills he set them aside and observed matter-of-factly, "These are pretty impressive figures. Is the bottom line equally impressive? How much will you personally be expected to pay out of your own pocket? I know you have medical insurance."

Although Christine's features were still pale, she appeared to be rallying. "You're right," she told him. "I do have very good insurance, for which I've forked over a small fortune in premiums over the years, though I've never made a claim. But even good insurance doesn't cover everything. As far as I can decipher, I now owe another small fortune—all because I demonstrated the poor judgment to actually become ill."

She paused, pouting. "Honestly, Clay," she muttered, "considering how much it costs to be sick these days, it's a wonder anybody ever does it."

Her attempt at humor failed to amuse him. "That's not funny, Christine," he said darkly.

She shrugged. "Believe me, I know."

They were both silent, then Clay asked bluntly, "Do you think you can afford to pay the bills?"

"I can hardly afford *not* to," Christine retorted. Her eyes grew murky as she considered. "As it happens, I suppose I do have enough savings to clear these accounts. It may be necessary to dip into my retirement fund, but, thank goodness, at least I have the money available somewhere. Unfortunately this is just the tip of the iceberg. As long as my treatment continues, the costs are going to keep mounting—and after a while, paying them off may become a little tricky."

Promptly Clay told her, "You know I'll help any way I can."

Christine's eyes shimmered. Reaching up to stroke Clay's cheek, she whispered huskily, "Thank you. I appreciate that more than you'll ever realize."

For a long moment she gazed at him, her countenance vulnerable and adoring; then her face changed and she looked away. "Don't worry," she said thickly. "I'm grateful for your offer, but there's no need for you to hock the Harley just yet. By an amazing coincidence, this very afternoon I was presented with the opportunity to pick up a substantial amount of cash."

Clay heard the undertone in her voice, and he stiffened. "What are you talking about?"

With a raspy intake of breath, Christine announced baldly, "Reese has offered to buy my share of the restaurant. He wants me out of there."

She thought Clay would explode. "Because you have cancer?" he bit out. His eyes blazed; she could feel him shake with a fury so intense the very air seemed to vibrate. "That bastard! I knew he was a self-centered creep the first time I laid eyes on him. I should have decked him then and saved us all a lot of trouble. He can't do that to you, if for no other reason than because there are laws—"

Christine waved him to silence. For some reason Clay's fulminating anger made it easier for her to control her own indignation, to view her predicament objectively. "Reese says it has nothing to do with my health, and I'm inclined to believe him. The fact is that I hurt him, I hurt him a lot. Lately I've been so engrossed in you—and in my health—that I haven't given much thought to how Reese must be feeling. I should have realized how angry and humiliated he'd be, and how naive it was of me to assume he and I could continue to work together as if nothing had happened."

Clay refused to be mollified. "You cannot just let Reese Cagney push you out of your own business, no matter how guilty you feel. There's a principle involved. You need to talk to an attorney."

"Why? What good would it do?" Christine countered. "When one partner wants out of a business, there's not a whole lot that can be done to prevent the breakup. If Reese and I become involved in a legal battle, it's bound to affect the management of the restaurant. We could end up bankrupting La Courgette and putting our employees out of work—not to mention wiping out the only significant asset I possess. I don't think that's what Reese wants. I sure as hell know it's not what I want."

Reluctantly Clay nodded. "You really love that place, don't you?"

"I built it," Christine said simply. "Hurting it would be like hurting my own child."

Hugging her consolingly, Clay asked, "So if you don't want to sue Reese, what do you want to do?"

She sighed. "Apart from getting better and living happily ever after with you, you mean? I'm not sure. Before you came in, I was thinking that maybe the wisest thing for me to do would be to let Reese and his father buy my share of the restaurant, after all, and then use the money to start over again with some-place smaller than La Courgette, more personal."

"It sounds like a lot of work," Clay commented.

"Oh, it is," Christine said. "Opening a restaurant is just about the hardest work you can imagine. There are so many things you have to do, all the way from scouting out a good location and training employees to planning the menu and ordering the flatware. It's exhausting and risky and frustrating, one hassle after another." She hesitated, and as Clay watched, her eyes brightened. "Starting a business is always hard work," she mused, her face beginning to glow with enthusiasm, "but, you know, it's kind of wonderful, too. I've never forgotten how I felt when we opened La Cour-gette. I was working fourteen hours a day, but it didn't matter because everything was new, everything was a challenge—"

Suddenly she broke off. Staring at Clay with fur-rowed brows, she demanded, "Why are you looking at me that way?" She touched his mouth, which was stretched into a loopy smile. "You're grinning like that silly purple walrus you gave me."

Clay shrugged. "I guess I'm happy," he told Christine. "I'm sitting here thinking how beautiful you are and how much I love you—and how great it is to see you excited about something again. You've been so depressed."

"I guess I have been," she admitted ruefully, "but now, instead, I'm beginning to feel mad, damned mad."

"At Reese?"

She shook her head. "Reese hasn't done anything wrong. It's the cancer I'm mad at. Whenever I think about my illness, it makes me so furious I want to spit! How *dare* some stupid disease try to spoil my life? Especially now when I have everything to live for—when I have you."

Clay seemed dazed. "There have been times when I've wondered if you even see me," he murmured.

Christine gasped. "Oh, Clay! You're the only thing I've been able to see since I first met you." She pressed her palms against his chest. She could feel his heartbeat, the life force within him strong and vital. She needed to share that strength, that vitality. She needed him. Gazing up at Clay with love and gratitude, she whispered humbly, "Oh, my darling, thank you for being so patient with me. I know I haven't been very good company for you lately. It wasn't deliberate. I never intended to let cancer dominate me, yet somehow it has."

"It's an easy trap to fall into," Clay agreed tolerantly, "and lots of people do. But you can learn to avoid it. You just have to refuse to put your life on hold while you battle your illness. Life doesn't begin at some distant point after you finish chemotherapy—life is here, life is *now.*"

"Then it's time we started living again, isn't it?" Christine murmured, and winding her arms around Clay's neck, she drew his mouth down hungrily to hers.

CHAPTER NINE

LIBERTY ABRAMS stood on the flybridge of the Institute's research vessel, a converted trawler, and braced herself against the gentle yawing motion of the boat. Shading her eyes against the glare from the water, she scanned the ocean. "I don't see any sign of the guys yet," she hollered down to Christine.

In the stern Christine lounged in the shelter of a canvas awning, her feet propped up on the gunwale while she listened to one of Lib's old Doors tapes. She was gazing at a freighter stopped in the distance outside the Golden Gate, presumably waiting for the arrival of the pilot boat that would guide it into San Francisco Bay, when Lib spoke. Turning down the volume on "Riders on the Storm," Christine lifted her head to squint through her sunglasses. "They've been gone quite a while, haven't they?" she called back, her casual tone belying her anxiety.

Lib glanced at her watch. "Not too long. They should each have plenty of air left." Tossing her long graying braid over her shoulder, she descended the ladder from the bridge and plopped alongside Christine's chair. "Denny and Clay are both expert divers, practically half dolphin," Lib reminded Christine, patting her hand reassuringly. "They'll be back soon."

Christine tugged off her tinted glasses and rubbed her eyes. "Of course you're right. I don't understand why I'm so antsy all of a sudden. From the beginning I've known that Clay was a diver, and it's never bothered me before."

"It was probably actually watching him disappear over the side that frightened you," Lib told her. "That, and not being able to see what's going on down there. There's always something a little spooky about bobbing serenely on the nice, warm surface while people you care about are poking around in the dark and the cold, facing heaven knows what."

Christine shuddered. "Suddenly I wish I'd never read *Jaws*."

She expected the other woman to laugh, but instead Lib said seriously, "Your fears aren't all that silly. Diving is a dangerous business, and there are a lot of sharks around here. Still, Denny and Clay have been working in these waters for years without incident. They know how to take care of themselves." She considered. "For what it's worth, a diver in open ocean is usually in a lot less danger of shark attack than a surfer or some swimmer who's splashing around near a beach, where a great white might mistake him for a seal."

"That makes me feel *so* much better," Christine retorted with a smile.

Lib noted, "I can sympathize with your concern. I used to worry about Denny all the time, until he started taking me with him on some of his dives so that I could see for myself what it's like. You ought to ask Clay to give you a few scuba lessons. Do you swim?"

"I can splash around in a pool with relative safety," Christine said. "Unfortunately, even that's out of the question right now." She swung her legs down from the gunwale and stood with a languid stretch that caused her long-sleeved shirt to ride up. She dropped her arms and started to tuck the tail back into the loose waistband of her slacks. As she did, she noted dryly the difference between her attire and Lib's. The older woman was dressed very sensibly for boating, in a halter top and a pair of ragged cutoffs, bleached grayish white, that bared her tanned legs to the summer sun and the salt spray. Christine, mindful of Dr. Fong's warnings about the effects of ultraviolet rays on a system weakened by chemotherapy, was covered from neck to toe in a shirt and lightweight slacks, and whenever she stepped from beneath the shelter of the awning, she donned a floppy beach hat with the words Souvenir of Fishermen's Wharf stitched around the brim.

Slathering a fresh coating of sunscreen on her face and arms, Christine gazed out over the water with longing. "I'd love to go swimming," she said with a sigh. "I haven't really been out on the water in years, not since college, when I spent spring break on Catalina with my—with some friends." She paused, her expression wistful. "That seems such a long time ago," she murmured. "I was a different person then— carefree, absolutely certain that my whole life was going to turn out exactly the way I planned it."

"Times change, people change," Lib observed ironically. "You'd never guess it to look at me now, but I had my very own I. Magnin charge card when I was eleven. If I hadn't met Denny while we were at

Berkeley, these days I'd probably be wearing fun furs and hosting teas for opera mavens.''

As if to punctuate her remark, the Jim Morrison cassette switched off with a sharp click. Lib and Christine both laughed. ''Well, so much for my taste in music,'' Lib said, smiling. ''And speaking of teas, I don't know about you, but I'm getting hungry. The guys are bound to surface pretty soon, so why don't we go ahead and set out lunch? Do you prefer to eat here or in the cabin? The cabin is hot and stuffy, but there's a table.''

''If it's all the same to you, I think I'd rather stay out on deck,'' Christine decided. ''Just let me fetch the hamper and the ice chest from the galley.''

From the moment Clay first introduced Christine to his two best friends, Lib and her husband, Denny, a big, bearded bear of a man, had welcomed her warmly. They made it clear that because she was Clay's special lady, she was special to them, and Christine quickly became very fond of the Abramses. They were bright, well-educated people united by a love for the earth that was almost as intense as their love for each other. If their taste and appearance occasionally made the couple seem to have stepped through a time warp, the simple explanation was that during the sixties they'd settled into a life-style that suited them and had never seen any reason to change it.

One of the things Christine liked most about her new friends was the matter-of-fact way in which they regarded her illness, accepting its incursion into her life with a lack of overt pity that Christine found wonderfully refreshing. With the Abramses, she was actually able to forget about her health.

The two women knelt together and unpacked the luncheon Christine had prepared. After spreading a cloth over the decking, she set out plates and silverware from the hamper, then fished a small covered bowl out of the bottom of the chest. "I wondered what I'd done with this," she muttered, wiping off ice water. "Here, Lib, I have something I want you to taste," she said, unsnapping the plastic seal. "It's mushroom-truffle pâté."

Lib sniffed the aromatic mixture with pleasure. "I sure do like your idea of a picnic," she said with a chuckle. "If lunch had been up to me, I would have brought cheese sandwiches and carrot sticks."

"There's not a thing in the world wrong with carrot sticks," Christine told her. "I just felt like splurging." From the depths of the hamper she produced a box of water wafers. "Have some crackers and tell me what you think."

Lib sampled the mixture and shivered with pleasure. "This stuff is scrumptious—your recipe?"

Shaking her head, Christine said, "No, it's one of Amir's, the chef at La Courgette. He's very good."

"He's great," Lib amplified as she smeared pâté on another cracker. "You ought to swipe him for your new place."

Christine sighed. "I wish I could. I know he'd probably come if I asked him—at the moment he's not too happy with my ex-associate—but I can't ask him. When Reese and I dissolved the partnership, one of the provisions he insisted our agreement had to contain was my promise that I wouldn't hire away any of

La Courgette's principal staff for a period of two years."

Lib wrinkled her nose. "That sounds sort of...mean."

"Reese is a careful businessman," Christine explained. "He was just making sure that my leaving La Courgette wouldn't adversely affect the value of the restaurant. In his position, I'd probably do the same." She shrugged. "Of course, even if I was free to hire Amir, I probably couldn't afford him, anyway. For one thing, I'm sure he'd want his cousin to come along as his assistant, and heaven only knows how long it'll be before I could even dream about taking on the pair of them. At the moment my ambitions are a little more modest."

"So how are plans shaping up?" Lib asked.

"Slowly," Christine answered. "There's a tremendous amount of work and research involved in starting a restaurant. I did all this ten years ago, but things have changed a lot in the past decade. The demographics of Marin County are different, the laws and zoning ordinances are different, and of course everything costs so much more. With money as tight as it is these days, I may have to go far afield to get the small-business loans I'll need—not that I'm anywhere near the point of arranging financing yet. I'm still trying to figure out what kind of restaurant I could start that there aren't already dozens of."

Lib looked surprised. "I assumed it would be vegetarian."

"No, probably not," Christine said. "After all the years I invested in La Courgette, I'd feel I was competing with myself."

"It would be hard to compete with La Courgette," Lib conceded. "It's a great place, even if it is kind of off the beaten path. Den and I ate there on our anniversary once. It was awfully pricey, but the food was very good, and I loved the scenery."

Christine's lips twisted. "Veggies with a view—that's been La Courgette's big selling point from the beginning. I'm afraid that pretty scenery is one thing my new restaurant won't have. I'm looking for some location with lots of foot traffic, possibly a commercial area that needs a good spot for lunch. It'll have to be small enough for me to handle on my own. When I first open, I'll probably be chief cook and bottle washer."

"Maybe you should start with a deli," Lib suggested, "someplace with great pastrami."

Pretending to be shocked, Christine chided, "Shame on you, Lib. What would a nice vegan girl like you know about pastrami?"

The older woman smacked her lips reminiscently. "I can't help it if I come from a family of unenlightened carnivores. Denny hates me to talk about it, but, oh, my, when I think of the things my mother could do with a brisket...."

Christine said temptingly, "If I'd realized you felt that way, I would have packed something good and meaty for lunch. In the time Clay and Denny have been underwater, you and I could have eaten half a cow. If we threw the bones overboard, the men would never be the wiser."

Lib grinned. "No, throwing the bones overboard would attract sharks, and I'm sure the guys would notice dorsal fins circling the boat. Besides," she added, rummaging through the wicker hamper, fishing out a can of olives, ''I don't think you could fit another sandwich in here, much less a side of beef. I can't believe how much food you prepared.''

''Yeah, there's probably too much,'' Christine acknowledged offhandedly. ''I guess I felt like going all out for today because it's going to be a while before I'm in the mood to cook again or even eat very much.''

Lib looked up. All trace of humor had vanished from her face. She stared piercingly at Christine. ''What do you mean?''

''I'm scheduled for chemotherapy in the morning,'' Christine said.

The olives slipped through Lib's limp fingers. ''Good Lord,'' she gasped. ''Here you are, cracking silly jokes and blithely talking about your new restaurant, and all the while you know you're going to be having chemo *tomorrow?* How can you be so calm?''

''How else do you want me to be?'' Christine asked quietly. ''The treatment won't be any easier if I worry myself sick about it. Knowing that for a while I'm going to be more or less incapacitated makes me all the more determined to enjoy the good times—like today.''

Lib's eyes narrowed. ''You're a brave woman, Christine. If I were in your position, I don't think I'd be able to cope.''

''Sure you would,'' Christine assured her. ''You'd cope because that's all you can do. Anyway, whenever I walk into the clinic, I remind myself that each session means I'm one step closer to the end of them, to having all this behind me. There's a lot of strength in that knowledge.''

"How does Clay feel about the treatments?" Lib asked.

"They worry him," Christine answered grimly. "That's one reason I won't let him stay with me. He always offers, and I always tell him no." She lifted her thin shoulders. "We argue about it every time, but in the end I win. Clay drops me off at the clinic and then heads on to the Institute. By the time he returns to pick me up in the evening, the worst has passed and I'm able to face him again with a certain amount of dignity."

Lib looked confused. "I don't understand you at all, Christine. If Clay wants to be with you—and you obviously need him to be with you—then why do you insist on undergoing this torture alone?"

"Because I can't stand watching him ache for me!" Christine exploded, jumping to her feet, almost overturning the picnic hamper. "I can't bear to lie there helpless, knowing that everything I suffer, he's suffering, too." She scrubbed her face with her hands. "I try to spare him, Lib, really I do, but I'm not an actress and sometimes it's impossible for me to hide how I feel."

"But there's no reason that you should hide your feelings from Clay," Lib insisted. "I'm sure he wouldn't want you to. He loves you."

Christine bit her lip. "I love him, too." She turned her head to gaze across the water. Behind her the rolling peaks of the coastal mountains scalloped the horizon, but in the west, except for the cluster of small dark shapes that were the Farallon Islands, there was only blue-green ocean stretching endlessly toward blue-green sky, cloudless and tranquil. She wished she could tap into that tranquillity. "Loving each other the way we do is what makes it so awful," she said. "The most selfish thing I ever did in my life was to become involved with Clay McMurphy."

"Are you blaming yourself for falling in love?" Lib asked.

Christine reflected. "No. Falling in love with Clay was as inevitable as, I suppose, my contracting cancer was—but I had no right to expose him to my pain. There was a point very early in our relationship when he tried to let me go. It was wrong of me to come back to him."

She began to pace the deck, her usually graceful movements jerky and agitated. "I should have remembered what my father's illness did to my mother," she declared bitterly, "but I was only a kid then, and I blamed Mom, I thought she was weak. I didn't understand that cancer is like some monster malevolent sponge. If you're not careful, it can absorb every bit of joy from the patient's life. Worse, it sucks all the happiness out of the people around you, too. Clay was a different man before he met me, carefree, unencumbered. He had a job he loved, he could take off on that bike of his whenever the spirit moved him. Now, because of me, he drives my Nissan a lot more than he rides his bike and he misses so much work that any boss besides an angel like your Dr. Berlinger would have fired him long ago...."

Lib sighed. "I don't suppose it would do much good, would it, to point out that I've known Clay years longer than you have? Yes, he was a different man before he met you—he was an obsessed workaholic who tried to fill the vacuum in his personal life by listening to sappy Broadway musicals. He hadn't been involved in a serious relationship since he and his wife split up. Denny and I used to worry that some night he'd roar off on his motorcycle and just...never come back." She shook her head emphatically. "All that's changed now, Christine. You've brought stability and emotion into his life, you've given him purpose. You may think you're a burden to Clay, but what you really are is his anchor."

"Some anchor," Christine replied, deliberately misunderstanding her friend. "One good puff of wind would blow me away." She exhaled raspily. "I want to believe you, Lib, but the plain fact is that I know I've caused Clay a lot of grief, and I feel very guilty about it."

Lib suggested carefully, "Maybe you ought to consider talking to a counselor, to help you work through that guilt and all the other feelings you're obviously having trouble dealing with."

Christine stared at Lib. After a moment she nodded slowly in a gesture of surrender. "You're probably right," she admitted. "I'm seeing every other kind of doctor there is—why not a shrink, too? At any rate, it can't hurt." She gazed out at the dark, mysterious water. Somewhere beneath the surface was the man she loved. "I wish I could be with Clay right now," she murmured.

I WISH Christine was with me right now, Clay thought, gliding silently through the depths, the only sound the even, ever-present susurration of the compressed air he breathed. Shafts of sunlight filtered in gauzy curtains through the clear water as he and Denny, a few yards away, swam slowly in formation, methodically crossing and recrossing the quadrant they'd marked for the day's search. Their passing shadows startled a school of pilchards that darted up in a glittering silver shower, like coins tossed by some fabulous despot. Behind his mouthpiece Clay smiled, dazzled momentarily by the sheer beauty of the sight. Then his mood sobered. No matter how much he loved the ocean and longed to share its richness with Christine, he was not there to enjoy himself. He had a job to do.

He studied the seabed below him carefully. Limited in their search to comparatively shallow water, they were traversing a region where a whole maze of fault lines extended outward from the coastline. The area was crisscrossed with seismic fissures, some only centimeters wide, others gaping crevices dark and deep enough to easily hide a man—or barrels of toxic waste. As Clay studied the bottom, trying to peer through the sediment and the swaying vegetation, he admitted yet again how unlikely it was that he and Denny, two lone divers in a very big ocean, would ever find what it was that they were looking for—assuming they even knew what they were looking for. Government survey teams with deep-water submersibles and the most up-to-date sonar imaging equipment were only just now beginning to map the area, in hopes of eventually compiling a list of all the underwater dump sites, and even the federal agencies funding the inventory admitted that the magnitude of the task was almost beyond them. For Clay and his colleagues to imagine that they could succeed with perseverance and a couple of aqualungs gave whole new dimensions to the word chutzpah. Yet neither Clay nor anybody else at the Institute had ever suggested that he abandon his quest.

He glanced at the stopwatch on his diver's watch, noting that it was almost time for him and his partner to reverse direction and tack back across the search area. He signaled to Denny. At once the bearded man halted his forward movement and swam over to Clay, dragging a net of small plastic vials behind him. With hand gestures the two men confirmed that both of them had just enough air left in their tanks to complete another sweep, and then Denny opened one of the tubes to collect a water specimen, as he'd been doing at regular intervals throughout the dive. After capping the vial, with a grease pen he wrote a code number on it and returned the sample to his carrying bag. But when Denny tried to clip the pen back onto his utility belt, it slipped out of his fingers and drifted softly downward toward a rift directly below them on the ocean floor. Clay swooped to catch the pen—and that was when he spotted the gleam of metal deep in the crevice.

LIB REPLACED the Doors cassette with some vintage Jefferson Airplane, and she was lip-synching "White Rabbit" when the men finally returned. Their reemergence caught Christine by surprise. Lounging under the sunshade, she sipped mineral water and enjoyed Lib's good-natured Grace Slick imitation until all at once the older woman broke character and dashed to the side to peer overboard. Christine switched off the tape player. In the booming silence she could hear a peculiar bubbling sound. She joined

Lib at the rail just as Denny's ursine head broke through the surface.

Lib hollered to her husband, "It's about time you two showed up! We were beginning to think you'd had a close encounter with something predatory."

Denny removed his mouthpiece and gulped the fresh air greedily. "Sorry about that, babe," he called, treading water. "We kind of got distracted." He dog-paddled to the ladder and handed the mesh bag up to Lib, who carefully hoisted it onboard while her husband grabbed the middle rung on the ladder and started to scale it.

"But where's Clay?" Christine asked in alarm.

The big man pushed his mask over his forehead and smiled. "Don't worry, hon, he's right behind me. He has the camera and he wanted to use up the film." With grace surprising for someone hampered with massive air tanks and flippers, Denny climbed aboard. Water dribbled from his beard and sluiced down his wet suit in dank-smelling rivulets. He moved forward to avoid splashing the picnic cloth the women had spread out, and Lib began to help him with his diving gear.

Christine bent low over the rail, shading her eyes with her palm, trying to squint through the glare reflecting off the water. Finally, after what seemed like ages, a dark shadow appeared beneath the brightness, and a moment later Clay surfaced. As soon as he emerged into the open air, he spit out his mouthpiece and whooped with exhilaration.

Christine cried, "My God, what's happened?"

"Not sure yet," he gasped. Christine bent low over the side, and Clay handed up his thirty-five millimeter still camera in its bright yellow waterproof housing. "Be careful with that, darling, it's precious," he told her. Because of the compressed air he'd been breathing, his voice sounded raw.

Cradling the camera like a baby, Christine stepped out of the way while Clay hauled himself up the ladder and clambered onto the deck. When he ripped off his face mask, his eyes glowed. At once he began to divest himself of his heavy scuba equipment. As he slipped out of the harness for his air tank and he started to unbuckle his weight belt, his gaze darted to his diving partner. "You saw. What do you think?"

Denny, who was stowing gear in a locker, looked dubious. "It's hard to say, man. It could be anything. People have been dumping their garbage in these waters since World War Two."

"Whatever it is can't be legal," Clay agreed with a grimace. "I've checked records going back fifty years, and there's no mention of there ever having been any sanctioned dumping in this immediate area—"

With an eloquent snort, Denny countered, "You know as well as I do that most of the records from those days aren't worth diddly. Procedures were just as sloppy. Half the time boats started jettisoning their loads as soon as they went out of the Golden Gate."

"Too true," Clay muttered. He continued removing his gear with Christine's help. When she touched his arm, she realized that beneath the sleek black rubber wet suit, he was trembling.

"Good grief, Clay, you're shaking like a leaf," she exclaimed.

He captured her wrist and splayed her palm against his chest. "If you think that's bad, feel my heart," he murmured. "You should have been down there with me a while ago. Denny thought I was going to hyperventilate. He was afraid he was going to have to rescue me—weren't you?" Clay added, raising his voice so that his friend could hear.

The bearded man shrugged. "I don't know about actually having to rescue you, but I'll admit I've never seen you come as close to losing it as you did when when we first spotted those barrels."

Christine snapped up her head. "Barrels?" she echoed eagerly. "What are you talking about? What sort of barrels?"

Clay sighed. "It's hard to say exactly. From what little we could actually see through the sediment, they look like standard fifty-gallon metal drums—the kind industrial waste is stored in. I thought I could make out some sort of label painted on the side of one of them, but it was too corroded to read from a distance."

Christine frowned. "What do you mean, from a distance?"

"The barrels are lodged in a crevice, a few meters below the level of the ocean bed," Clay said. "If the sun hadn't happened to be shining at exactly the right angle, and Denny and I hadn't happened to pause in just the right spot, we might never have noticed anything." He paused. "I'll have to make sure I carry plenty of light with me when I try for a closer look," he appended mildly.

Clay's insouciant tone failed to disguise the significance of his words. Christine stared at him in horror, all her fears returning in full force. "A closer look?

You mean you're planning on diving down into some sort of—of crack in the ocean floor?''

With a winning smile, Clay tried to reassure her. ''It's only a little seismic fissure, love, not some abyssal trench. The spot where the barrels are lodged isn't as wide as this boat. I'd have gone in today, but Denny wouldn't let me. He was right, of course. We didn't have enough air, and besides, there's other equipment we'll need before we can document our find properly—lights, a vacuum to suction off the sediment, a videocamera . . . So we set out markers, I finished off the roll of film in the thirty-five, and then we surfaced.''

Christine bit her lip, struggling to understand. ''And you think that whatever's in these metal drums you found is what has poisoned your elephant seal, is that it?''

Clay smiled ironically. ''Well, to be perfectly honest, we haven't yet *proved* that Moonie's paralysis was caused by pollution at all. But the signs seem to point to some water-borne agent, and if those barrels are leaking chemicals, the currents in this area could conceivably carry the contamination toward the spot where the seal was beached. So we have to find out what's in the barrels. Once we know, we can look for traces of those chemicals in the seal's bloodstream. . . .''

His fingers tightened around Christine's. ''It's a long shot, like winning the lottery. Denny's right when he says that the storage containers we stumbled across down there could be anything, including totally innocuous. That stuff probably has nothing at all to do with what's wrong with the animal at the Institute, and yet I can't shake this gut feeling that this is it, that we've finally found it."

Christine nodded confidently. "Trust that feeling, Clay. You and Denny have been working too hard to be misled now. And the way you guys just happened to stop in exactly the right spot—well, it sure sounds like fate to me."

"We could use a little divine intervention," he conceded, his tone almost whimsical. After a second he sobered. "Time's running out, Christine. If somebody doesn't discover what harmed Moonie in time to prevent it from spreading south to the breeding grounds at Año Nuevo, there could be ecological disaster. Seventy years ago elephant seals were almost extinct, less than a hundred of them left in the entire world. Now there are eighty thousand—but with a little carelessness, mankind could still wipe them all—"

Denny and Lib began to clap.

Clay broke off and turned to stare at his friends, who were perched together on the gunwale beneath the canopy, watching him with almost identical wry grins.

"Great speech, man," Denny drawled with good-natured insolence. "We could have used you in People's Park in '69."

Clay felt his face burn. Raking back his wet hair with his hands, he admitted abashedly, "Well, Dr. Berlinger did accuse me once of imagining myself as David, squared off against the Goliath polluters of this world. I guess he wasn't kidding."

"Personally I think you both have earned the right to feel impressed with yourselves," Christine told the men stoutly. "You certainly have impressed *me*. I know what you're doing is important. I just wish it wasn't so risky."

"But it's a risk worth taking," Clay said. He stroked Christine's pale cheek. His expression grew tender. "All important things are dangerous," he reminded her with a smile, "even love."

That smile warmed Christine while Clay and Denny put away their diving gear and the party settled for lunch. Fishing around in the cooler, Christine pulled out cans of soda. "An occasion like this calls for a toast. I wish I'd brought something festive."

Lib laughed. "You mean you don't have any champagne in that ice chest? You seem to have everything else!"

"Alas, not," Christine declared. "I'm afraid we'll have to settle for diet soda." She handed out the soft drinks and glanced at Lib. "Will you do the honors, please?"

The older woman nodded. She gazed at the men with warm eyes and addressed them fondly. "You know, you two, by tonight I'm probably going to think of half a dozen nice, pithy quotations from Shakespeare or the Bible that would be appropriate for a moment like this, but of course right now my mind is a blank. So I guess all I can do is tell you both, on behalf of Christine and Moonie and me—and a world that unfortunately will probably never appreciate what you've done for it—is that we love you and we're very, very proud of you. Congratulations, Denny and Clay, and thanks."

"Amen," Christine murmured sincerely, lifting her drink in salute. Despite the absurd picture the four friends made, sprawled on the deck, waving soda cans in the air, Christine felt her eyes swim with happy tears.

Clay and Denny tried to do justice to Christine's lunch, but soon they produced oceanographic charts and began telling the women all about the search, too absorbed in their discovery to pay more than scant attention to the food they were downing. Christine watched with some chagrin as the pâté and other delicacies she'd prepared so carefully disappeared without notice, and yet it was impossible not to share Clay's excitement, his triumph. She'd never really understood how much his work meant to him. During that first night they spent together, he had told her he was involved in some quixotic quest to track down the source of the pollution that was poisoning the marine mammals he loved so passionately, but only now, seeing the triumph gleam in his eyes, feeling him literally shake with excitement, did she begin to comprehend the power of the forces that drove him.

Ducking her head so that her expression was veiled by the drooping brim of her hat, Christine gazed longingly at Clay. He'd changed from his wet suit into a T-shirt and brief shorts. She felt her breath quicken at the sight of his broad shoulders stretching the soft cotton shirt, the bare brown legs and heavily muscled thighs that she knew so intimately. He looked casual and vibrant and sexy. As much as she was enjoying this time with their friends, she wished she and Clay could be alone so she could show him exactly how happy she was for him. . . .

Denny laughed. "Hey, Christine, could you please pass us the Greek salad, or have you decided to eat it all yourself?"

Christine jumped. "Wh-what did you say?" she stammered, blushing.

Lib eyed her knowingly, and it occurred to Christine that the other woman might be in a similar mood for privacy with her husband. "We asked if you could pass us the salad so that we can have seconds," Lib repeated patiently. "I'm still trying to figure out what gives that special zip to the dressing."

Hastily handing over a bowl of marinated vegetables and feta cheese that had somehow been pushed behind her, out of reach of Clay and the Abramses, Christine said, "You're probably tasting the lemon. I always substitute a little fresh lemon juice for part of the wine vinegar."

"Well, whatever it is, it's great," Lib said. She began dishing salad for herself and her husband.

Clay gazed thoughtfully at Christine. "Are you all right?" he asked in an undertone. "You look a little flushed."

Christine felt her cheeks grow even warmer. "I'm fine."

"You're sure?" Clay pressed. "You're not getting too much sun, are you?"

She smiled. "I told you, I'm fine, darling. If I'm getting too much of anything, it must be sheer joy. This has been a wonderful, exciting day."

"If you think today was exciting, just wait till tomorrow," Denny boomed jovially. "Can you imagine how Dr. Berlinger's going to react when we tell him what we found today?"

"I guess he'll get pretty worked up," Christine allowed.

Denny guffawed. "'Worked up' is putting it mildly! Do you have any idea how much Dr. Berlinger has invested in this search we've been carrying on these past months? Not just money—though he's spent a fortune—but his life's work and the reputation of the Institute are at stake. If the water samples we collected near those barrels show any sign of contamination, he's going to drag us back out here tomorrow with videocameras and salvage equipment and probably a brass band, if he can fit it on the boat."

"It sounds fantastic," Christine said. "I don't suppose there's any way I could tag along with you guys, is there?"

Clay considered. "Well, we could try to—" Suddenly his expression changed. "Not tomorrow, darling," he reminded her gently.

Christine caught her breath as if she'd been punched. She'd been so enrapt in Clay's discovery that she'd forgotten her appointment at the clinic the following morning. She hadn't believed there was anything that could make her forget chemotherapy. Gulping back her disappointment, she muttered, "Oh, of course. Well, I guess I'll have to settle for being with you all in spirit when you show your find to Dr. Berlinger."

Scowling, Clay offered, "I suppose we could postpone the return trip for a few days."

Denny blustered in confusion. "What do you mean, postpone it? For God's sake, man, this project means even more to you than it does to me, so why, after all this time—" He swallowed his words with a strangled gulp when Lib suddenly jabbed him with her elbow.

Stunned by the magnitude of the sacrifice Clay was offering, Christine looked away, so filled with emotion that she was unable to face him. Gnawing her lip, she recalled how, that stormy evening when he found her parked by the ocean, he had referred to himself scornfully as a knight in shining leather. He had meant the words to be sarcastic, yet in a peculiar way they had turned out to be true. Clay was an odd sort of knight, on an odd sort of quest. Locating a toxic waste dump might not be everybody's idea of a chivalric crusade, but it was Clay's, and now, just when his Grail was almost in reach, he was proposing to delay his moment of triumph—because of her.

Christine gazed at Clay, and her eyes brimmed with love. "No, Clay," she declared firmly, "you are not going to postpone your trip even for a day. Your work is too important. Even though I'll be disappointed not to be with you when you show your find to Dr. Berlinger, I'd be a lot more disappointed if you waited on my account." She grinned. "So there."

Clay looked quizzical. "You're sure you'll be all right?"

"Yes, darling, I'm sure I'll be all right," Christine told him. "Knowing how much this discovery means to you, I'll be better than all right." She stretched out her hand to him. "Regardless of whether or not I'm with you, I want you to savor every moment, Clay. You've earned it. I want people to cheer and throw confetti, I want you to feel just as proud and delighted for yourself as I am for you. And in a few days, as soon as I'm feeling up to it, you and I will open a bottle of champagne and have our very own private celebration at home. Is that a deal?"

"You'd better believe it, lady," Clay said, clasping her fingers in his big, warm palm, the sapphire glint in his eyes brilliant with promise.

Christine couldn't remember when she'd last felt so happy.

CHAPTER TEN

"I LOVE YOU, too, Mom. Kiss Jeff and Adam for me. Bye."

Christine listened until she heard the soft click signaling that her overseas telephone connection was broken. In the quiet house the faint noise seemed to boom. When she tried to hang up the receiver, her fingers felt clumsy, and she had to watch to make certain she replaced the handset securely in its cradle. Then, with a sigh, she switched off the table lamp and stared blindly into the darkness.

She had no idea what time it was—obviously either very late or very early. There were no sounds of traffic out on the highway, no canned laughter from a neighbor's TV. Even the ocean seemed silent. When Meg answered the telephone in Germany, she had mentioned something about just preparing lunch for her son. The offhand comment had caused a vision to flash through Christine's weary mind, an unbearably poignant image of her adored little brother settling down to milk and peanut butter at the kitchen table. Christine's eyes burned. She wondered if her mother still trimmed the crusts off sandwiches.

Whatever the hour was, Christine acknowledged that she probably shouldn't have telephoned her mother just then. Meg was perfectly capable of calculating the time difference between Europe and California, and when she had realized that Christine was calling in the middle of the night, she'd become very upset. With doubtful success Christine had tried to reassure her mother that she bore no bad news, that she'd merely been feeling restless, in the mood to talk to her family. She promised Meg that nothing was wrong, that she was recuperating as expected from her latest chemotherapy treatment, already past the most inconvenient side effects and ready to resume normal activities. She gave her mother an update on her search for a site for the new restaurant, she regaled her with an account of the cruise with Clay and the Abramses, and its interesting conclusion. Christine told Meg everything she could think of that would make her life sound busy and exciting and carefree—and when the conversation ended, she had known that her mother remained unconvinced.

The cool night air seeped through Christine's thin cotton gown, and she shivered in the darkness. Tucking her bare feet beneath her, she curled up on the couch and tugged her angora bed jacket tighter around her shoulders. When she turned up the collar, she nuzzled her cheek luxuriously against the delicate knit fabric. The jacket was a present from Clay's mother. Progressive chemotherapy treatments were beginning to affect Christine's sense of touch in bizarre ways, numbing her fingertips yet occasionally making the rest of her skin so hypersensitive that heavy clothing could be almost painful to wear. Christine had tried to hide the problem from Clay, but his eyes were too sharp; he noticed her wincing when she donned her bathrobe, and he demanded an explanation. Later, after he mentioned the situation during a phone call to his parents, Hester McMurphy had responded at once. When Christine opened the mysterious package from Florida and discovered a beautiful handmade bed jacket, lightweight yet warm and as caressingly soft as a summer breeze, she had started to cry, moved by an act of loving generosity from a woman she'd never met.

As Christine sat in the darkness, too agitated to unwind, she stroked the jacket and mused about the kindness of strangers. Although Christine knew that her own mother would never refuse charity to someone who needed it, she couldn't quite imagine Meg going to the trouble of knitting a sweater for Clay. Hester's gift, spontaneous and from the heart, touched Christine deeply. She thought it gave her some insight into how Clay had become the special man she'd always known him to be. She just wished she could figure out how on earth she was ever going to live up to his example.

Yawning windily, Christine reminded herself that she needed rest. She was supposed to talk to a real estate agent the following afternoon, regarding some rental properties that might be suitable for a small lunchroom. But Christine could not sleep. When she and Clay had first retired for the night, she'd actually dozed off for a short while, but then she woke again suddenly, jolted by some feeling of panic too formless to be called a nightmare. Motionless except for her racing heart, she lay in bed for an hour, gazing at the dark ceiling while she prayed for the repose that eluded her. When she finally accepted that sleep was impossible, she crept from Clay's side and went into the liv-

ing room, where impulsively she telephoned her
mother. Now, aching with fatigue, she told herself that
it was time to return to bed. If she could not relax, at
least she could draw comfort from the warmth and
security of Clay's large, slumbering body.

Padding barefoot down the dark hallway, Christine
paused at the bathroom door. She grimaced at the
sour taste tension had left in her mouth. Stepping into
the bathroom, she flipped on the light switch. The
sudden glare dazzled her, and she squinted tightly
while she fumbled for the toothpaste. By the time she
finished cleaning her teeth, her eyes had adjusted to
the brightness. She returned her brush to its holder
inside the medicine cabinet, closed the mirrored
door—and stared directly into her reflection.

Suddenly she saw gawking back at her the image
that had jarred her from sleep: a woman's face, chalky
and emaciated beneath a mop of drab, stringy hair,
with huge, feverish-looking eyes set deep in bruised
hollows above sharp cheekbones. A pitiful, ravaged
face.

Her own face.

Christine flinched. Lowering her lashes, she inhaled raspily, refusing to believe the evidence before
her. This was only a waking nightmare, she reassured
herself stoutly; an unpleasant fantasy triggered by the
remnant of the poisons still circulating through her
bloodstream after her last chemo. If the pathetic,
wasted creature she saw in the mirror was real, she
ought to have noticed the difference long before now.
Such profound changes did not happen overnight. Of
course she knew she'd lost weight, but that didn't
mean she'd lost her *looks,* as well....

With dread Christine opened her eyes again. The white-faced woman was still there. Cautiously Christine reached up to touch the surface of the mirror. She watched the reflection of her fingers recede slowly until they lay across thin, chapped lips that moved in mute melancholy. The fingers advanced again, and this time when they met their twins in the cold glass, there was a sheen of moisture on them, like tears.

For months she'd been telling herself she was improving. She'd convinced herself that her treatments were working, that each session of chemotherapy was only an unpleasant but necessary step on the path to recovery and renewed health. Like the patients of that quack psychologist who'd flourished in the twenties, she'd all but chanted, "Every day, in every way, I am getting better and better." In time she'd come to believe the singsong words.

But now, suddenly seeing herself—really seeing herself—she had to ask the terrifying question: *what if she was wrong?*

All at once Christine's legs were too weak to support her. Limply she stumbled backward, feeling behind her to brace herself as she sank onto the ledge of the bathtub. When she knew she would not fall, she dropped her head into her hands and trembled.

"Christine."

She sensed his presence before he spoke. Sunk in misery, her body still quickened at his nearness. Alerted by a creaking floor plank, or his musky masculine scent faint in the air, or perhaps simply the electric aura he radiated, Christine knew the exact instant Clay loomed over her. Without glancing up, she murmured, "I'm sorry. I didn't mean to wake you. I couldn't sleep, so I decided to telephone my mother, instead.''

His voice was gravelly with concern. "Is something wrong with your family? Is that why you're crying?"

"They're all fine," Christine said. Slowly she lifted her face from her palms. Clay stood framed in the bathroom door, his hastily donned robe gaping open, revealing most of his long, tanned body. From his spatulate toes to his thick, wild mane, he was strong, sexy... healthy. She almost could not bear to look at him. She glanced down at her hands. Broken tendrils of hair, as dry and brittle as straw, were twined around her fingers. She held up the lackluster strands like an offering. "I used to have nice hair," she whispered.

Clay blinked. She saw a gray line of strain appear along the edge of his jaw. "You had beautiful hair," he said quietly, firmly. "You will again. Once you've finished your treatments, after all of this is behind you, everything you think you've lost will come back to you, as good as new. I mean it."

Christine's lips twisted. "Cross your heart and hope to die?" she mocked, her sarcasm edged with despair. She dusted her hands on her gown and stood up stiffly. Clay held out his arms to her, and she went to him like a lost child.

In the granite cradle of his embrace all things were permissible—even the truth. Listening to his heart thud beneath her ear, she confessed, "Oh, darling, sometimes I don't know who I am anymore. I feel as if I've completely lost control of myself, of my emotions, my appearance, everything. I don't think I've ever been a particularly conceited person, but people have always said I was attractive, and I've always liked what I saw in the mirror. But now when I look, some strange woman stares back at me, someone thin and frail and pasty-white. I touch my face to prove it's me, but my fingers are numb, and it feels like I'm touching a wax doll. And my hair—oh, God, my hair..." She shuddered. "I know it's vain and shallow to be upset just because my hair looks so ugly. At least I didn't go bald, the way poor little Samantha did. And even if I had, so what? I mean, the whole point is for me to get better, isn't it? Only a truly narcissistic person would even think about something as unimportant as her personal appearance, when it's her *life* that's at stake—"

Clay cut in staunchly, "Your personal appearance is not unimportant, Christine. I don't mean that it matters whether or not you're beautiful—you'll always be beautiful to the people who love you. What matters is whether you're beautiful to yourself. It's important for you to feel comfortable with your self-image."

"Well, I'm not comfortable with it!" Christine snapped. All at once the anguish that had been welling in her spilled over, pouring from her in a bitter torrent. "I hate that face I see in the mirror!" she sobbed. "I hate being sick! I hate the pain and the weakness and the mood swings. I hate never knowing from one day to the next if I'm going to feel good enough to get up and go about the business of living. I hate wondering whether or not a year from now I'll even *be*—"

Suddenly she broke off, unable to speak the fatal words, and the agonizing litany ended in a strangled cough. Clay held her tightly, rocking her in his arms while he crooned soothingly and stroked her flaccid hair.

Then he said, "Let me give you a shampoo."

The quietly uttered statement caught Christine by surprise. Choking back her grief, she craned her neck to peer at him. "What did you say?" she mumbled.

Framing her face with gentle hands, Clay repeated, "Let me give you a shampoo. Maybe it sounds silly, but..." Sheepishly he explained, "When I was a tiny child, little more than a toddler, my mother was ill. Years later I learned that she'd had a tubal pregnancy—which, incidentally, happens to be why I'm an only child—but of course I didn't understand any of that at the time. All I knew was how fragile my mother seemed, and how lovingly my father looked after her. One day I woke up from a nap and went into the bathroom, and there I found Dad washing Mom's hair for her, because she was too weak to wash it herself. The sight of them together made an indelible impression on me. My father has never been the kind of man who feels comfortable doing 'womanly' things, but I've always remembered how tender he seemed...." Clay's voice trailed off, and he shrugged. "So just now, when you were so upset about your hair, all of a sudden I wondered if you'd like a shampoo," he finished lightly. "I guess it's a stupid, sentimental idea—"

"It's a perfectly beautiful idea," Christine told him huskily. "Thank you."

Clay's cheek twitched. "Maybe you'd better save your thanks until after I've finished. I can warn you right now that I'm no Vidal Sassoon."

"Doesn't matter," Christine murmured. "I'm all yours."

He arranged one of the dining chairs in front of the sink and draped a towel over the edge to cushion Christine's neck. She slipped the bed jacket down off her shoulders and shivered as she seated herself. Clay could feel the tension in her slight shoulders when he helped her arch backward so that her hair dangled over the bowl. With hooded eyes he glanced downward, noting the deep hollows in her throat, the small breasts half bared by the drooping neckline of the too-loose nightgown. Through the gauzy cotton her nipples pressed, pebble-hard in the cool air. Clay swallowed thickly. "You look chilly. Shall I fetch the afghan off the couch for you?" he asked.

She shook her head. "I'm fine."

Clay turned on the faucet and tested the water temperature with his fingers. "Well, you'll have to let me know if I do something wrong," he told her. "This is a first for me."

Christine frowned. "You never gave your wife a shampoo?"

"No, love," Clay said, gazing down at her with fond irony. "Only you."

"Oh." The idea seemed to bemuse her. She closed her eyes and gave herself up to Clay's ministrations.

He did not recognize the brand name of the shampoo Christine used, but when he squeezed the thick gel into his palm, it released a dry, tantalizing herbal perfume that made Clay think of a field of sunflowers on a hot summer day. The fragrance lingered as he worked the shampoo into silky lather and smoothed it onto Christine's wet tresses. With long, deliberate

strokes he massaged the soap into her scalp, sleeking
back her hair, tracing the delicate whorls of her ears,
lacing his fingertips through the wet-dark strands to
shape her fragile skull. She had such wonderful, classic bone structure, he thought; the kind that age and
fortune could never destroy. He wished he knew how
to convince her that even when she was an old, old
woman, in some ways she would always be beautiful.

Her eyes were closed as if she slept, her long lashes
dark against her bloodless cheeks, but when Clay
cupped her nape in his palm so that he could pour
warm rinse water over the back of her hair, he could
feel the tendons still corded with stress. "Hush, love,
it's all right," he murmured, hoping she would respond to his measured tranquil tones. She stirred, and
he thought he felt some of the tension begin to leach
out of her.

When all the shampoo had been rinsed away, leaving behind only its summery scent, and strands of
Christine's hair squeaked with cleanliness, Clay picked
up one of the velvety thick towels he'd bought when
she moved in, and he swathed it around her wet head.
Then he swung Christine into his arms, ignoring her
wordless protests muffled against his chest, and he
carried her into the living room. Still holding Christine in his lap, he sank onto the sofa and began to
towel-dry her hair with caressing gentleness. All the
while he talked to her in a low drowsy monotone that
was almost a lullaby, and by the time her hair was dry
and fluffing freshly around her face, Clay saw with
relief that Christine had finally fallen asleep.

Taking care not to disturb the woman dozing in his
arms, with a weary sigh Clay tossed aside the damp

towel. As he did so, he glanced around and noticed
with surprise that he could see a sliver of dim, pearly
light peeking through the curtains on the dining-room
window. Dawn approached. The long night was almost over. He gazed down at Christine, resting so
sweetly with her head on his thigh, her fair hair curl-
ing in baby-soft ringlets on her cheek. Sleep had
brought with it temporary respite from anxiety,
smoothing lines, erasing shadows. Just for a moment
she looked as peaceful and carefree as a child.

But Christine was not a child, Clay acknowledged
ruefully, and it had been many months since she'd experienced anything approaching peace. She was a
brave, valiant woman. From the beginning she'd
demonstrated remarkable fortitude, but now, at long
last, she was losing heart. He shuddered to think what
would happen to her if the agonizing treatments she'd
endured failed to bring about a cure, or even remission. If Christine's oncologist wanted her to continue
chemotherapy beyond the course originally prescribed, Clay was very much afraid she'd simply refuse.

Moving with great care, Clay sank down alongside
Christine, sheltering her with his body. He dragged his
mother's mohair afghan off the back of the couch and
draped it over them both. The sofa was lumpy and too
short for him, and he thought longingly of his bed. He
felt certain that the woman in his arms would also rest
more comfortably if he carried her back into the other
room, but now that she was finally asleep, he did not
want to disturb her. Daylight might be breaking outside, but when Christine awoke, she would be lost

once more in the black night of her soul. Clay prayed she'd be able to survive the darkness.

"So HOW DO I LOOK?" Clay asked, stopping at the Institute parking lot to tug at his tie for the dozenth time.

Christine smiled encouragingly, a little puzzled by his nervousness. Considering how long Clay had been rehearsing for this moment—months, literally; ever since the paralyzed elephant seal had been discovered beached at Half Moon Bay—the last thing she'd expected of him was an attack of stage fright.

She reassured him, "You look very handsome, very scholarly—Dr. McMurphy to the hilt." She patted his shoulder, and she could feel the tweed fabric of his sport coat stretched tautly over his heavy deltoid muscles. "I do think, however," she noted dryly, "that if you plan to start making public appearances on a regular basis, you ought to consider buying a jacket that fits better."

Clay groaned. "I sincerely hope that this is the only press conference I will ever be called upon to preside over. I loathe speaking to crowds."

Christine looked surprised. "Oh, really? That sounds pretty funny, coming from a man who used to be a university lecturer."

"In school the students were trying to impress *me*," Clay reminded her. "Here the situation is reversed."

"I see," Christine murmured with a sympathetic pang. She thought she began to understand his quandary. For the better part of a year Clay had dedicated himself to tracking down the mysterious agent that had injured one specific animal. That was a long time—long enough for him to begin fretting about how the rest of the world might react to his single-minded quest. What if the government and scientific communities that he wished to persuade thought his actions were fatuous, his conclusions crazy—or worse, what if they didn't think of them at all? Suppose he gave a press conference and nobody came?

Christine said loyally, "I have complete faith in you, darling. I've read your notes and I've watched your videos, and I know you're going to wow everybody who hears you today." Rising on tiptoe, she kissed his cheek lightly.

Clay's hands spanned her narrow waist, and he pulled her close. "I wish you were going to be able to stay for the reception afterward," he said gruffly.

"I'll hang around as long as I can before I have to leave," Christine promised, "and then I'll come back once my appointment is over. But in any case, I'll be here for your speech. That's the important part." She made a face. "It's just damned bad luck that our schedules conflict on this one day of all days. I did try to shift mine, but the secretary at the bank said that if I didn't see the loan officer this afternoon, it might be weeks before he'll have time for me. I guess when you're trying to talk someone into giving you money, you're pretty much obliged to do it at their convenience."

She thought about the location she'd discovered that seemed ideal for a small, homey restaurant, a corner site in a growing industrial park that ought to generate lots of lunch trade. The rent was not unreasonable, but the owner was insisting on a year's lease, payable in six-month installments, before he'd agree to the capital improvements she asked for. She said, "Now that I've finally found the spot I want for my new place, I can't take a chance on losing it. It would be awful to have my plans collapse at this late date, because of some glitch in arranging financing."

Clay searched her face worriedly for signs of strain. Despite the depression that had been troubling her on occasion, Clay thought Christine looked a little more like her old self. She was wearing a new dress, something bright and becoming that disguised her thinness, and she'd applied cosmetics and arranged her hair with special artistry. "I realize you have a lot riding on this appointment, but are you sure you're really up to it?" he probed.

Christine nodded. "Actually I feel pretty good—all the adrenaline pumping through my system, I reckon. This is an exciting day for both of us."

"Well, just don't get too excited," Clay said darkly. "You know Dr. Fong doesn't want you stressing out."

"I'm going to be fine," Christine promised him. "At that meeting I'll be equipped with bank statements, income tax returns, character references—every kind of ammunition I could possibly need to convince the loan officer that I'm a worthy credit risk, not somebody who'll take his money and abscond to Aruba." Straightening the tie Clay had tugged out of position, she said, "Don't worry about me so much, sweetheart. Worry about your own presentation."

"I am," he conceded resignedly. "It's not that I'm not prepared for it. I think I have all the evidence I'll need to prove my position. I just wish I could get over this feeling that I'm about to dive into the middle of a swarm of great whites—without a shark cage." With a mordant laugh he looped Christine's arm through his, and the two of them marched through the gates to the office building where Clay was scheduled to impart his findings to a waiting world.

If Clay was afraid that he'd be delivering his announcement to a nonexistent audience, Christine thought wryly, his fears were certainly proved groundless. Well before the scheduled hour, the conference room began to fill. Many of those who arrived earliest were his colleagues and friends, but they were soon joined by other people Christine did not recognize, people whose name tags identified them as representatives from universities and government agencies, commercial fishermen's associations. Christine overheard one man introduce himself as an assistant manager for the marine sanctuary that surrounded the Farallon Islands, and an intense-looking young woman was attending on behalf of the National Oceanic and Atmospheric Administration. In the doorway, Dr. Berlinger and one of the guests were conversing in a language that sounded like Japanese. There were also a couple of newspaper reporters.

Christine stood on the sidelines, beaming bracingly whenever Clay happened to glance in her direction, but as the time for his opening statements neared, he became more preoccupied, less aware of her. He and Denny huddled, consulting earnestly about something that seemed to have to do with the oceanographic charts that festooned the walls behind the podium, and when Lib carried in the stack of neatly bound reports she'd assembled for handouts, Clay picked up one and stood riffling the pages as if they were a deck of cards.

Newcomers continued to crowd into the room until there were no more seats available. The atmosphere felt close, and the air reverberated with the din of chattering voices and scraping chairs. But when Clay stepped to the microphone, the audience fell silent at once.

"Good afternoon, ladies and gentlemen," Clay began, his tone steady and assured, giving no hint of the last-minute jitters he'd suffered earlier. "I'm Clay McMurphy, and on behalf of Dr. Henry Berlinger and the staff of the Berlinger Institute, I'd like to welcome you here today. As you know from your invitations, the purpose of this meeting is to discuss our findings in regard to the bull elephant seal that was beached at Half Moon Bay early last spring and to alert the public to what we feel is a potentially very dangerous source of pollution in the Gulf of the Farallones—"

Christine listened, deeply affected, as Clay spoke. For a man who claimed to detest public appearances, he handled himself remarkably well, delivering his talk with skill and conviction, presenting each point so clearly that even Christine, arguably the person in the room least knowledgeable about marine ecology, could follow the gist of his argument. It occurred to her that when Clay traded in his Saab for a Harley-Davidson, the academic world had lost a very good teacher.

The other people in the audience seemed as impressed by Clay's speech as Christine was. He concluded the presentation with video footage of the suspicious metal drums deep in their underwater crevice—a sight that made Christine shiver, no matter how many times she viewed the tape—and then he opened the floor for discussion. At once a dozen voices assailed him.

"Dr. McMurphy, when you mentioned the empirical evidence that led you to suspect—"

"Dr. McMurphy, how do you reconcile these findings with the paper you published on—"

"Dr. McMurphy, what do you propose—"

"Dr. McMurphy—"

The questions came with bewildering speed, but Clay took pains to reply fully to each one. Seeing the care and respect with which the audience recorded his answers, Christine suddenly realized something she'd never quite appreciated before: Clay McMurphy might not be rich or famous, but he was a man held in high esteem by the members of his own profession. Now, watching him in his moment of triumph, her heart swelled with joy for him.

The formal presentation ended with a round of applause, and Lib stepped to the microphone to remind the assembly that light refreshments were waiting in an adjoining room. The audience stirred. Christine glanced at her wristwatch and noticed it was almost time for her to leave for her appointment. Wanting to say goodbye to Clay, she turned in his direction, but he was surrounded by people who were bombarding him with questions. She wondered if maybe she just ought to leave without bothering him.

Then he looked at her. Lifting his head, Clay's gaze sought out and locked with Christine's. She beamed. "You were wonderful," she mouthed, knowing he'd be able to read the smile on her lips, if not the words. "I love you." For a moment their thoughts drowned out the din, then one of the reporters demanded Clay's attention, and reluctantly he turned away.

Christine sighed and slipped out of the conference room.

WHEN DENNY wheeled his pickup into the driveway at the rear of Clay's house, Clay saw with relief that Christine's Nissan was parked in the garage. His tension eased. "Well, at least she made it home safely," he told the Abramses. "When she didn't come back to pick me up after her appointment, I was afraid something might have happened to her."

Lib, who sat between the two men on the narrow bench seat, smiled reassuringly. "I'm sure that in all the excitement, Christine probably just forgot you didn't ride the Harley to work. Things have been hectic today."

"I'll say," Clay agreed. Twisting his neck stiffly, he dug his fingers beneath his loosened collar and massaged the muscles knotted at his nape. Then he picked up his jacket and the tie wadded on his lap and he gestured toward his house. "Would you two like to come inside? We can dig up something to eat. I'm not sure what's in the refrigerator, but Christine's leftovers are better than most people's company dinners."

Denny and Lib glanced at each other. "I don't think so, Clay, not tonight," Lib told him. "It's been a long day for everyone, and you and Christine will have a lot to talk about."

Nodding, Clay agreed, "Yeah, you're probably right. I expect she's anxious to tell me all about her meeting with the bank manager. Before she left me this afternoon, she was pretty hyper." He paused again, then held out his hands to his friends. "Well, thanks for the ride. Thanks—thanks for everything."

"You're the one who deserves all the thanks," Denny said quietly. "You did it, man. It was your hunch, your determination—your triumph."

Beaming, Lib concurred, "We're very proud of you, you know. You may have actually made a difference in the world."

Clay gazed fondly at the couple. "You guys... Have I told you lately how much you two mean to me?"

"You mean a lot to us, too," Lib said, "you and Christine both. Now, why don't you go and share the good news with her?"

When Clay opened the back door, Christine was in the kitchen. She'd donned an apron over her new dress, and she was standing in her stocking feet at the sink, carving radish roses as if they were Italian cameos. Neither one of them particularly liked radishes. The door hinges creaked, and Christine jerked her head in Clay's direction. Dropping her paring knife into the salad drainer, she stared at him with stricken eyes. "Oh, no," she gasped. "I was supposed to go back and pick you up. I'm so sorry!"

Clay tossed his sport coat and tie over the back of a chair and pecked Christine's cheek. "It's all right, love," he told her soothingly. "Denny and Lib gave me a lift home."

She frowned. "Was that their truck I just heard on the street? It's certainly a long detour for them to drive all the way down here. Why didn't you invite them in for dinner? It'll be ready in just a minute, and we have plenty."

Clay eyed the variety of dishes arranged on the countertop, enough food for a buffet. The overabundance troubled him. The only time Christine cooked compulsively was when she was very happy—or very unhappy. Clay said, "Of course I asked Denny and Lib if they'd like to eat with us, but they seemed in a hurry to get home. I guess they're just tired. It's been a hell of a day for everyone."

"I see," Christine muttered. She turned away from Clay to finish arranging trimmed vegetables on chilled plates. After drizzling vinaigrette in a golden stream over the two salads, she carried them into the dining room, trailing the pungent scent of balsamic vinegar in her wake. Clay followed her. As Christine set down the plates, she asked, "How did the reception go? Was it as much a success as your talk?"

"It wasn't bad," Clay replied. "Everybody seemed to agree that we're on to something. I heard the woman from the government agency telling Dr. Berlinger that she's coming back next week with some more of her people, to take a look at our raw data."

Christine nodded. "That's great. I can't tell you how happy I am that things are finally beginning to come together for you. You've worked so hard."

"Everybody at the Institute has worked hard," Clay said, "which reminds me—Dr. Berlinger told me that after things have settled down a bit, he'll throw a celebration out at his place for all the staff and volunteers and their families. That way, we can all share in the fun."

"Great," Christine declared. "I'll look forward to it. I really hated missing out on the reception today."

Clay laughed. "Well, I guarantee that a party at Dr. Berlinger's will be more fun than a formal reception. He has a beautiful ranch up the coast a way. I've been hoping you'd get a chance to see it."

"Sounds fantastic," Christine agreed, lighting a pair of tall tapers.

Then Clay asked, "And how did your meeting with the banker go this afternoon?"

Suddenly Christine gripped the edge of the dinner table as if her legs would not support her. The wavering candlelight cast dark shadows over her white, set face. "I didn't get the loan," she whispered hoarsely.

Clay cursed. He'd guessed already, of course. He'd known the instant he opened his back door and saw her moving mechanically around the kitchen like some robot Julia Child. "I'm so sorry," he said. "Is there anything I can do?"

"Hold me?" Christine suggested diffidently.

At once Clay dragged her slight body into his arms. She was trembling violently. Standing in her bare feet, the top of her head only just reached his chin, and when she burrowed her face against his chest, her hair tickled his throat. She felt tiny, defenseless, utterly vulnerable. With an effort, Clay asked, "So what happened? What about all those papers you took to show the loan officer?"

"He wouldn't even look at them," Christine said, choking on her bitterness. "Everything's meaningless now—my restaurant experience, my credit history. The only thing that matters is that I have cancer."

Gritting his teeth, Clay persisted, "Did you explain to the banker that you've almost completed the course of treatment your doctor prescribed?"

Christine nodded. "He was very polite—he wished me all the luck in the world—but he maintained that, according to bank policy, my medical records would have to show I'd been 'clean' for at least five years before he could even consider loaning money to me." She shuddered. "*Clean.* Oh, God, Clay, I don't think I've ever felt so angry and humiliated in my life! He made me sound as if I were a junkie or—or a leper...."

Struggling to cap the rage that welled in him, Clay prayed he would never meet the person who'd so upset Christine. With spurious calm he reminded her, "There are other banks."

"But that won't make any difference. Because of my medical condition, I'm considered such a bad credit risk that even the average loan sharks would hesitate to advance me any money."

"Loan shark? Good Lord, Christine, you wouldn't—"

"No, I wouldn't," she snapped. "I've lost my health, not my mind." She took a deep, bracing breath. "No matter how furious and frustrated the situation makes me, I know that getting mad is just a waste of energy, so instead I've been thinking about my options," she told him. "That's why I forgot to pick you up. I was so absorbed in trying to figure out what I'm going to do that for a while there, everything else went out of my mind—not that that's any excuse, of course."

Clay muttered, "Don't worry about it. The important thing is that you're doing something positive. Did you come to any decisions?"

"Well, the first thing I decided was that giving up on starting a new business is *not* an option!" Christine declared fiercely. "I want that restaurant, and one way or another, I mean to have it."

Hugging her, Clay cheered, "Good for you, darling. I love it when you're spunky."

Christine giggled dryly. "Spunk I have tons of. It's cash I need right now." She sighed. "The money I got from La Courgette—I can't touch that, because I need it for medical and living expenses. And I refuse to ask for handouts from friends or family. So far as I can tell, if I want to raise enough capital to open a new restaurant, I'm left with only one alternative."

"And what's that?"

Christine lifted her head to face Clay, her expression determined. She said, "I'm going to have to sell my home."

He stared at her. "Your home?" he echoed blankly. It took a fraction of a second for him to remember the elegant little suburban bungalow with English floral wallpaper in the bedroom. Christine's house. She had moved into Clay's beachfront dwelling with such apparent ease, merging their disparate life-styles as harmoniously as if they'd lived together for years, that Clay tended to forget she even owned another residence. In all the months she'd stayed with him, she'd never once mentioned moving back to her own home, and yet he knew that the house in Mill Valley held some mystical significance for Christine that he'd never quite comprehended. Cautiously he pressed, "You're thinking about selling your house? That's a big decision."

"I know it is," Christine said. "I sweated and scrimped to buy that place, all by myself. Reese thought I was nuts. He wanted me to move into his

condo with him, but I said no, I had to have a house
of my own, I had to replace the home my mother and
I lost after Daddy died...." She smiled sardonically.
"I guess it's pretty ironic that the same disease that
robbed me of that home is going to take this one, as
well."

"Christine—" Clay began thickly.

She shook her head. "Please don't say anything.
I've made up my mind. I'm an adult, and I know that
sometimes when you want something badly, the only
way to get it is by sacrificing something else that's
equally precious to you."

Clay scowled in frustration. "I wish I knew some
way to help you."

Wetting her lips with a flick of her tongue, Christine murmured. "There is one thing...." Her voice
trailed off.

"Yes?" Clay prompted.

She swallowed hard. Peering up at him through her
lashes, she asked in a soft voice, "Make love to me
tonight? I love you so much, and lately we've both
been so busy.... I can deal with losing my job and my
home—even my looks—but I couldn't bear to think
I'd lost you, too—"

Before the words could slip from her mouth, Clay
was kissing Christine fiercely. "You haven't lost me,"
he growled against her lips. "You're never going to
lose me! And you're never going to lose your home,
either." With an intensity that was almost cruel, he
declared, "There's something I want you to remember, Christine—that bungalow in Mill Valley is only a
house. Whether you keep it or sell it or a typhoon
comes along and blows the damned thing into the bay,

you have not lost your *home*. Your home is here with me!''

Then he scooped her into his arms and carried her into the bedroom.

CHAPTER ELEVEN

GNAWING HER LIP, Christine gazed across the desk at her oncologist. "So that's it?" she asked, almost afraid to hope. "I've really finished with my treatment? No more—no more chemotherapy?"

Patricia Fong nodded gravely. "That's right, Christine. Unless there's a recurrence of the disease, some evidence of metastasis—which in your case I consider unlikely—you won't be having any more chemotherapy."

"Oh, thank God!" Christine cried. She gripped the arms of her chair, shaking with emotion until she thought she might slither off the seat. "Oh, thank God," she repeated hoarsely. She gulped as she admitted, "I never told you this, Patricia, but there were moments when I didn't believe this day would ever come."

"I know," the doctor said gently. "Everybody feels that way at times."

She paused to give Christine a chance to collect herself, then she picked up the thick medical file lying on the desk in front of her. Briskly she announced, "Christine, I want to make sure you understand that even though the chemotherapy may be behind you, you're not free of me yet. Careful follow-up is absolutely vital to your recovery. I'll want to see you on a monthly basis for chest X rays and blood work. At the end of a year we'll do another CAT scan, and after that you'll need a checkup every three to six months. If you remain symptom free for five years, well, then—"

"Then I'll be...cured?" Christine whispered, wary of tempting the fates by speaking the word aloud.

Dr. Fong smiled. "It has a nice ring to it, doesn't it?"

Inhaling deeply, Christine garnered her courage. When she felt she was braced for the oncologist's possible response to her question, she ventured, "Patricia, there's something I have to ask, and I want you to please be honest with me."

"Ask away," the other woman said.

Christine said, "I'm almost thirty-three years old. Will I ever be able to have children?"

The physician did not hesitate. "I don't know," she answered frankly. "After the continual shocks your body has suffered during the past months, it's impossible to predict whether or not your system will return completely to normal. Many women in your position are able to conceive and have perfectly ordinary pregnancies. Others aren't. Certainly the excellent health you enjoyed before you become ill is a factor in your favor, and the fact that you've responded so well to treatment is an encouraging sign. But even though I know how eager you must be to put this behind you and get on with your life, at the moment all I can do is advise you to be patient. You have time."

"Time," Christine murmured, and the word trembled on her lips. She had time. What a lovely, lovely thought.

On her way out of the doctor's office, Christine stopped by the receptionist's desk long enough to schedule the first of her follow-up appointments. When she turned again to head toward the clinic exit, someone called her name.

Puzzled, Christine paused and glanced back. A brown-haired girl in a high-school drill-team uniform was advancing toward her, a grin splitting her round face. "Hey, it's great to see you again," the teenager greeted. "I was hoping we'd bump into each other one of these days when I came in for a checkup."

Christine frowned blankly. "Hello?" she murmured, trying to place the big dark eyes and the cap of shining, chestnut-colored ringlets.

The girl giggled. "You don't recognize me, do you?" she teased triumphantly. "Is that any way to treat your old roomie?"

Christine stared in disbelief. "Samantha?" she gasped, unable to equate the pretty, plump-faced young girl with the rake-thin waif who'd once shared her hospital room. "Good heavens, is it really you?"

Samantha's smile stretched still wider. "Yes, it's me, chipmunk cheeks and curls and all." She tousled her short hair with her fingers. "As you can see, it didn't come back flaming red, the way I'd hoped, but I guess I can put up with it."

"Oh, Samantha, you look beautiful," Christine exclaimed. "How do you feel?"

The girl shrugged. "Good. Alive." Her gaze flicked over Christine, and her expression grew sober, taking on a maturity that sat oddly on her young features. "What about you?" Samantha asked quietly. "How are you doing?"

With a grin Christine told her, "Well, Dr. Fong has just informed me that chemo is behind me, so I guess I must be doing okay."

"That's great," Samantha said. "I remember how I felt when she told me the same thing. It's like your own personal miracle, isn't it?"

"Yes, it is," Christine said thickly. "That's exactly how it feels."

The receptionist called Samantha's name. "Sorry, gotta split," the girl said. She took a step toward the front desk; then suddenly she turned back and flung her arms around Christine. "I'm glad I saw you today," Samantha whispered as she hugged the older woman tightly.

Christine felt her eyes fill. "I'm very glad I saw you, too." She waited until Samantha disappeared through the door leading back to the examination rooms before she headed on out of the clinic.

WHILE CHRISTINE leaned over the sink, carefully applying her makeup, she could hear Clay rummaging around in the bedroom. The closet door creaked. Something that sounded like a cardboard carton thudded to the floor. Clay called, "Darling, I have a surprise for you."

"That's nice," Christine muttered, too intent on filling in the bow of her upper lip to pay much attention to the noise he was making. They would be leaving soon for the celebration Dr. Berlinger was hosting for the Institute staff, and even though dress for the event was casual, Christine was determined to look her best. She was wearing white denims and a soft blouson top in a becoming rose color, and to disguise her hair's limpness, she'd tied it back with a bright scarf. But when she peered anxiously at her image in the bathroom mirror, she was not really checking to make sure her eyeliner hadn't smeared. Against the advice of her physician, Christine was searching her face for signs of improvement.

Christine's doctor had warned her not to expect overnight changes. The healing process, when it began, would evidence itself in infinitely small ways, Patricia explained—the merest blush of pink on a sallow cheek, a strain line that no longer looked quite so pinched, an extra fraction of an ounce registering on the digital readout when Christine stepped on the scale. Dr. Fong admonished her patient not to allow her mood to be dictated by routine daily fluctuations of weight and well-being—but Christine, eager for hard evidence that she was getting better, found it impossible to heed the oncologist's advice.

She heard Clay approach. "Hey, lady, don't you like presents?" he asked from the door.

With a chuckle Christine laid down her lip brush and turned to face Clay. He stood framed in the bathroom door. His hands were hidden behind his back, and he grinned like a little boy—a very sexy little boy, Christine amended, allowing her gaze to drift upward over the long legs in tight jeans, the broad, muscular chest outlined explicitly by a black *Phantom of the Opera* T-shirt. Christine smiled indulgently. "Sure, I like presents," she said. "What's the occasion?"

"No particular occasion," Clay murmured mysteriously. With a courtly flourish, from behind him he whipped out a glitter-flake blue crash helmet with a wraparound sun visor.

Christine stiffened. "What's that?"

Clay's eyes glinted. "What does it look like?"

"It looks like a motorcycle helmet," she replied cautiously, "but you already have one."

"I told you, this is a present for you. Want to try it on?" When Christine said nothing, regarding the headgear with stern suspicion, Clay explained lightly, "It's a beautiful day, and the ride out to Dr. Berlinger's ranch is such a pretty one that I thought that instead of driving your car to the party, we'd take the Harley."

Christine felt the blood leach from her face. Fumbling for the edge of the sink to steady herself, she reminded him, "Clay, I have never been on a motorcycle in my life."

"Then it's about time you started, isn't it?" he shot back smugly.

"But you know how I feel about those—those things...."

Suddenly the humor vanished from Clay's voice. "Christine, do you trust me?" he asked flatly.

She blinked. "Of course I do."

"Then trust me on this," he said. "You know I'd never take a chance on hurting you. I'm quite sure that once you've actually ridden on the bike with me, you'll realize there's nothing to be afraid of."

Christine snorted. "Don't try to cajole me, Clay. If there's nothing to be afraid of, then why do you want me to wear a crash helmet?"

Tipping his head in acknowledgment of her riposte, he admitted wryly, "I want you to wear a helmet because any reasonable, intelligent person knows that in the unlikely case of an accident, a helmet can save your life.''

He waited. He could see the conflicting emotions that passed over Christine's face as she glanced at the helmet, alarm battling with something that might have been temptation. He urged her quietly, ''Please, sweetheart, this is important to me. I love riding motorcycles, and I want you to be able to share in my enjoyment. I'll never force you to do anything that genuinely frightens you, but it would mean a great deal to me if you'd at least give it a try.''

After a long, anxious moment, Christine let out her breath with a hiss. Reluctantly she conceded, ''I guess it's not asking very much of me just to give the Harley a try. Considering all the other things I've survived lately, I don't see why I should be upset by the prospect of a simple ride in the country.''

''That's my brave girl,'' Clay said with approval. Setting down the helmet on the ledge of the bathtub, he drew Christine into his arms and proceeded to smudge her freshly applied lipstick.

Dr. Berlinger's ranch was located in a remote portion of the Marin peninsula, rural and secluded, light-years removed from the eastern half of the county, with its trendy bedroom communities clumped densely along the upper reaches of San Francisco Bay. To reach the ranch, Clay and Christine drove westward along Highway 1 through the Point Reyes wilderness area. They skirted sandy beaches and shallow mud-flats on which spidery walkways stretched out to dilapidated boathouses perched on piers above the high-water mark; they wound through grassy, rolling hills where sheep and white-faced cattle overlooked the Pacific while they grazed.

The course was an easy one, picturesque and not nearly so rugged and twisting as the more familiar route between the Institute and Clay's beach house, but almost as soon as he pulled the Harley out of his driveway, he began to wonder with compunction whether he'd made a serious mistake. Perhaps he shouldn't have goaded Christine into riding the motorcycle. Perched on the seat behind him, she said nothing, but even at the sedate pace he set, she clutched his waist bruisingly, and she held herself with such preternatural stiffness, fighting the instinct to lean into the turns, that once or twice she almost threatened to unbalance them.

"Relax, darling," he called back over his shoulder, but the wind blew the words away. Through the vibration of the engine he could feel her tremble. Telling himself that they'd gone too far to turn back now, Clay drove on—and eventually he was rewarded when he sensed her slender body begin to sway with the movement of the bike. When she actually loosened her killer grip to point out a flock of long-legged egrets feeding in a salt marsh alongside the highway, Clay knew she was going to be all right.

Just before they reached the turnoff to Dr. Berlinger's ranch, Clay pulled the motorcycle off onto the shoulder of the highway, rolling to a halt on the gravel as he switched off the ignition. The engine sputtered explosively and died, and in the sudden booming silence, he could hear the weird, metallic cry of sea gulls circling a fishing boat far out on the water. Clay took off his helmet, swung his long legs off the bike, then turned to lift Christine down from the saddle. When her feet touched the ground, her knees seemed to wobble, but by the time she unsnapped the chin strap and removed the heavy helmet, she was steady again. Tossing back her hair, she glanced around and inquired, "Why have we stopped here? Is something wrong?"

Clay shook his head. "Nothing's wrong. We're less than a mile from Dr. Berlinger's place, and I thought we'd take a minute to catch our breath before we head on."

"Sounds good to me," Christine muttered. She gazed toward the beach. Just beyond the shoreline waves broke against a cluster of jagged rocks, spraying the air with misty rainbows in the bright afternoon sun. "This is a pretty spot," she noted.

"Yes, I've always liked this stretch of the coastline," Clay said. "It seems so isolated and unspoiled—although supposedly some of the little beaches and inlets around here were very popular with rumrunners, back in the days of Prohibition."

Christine's brows quirked. "Oh, really? I didn't know that." She lifted her chin, letting the cool offshore breeze bathe her face and the hollows of her throat. "It was sweltering inside the helmet," she told Clay. "I hope it didn't make my mascara run."

"You look just fine," he assured her, "very fresh and collected." He paused. "Actually the main reason I stopped here, instead of going straight on to the ranch, was to find out how you're doing. When we first started out from home, you seemed a little—uneasy. Are you okay now?"

She considered. "I guess so—apart from the fact that my insides feel as if I just stepped out of a blender. The ride hasn't been as bad as I expected. It's terrifying, but sort of interesting, too. After a while I began to notice this strange sensation you get when there's no car separating you from the world around you. In a way, it was rather liberating," she mused.

"Does that mean you think you might actually learn to enjoy motorcycles?" Clay asked eagerly.

"I'm not sure yet," Christine admitted. "I'll have to think about it. But I can't honestly say I'm sorry you pressured me into taking this ride."

Clay stared at her. "If I'd realized how easy it was to coax you into attempting things you're afraid of," he murmured enigmatically, "I might have tried applying pressure a long time ago."

Christine frowned. "What on earth are you talking about?"

Shoving his hands into the pockets of his jeans, Clay rocked on his boot heels and said airily, "Well, I was thinking—now that you've trusted me enough to ride my motorcycle, how about trusting me enough to marry me?"

The words were uttered lightly, almost frivolously, but Christine felt as if she'd been poleaxed. Despite Clay's insouciant tone, she knew better than to assume he was joking. Struggling to remain calm, she pointed out uncomfortably, "Clay, darling, it's a quantum leap from jumping on a Harley to jumping into matrimony. What's happened to make you suddenly decide that we ought to get married?"

Clay swiveled his head to gaze levelly at her. Beneath his straight brows his eyes were piercing.

"There's nothing sudden about it," he said. "I've wanted to marry you ever since I first met you. I haven't said so straight out because I realize that for some reason the very idea of marriage makes you skittish, but I've tried in as many ways as I know how to tell you that I think we belong together forever."

Christine bit her lip. "That's a lovely, precious sentiment," she told him, "but you're forgetting something. Even though the odds are that I've licked this disease, there's always a faint possibility of recurrence. We have no idea how long forever would be."

Clay motioned impatiently. "Nobody ever knows how long forever is, Christine. We could get hit by a truck this afternoon. There could be another earthquake and California could drop into the ocean. None of it matters. I want to marry you. I want to spend my life with you, and whether it's for one year or fifty, I want the world to know that we're pledged to each other, legally and emotionally, body and soul."

"But what about children?" Christine asked quietly. "Even assuming I'm completely cured, Patricia says there's no way to tell whether or not I'll ever be able to have children. And if I can't, then with my health history it's a pretty safe bet that no agency will ever let us adopt."

Staring blindly toward the horizon, Clay listened in intent silence while Christine spoke. When she finished, he kicked at the gravel with the steel toe of his boot, sending a small stone arcing across the pavement. "I wouldn't mind having kids, especially if they're yours, but my life won't be incomplete without them. If the fates are unkind to us, I suppose we can always pretend the animals at the Institute are our children. Moonie needs someone to love him. How would you feel about a three-ton baby?"

In spite of herself, Christine felt the corners of her mouth twitch. "You have an answer for everything, don't you?"

"Everything except why you're avoiding agreeing to my proposal," Clay murmured.

Her faint smile vanished. "Please, Clay. You know I love you. I started falling in love with you the day you staggered into La Courgette and tracked mud and blood all over the pink terrazzo."

His brows shot up. "Lady," he said in clipped tones, "you have a very peculiar notion of romance."

Gesturing helplessly, Christine admitted, "I know it sounds silly, but you made a tremendous impression on me then. You were dazed and in pain, and you were trying to act so tough, yet you worried more about inconveniencing me than you did about the fact that your face was bleeding. Somehow that really got to me...." She laid her hand on his jacket sleeve. Through the scarred leather she could feel his muscles, iron-hard with tension. She said earnestly, "Nothing that's happened since has ever detracted from the impact of that first moment, Clay. I love you with all my heart, and I keep loving you more each day."

"Then prove it by saying you'll marry me," Clay said roughly. "If you love me, Christine, prove it by making a commitment."

She closed her eyes. *Commitment*, she thought; Clay wanted a commitment from her. She'd assumed he knew he already had one. How amazing—and troubling—it felt to realize that Clay still doubted her devotion.

Even though Christine thought it seemed redundant to insist on a public avowal of something that already existed between them, she acknowledged that Clay asked very little of her, yet gave so much.... She made her decision. Lifting her lashes again, she smiled up at her lover and said serenely, "Okay."

Clay grew very still. The planes of his face were taut with strain as he regarded Christine incredulously. "Okay?" he muttered gruffly. "After all this time, just *okay?*"

Christine lifted her shoulders. "I'm a cook, dear, not a poet. When we get home from the party, I'll prove my sincerity by making you a soufflé, but for now, all I can do is say, yes, I'll marry you."

His nostrils flared. "When?"

"Whenever you want, I guess," she said.

Clay glanced at his wristwatch. "Damn," he grumbled. "I don't know what inspired me to propose to you on the day of Dr. Berlinger's big bash. If we skipped it, we could be in Reno in five hours . . . less if you'd let me take the Harley—"

Stunned and alarmed by his precipitate plans, Christine held up her hand to halt him. "Hey, guy, slow down a little, will you?" she broke in with an uneasy laugh. "I don't know about you, but I have no intention of making my vows in some tacky open-all-night wedding chapel in Nevada. If we're going to get married, let's do it right. The ceremony doesn't have to be in a church, but I want it someplace beautiful, where we're surrounded by my family and your family and all the people we care about. Surely you'd prefer that, too?''

A little crestfallen, Clay nodded. ''I suppose so,'' he admitted grudgingly. ''Belinda and I eloped, and I know my parents would never forgive me if I cheated them out of another wedding.''

''Then you'd better do it right this time, because you're not going to have a third chance,'' Christine retorted tartly. She paused, studying his features. ''Why are you in such a hurry, love?'' she asked seriously. ''I've said I'll marry you, but what's the point of this sudden rush to the altar? I mean, it's not as if we were a couple of kids waiting for legal permission to hop into bed together.''

''No, but—'' Clay grimaced. ''Oh, hell, Christine, it's difficult to explain,'' he declared shortly, ''sort of a premonition. Maybe I'm afraid that if I give you time to reconsider my proposal, you'll change your mind.'' He shook his head. ''Sometimes you can seem so bloody elusive.''

Christine stared at him. Rising on tiptoe, she wound her arms around his neck and arched against him provocatively. As she wove her fingers into his windblown curls, she promised, ''Well, I'm certainly not eluding you any longer.''

''Thank heaven,'' Clay growled, and he lowered his mouth to hers. They did not break off the embrace until they were startled by the raucous blare of an automobile horn, almost underfoot. They jerked apart just as a carload of student volunteers from the Institute sped past on the highway, hooting and waving.

Christine glanced sheepishly at Clay. Her face felt flushed, and her body tingled with the imprint of his need. "They're expecting us at the party," she reminded him huskily. "Dr. Berlinger will be hurt if we're late."

Clay's expression was sardonic. "For the first time ever, I almost don't care how Dr. Berlinger feels," he muttered wryly, gazing at Christine with hooded eyes. "But I guess you're right—duty calls."

He picked up Christine's motorcycle helmet and helped her fasten it securely before donning his own. Oddly subdued, they climbed back onto the Harley and proceeded at a decorous speed the rest of the way to the ranch.

Most of Dr. Berlinger's property was leased out for grazing, but his big white Victorian farmhouse stood on a knoll covered with flowers, and a lush green lawn swept unobstructed to the lip of a high bluff overlooking the sparkling Pacific. When Clay and Christine parked the motorcycle among the automobiles and pickups jam-packed in the circular driveway, they could hear music and the high-pitched squeals of children. Strolling after another couple, they followed the noise around the side of the house to the backyard, where the party was being held. Their path took them through a kitchen garden. Bees buzzed drowsily among the tomato vines, and the warm air was perfumed with the spicy scents of mint and basil. Christine inhaled deliciously. "What a wonderful place this is," she exclaimed. "Your boss must hate having to leave it to go to work each day."

Clay said quietly, "In point of fact, Dr. Berlinger doesn't *have* to go to work at all—officially he's retired. But I think the reason he spends so much time at the Institute, apart from the fact that he believes in what we're trying to accomplish, is that he gets lonely out here. His wife died many years ago, and he has no children.''

''Oh, I didn't realize,'' Christine murmured sadly. ''No wonder he enjoys being surrounded by young people.''

''Well, he should be in his element today,'' Clay told her as they rounded the corner of the house. ''Lib said she mailed out invitations to all the staff and the volunteers and just about anyone who's ever made a donation or expressed interest in the Institute's work. If even half those people show up with their families, the place is going to be a regular circus.''

''I think it sounds like fun,'' Christine said, hugging Clay's arm. ''I can't remember the last time I went to the circus.''

When they stepped through a gate into the backyard, Christine's spirits soared. She surveyed the scene before her with delight. Scores, hundreds of people of all ages milled about, laughing and shouting. On the patio next to the house, a small rock group struggled valiantly to be heard over the noise of the crowd, but most of the guests were too engrossed in conversation to listen, or else were watching a pair of clowns entertain a group of children with a comedy juggling act. Picnic tables dotted the lawn, and on the far side of the grassy expanse was erected a commodious food-service tent, its candy-striped canvas sides rippling in the soft breeze.

Although dinner would not be served for several hours, Christine could see people bustling busily inside the tent, setting up a buffet. ''I wonder who's doing the catering," she murmured with professional interest, but Clay shook his head.

"Nobody's said—or if they have, I wasn't listening," he told her. "With all the reports and depositions I've been stuck preparing lately, the last thing I've had time to worry about is this party. But I'm sure whoever Dr. Berlinger hired to handle the food is very good. He never scrimps where his friends are concerned."

"Obviously not," Christine agreed dryly. Scanning the crowd for a glimpse of their host, she asked, "Do you see Dr. Berlinger anywhere? We ought to let him know we're here."

"We'll bump into him eventually," Clay assured her. "Just now I think I spotted Denny chatting with the guys in the band. Maybe he knows where Dr. Berlinger is."

Clay and Christine wended their way toward the patio, pausing repeatedly to speak to acquaintances who called out greetings from every side. When a pair of small children playing tag darted between them, the couple became separated, soon losing track of each other in the crush. Somebody shoved a soft drink into Christine's hand, and she started to meander idly through the crowd, content to enjoy the sheer zest of the people eddying around her. Her innocent pleasure lasted until, out of curiosity, she wandered over to the entrance of the catering tent—and ran into Tish, the waitress-turned-hostess from La Courgette.

The girl's vision was impaired by the bulky cartons of napkins she was unloading from the back of a van, and when she rounded the corner of the tent and stumbled into Christine, at first she did not see who it was that she'd collided with. "Excuse me, please," Tish muttered distractedly, sounding harried as she struggled not to drop the two large boxes balanced precariously in her arms.

Christine halted her. "You should know better than to try to carry both those cartons at once, Tish," she admonished her sternly, and the girl glanced up in amazement.

"Ms. Dryden?" she exclaimed, gawking at her former employer. "What are you doing here?"

"I'm a guest," Christine said mildly. "What about you? Why are you lugging boxes like a busboy? Have you switched jobs or something?"

Tish looked uncomfortable. "No, I—I still work at La Courgette," she stammered. "We—the restaurant—have recently started doing a little catering. This is the biggest affair we've handled so far, and we're kind of disorganized."

"I see," Christine murmured, flustered. Half the people who worked at the Institute were practicing vegetarians, so she supposed it was no startling coincidence that Dr. Berlinger had hired La Courgette to cater his party, but she found it less easy to accept that in her absence the business she'd founded was now branching into activities she knew nothing about. For the first time she began to realize that her connection with the restaurant was well and truly severed. "I see," she repeated hollowly. "That's . . . nice."

Tish frowned worriedly at her. Gnawing her lip, she began, "Ms. Dryden, it's been real nice to see you again, but—" Her words were interrupted by a familiar masculine voice shouting impatiently from outside the tent.

"Tish!"

Christine stiffened. "Forgive me, you have work to do," she muttered hastily to the girl. "I'll get out of your way." She whirled away to leave, but too late. Her path was blocked by a tall man stalking toward her, his pale hair in disarray.

"Tish, where on earth did you disappear to with those napkins?" he demanded. "Why aren't they—" He broke off with a gasp of shock and disbelief. Christine ducked her head and prayed for strength. When she thought she had control of herself, she slowly looked up again and found herself gazing directly into Reese Cagney's horror-stricken face.

They had not seen each other in months, not since Christine had signed the papers dissolving her partnership in La Courgette. As Reese stared at her with consternation, his fabled composure absent for once, Christine tried to recall exactly how much weight she'd lost since then.

"My God, Christine," he croaked, averting his eyes, struggling to hide his pity and dismay, "you—you..." His words faded away impotently.

Christine felt very cold. All her happiness, her pleasure in the afternoon, was gone, erased instantly by Reese's unguarded reaction to her appearance. This was a man who for ten years had told her she was beautiful, and now she repelled him.

With stony precision Christine said, "Hello, Reese. I certainly didn't expect to see you here today."

She gave him credit for recovering quickly. Taking his cue from her, Reese declared brightly, "Yes, it is a surprise to find you here. I didn't realize you were connected with the Berlinger Institute."

"Clay works there. I thought you knew," Christine reminded him.

He considered. "Of course, now I remember. I guess it hadn't occurred to me that you and your... friend would still be together."

"We're engaged," Christine said.

Reese nodded. "That's a coincidence," he said. "I'm married."

The terse announcement staggered Christine. Forcing her numb lips into a smile, she chirped, "Oh, really? What a surprise. Who's the lucky woman—anybody I know?"

"No. We only just met in the wine country late last spring," Reese told her, intently watching her reaction. "I guess you could say it was love at first sight. At any rate, we didn't see much point in dragging things out, so we got married on the Fourth of July."

After all the years she'd strung him along, Christine supposed that her ex-fiancé had earned the right to sound smug. With the petrified grin still firmly in place, Christine said, "That's nice, Reese. I hope you'll both be very happy."

Her graciousness seemed to touch him. Relaxing a little, Reese said seriously, "Thank you, Christine. I'm sure we will be happy. She's a lovely girl." He peered over Christine's shoulder toward a group of people setting up a steam table on the far side of the catering tent. "Here, you can judge for yourself," he murmured. Beckoning with his hand, he called, "Darling, could you come here a moment, please? There's someone I want to introduce to you." At once a dark-haired woman enveloped in an apron trotted to his side. She was tall and stately, and she looked about twenty-five. When she slipped off the insulated oven mitts she was wearing, Christine spotted shiny new rings glittering on her wedding finger.

Reese's wife glanced blankly at Christine before returning her adoring eyes to her husband. Quietly he told her, "Sweetheart, this is Christine."

The new Mrs. Cagney's initial reaction was just as appalled as Reese's, but she hid it better. "Christine? Really? How—how very nice to meet you," she declared, holding out her hand. "I've heard so very much about you."

"All of it bad, I'm sure," Christine quipped, accepting the younger woman's salute. Her grip was firm, almost too firm for Christine's fragile fingers. Wincing, Christine said, "I was just telling Reese that I hope you'll both be very happy."

"Thank you. I'm sure we will be, especially now that—" Reese's bride smiled fondly at her husband. "I know you wanted to keep our news a secret a little longer, but it's all right for us to tell Christine, isn't it?"

Reese beamed. "Whatever you want, dear."

Christine's gaze flicked between the two luminous faces, and something twisted inside her. *A baby,* she thought. *Reese's wife is going to have a baby.* Swallowing hard, Christine said, "I don't think anybody has to betray any secrets. All I have to do is look at you two to see that congratulations are in order. That's wonderful. I'm delighted for you both." She paused, elaborately consulting her wristwatch. Briskly she announced, "Well, I hate to run, but I'd better say goodbye. I really must go find out what Clay is up to.

Reese, the next time you talk to your parents, please give them my best."

Nodding, Reese said, "Of course. You must remember me to your folks, too." He watched Christine walk away. When she reached the exit to the tent, he called her name. She looked back. Reese's arm was wrapped protectively around his wife. His expression was sober. His glance slid over Christine's thin body, returning to her face, and he said awkwardly, "I just wanted to tell you—well—*vaya con Dios,* Christine."

She nodded. "Thank you, Reese. I appreciate that." Squaring her shoulders, she marched out of the catering tent and returned to the party.

Skirting the edge of the crowd, Christine picked her way across the lawn until she found a little wrought-iron bench surrounded by rosebushes, at the top of the knoll. Sinking onto the cool metal seat, she gazed down at the ocean, lost in thought. She had no idea how long she'd been sitting there when Clay discovered her.

"Where did you disappear to?" he asked with good-humored impatience. "I've been looking all over the place for you. We're in for a treat. Lib says the band has agreed to let Denny sing."

Blinking dazedly, Christine asked, "Denny sings?"

Clay grinned. "As a matter of fact, he's classically trained. His father was a cantor in New Jersey, who had hopes of his only son following in his footsteps. Of course, by the time Denny made it to Berkeley, his taste in music had changed radically. His idea of a classic now is Joe Cocker singing 'With a Little Help From My Friends' at Woodstock...."

He reached down to grasp Christine's hand. "Come on, darling. It'll be fun to listen to Denny, and afterward, Dr. Berlinger is going to talk. A lot of the guests here today haven't been at the Institute lately, and he's going to update them on the progress we're making. Some people may not be aware that the government has actually identified the company that dumped those barrels we found, or that plans are already afoot to retrieve them. I know that news will get a cheer from the crowd!" Clay paused, smiling tenderly at Christine. He murmured, "Then I was thinking that if you don't mind, maybe while Dr. Berlinger has everybody's attention, we could get him to announce our engagement."

Christine froze. "No, Clay."

"No?" Clay looked quizzical. "Well, it seems to me that it would be an ideal opportunity to let all our friends know, but if you'd prefer to make the announcement yourself—"

She shook her head stiffly. She said, "I mean *no,* Clay. I don't think we should announce our engagement at all, not—not yet, not until I'm completely better."

Clay's coaxing smile vanished. "What the hell are you talking about?" he demanded grimly.

Christine sighed. Pulling her hand from his grasp, she laced her fingers into a knot and stared at her white knuckles while she explained dully, "You asked me where I was just now. I was in the catering tent. You'll never guess who's providing the food here today—La Courgette. I was in the tent, talking to Reese."

"Yes?" Clay prompted. The very blandness of his tone made Christine's neck tingle.

She said, "I was talking to Reese and his new wife—his *pregnant* wife."

Christine felt rather than saw Clay's startled reaction. "My God, woman," he choked, sinking onto the bench alongside her, "you can't possibly be trying to tell me that you're still in love with that arrogant bastard. Not after the way he treated you, the way he forced you out of your own business—"

"No, that's not what I'm saying!" Christine shot back in disgust. "What kind of a doormat do you think I am?" She turned her head to glance sidelong at Clay, letting her eyes skate over his body with deliberate intent. She told him, "I looked at Reese and I felt nothing. We were lovers for ten years, and now there's nothing, nothing on his part, either, except—" she sniffed "—except distaste. I guess he's decided he prefers voluptuous brunettes to scrawny blondes with bad hair."

Christine shrugged. "But it doesn't really matter what I look like, because it only took one glimpse of Reese and his new wife together for me to realize that he's happier with her than he ever was with me, or than he ever would have been with me. They're going to have a bright future, with joy and laughter and probably a houseful of kids. That's what a good marriage should be, Clay, that's what everyone should have—and that's what you may not have if you marry me."

"Christine—" Clay rasped.

She ignored him as she forged on resolutely. "No matter how hard we try to pretend it's not so, the fact remains that I have been a very sick woman, Clay, and it will be literally years before I'm officially cured. You say it doesn't matter to you—but it matters to me.''

Laying her hand on his thigh, Christine said, "More than anything in the world I want us to be together forever, but I love you too much to let you tie yourself to me when we have no idea what the future will bring. I'd rather suffer alone than hurt you. I don't want you to be emotionally devastated, the way my mother was when my father died. I don't want you to end up old and alone, like Dr. Berlinger. Whatever happens to me, I want you to be free to walk away if the situation becomes unbearable—just the way you walked away from your old life at the university years ago.''

The muscles beneath Christine's hand vibrated with emotion as Clay declared quietly, ''Bull.''

She scowled uncertainly at him. ''What?''

He exploded. Leaping to his feet again, his eyes blazing, he cried, ''You heard me, Christine! This noble talk about being self-sacrificing and not tying me down—it's all bull, and I'm sick of it. The truth is that you're giving up—on me, on life, on everything—and you don't care a damn what your selfish emotional cowardice is doing to the people who love you!''

He gestured wildly. ''If you had any gumption at all, woman, you'd keep on fighting. Hell, even that crippled elephant seal in his concrete cage is showing more guts than you do! Pathetic old Moonie may not be able to swim or mate anymore, but he's growing and getting stronger, and when someone threatens him, he bellows and snaps right back. You make all the right noises, you say you're going to get on with your life and start a new business and marry me, but now when it comes to the crunch, you're backing down, because it's easier to cringe and whimper than it is to help yourself."

Clay paused to gasp for breath. Glaring into her stunned face, he said hoarsely, "I'm sorry for you, Christine. I love you and I've done everything I know how to help you—but if you refuse to help yourself, then there's nothing more I can do. So from now on you're on your own." He whirled away, trampling roses, and started to stalk down the hill.

Christine tried to stand, but suddenly her legs felt too rubbery to support her. "Where are you going?" she cried.

"Somewhere where I know I can make a difference, damn it!" he shouted back over his shoulder. Then he disappeared into the crowd.

Levering herself to her feet, she stumbled after him. By the time she reached the parking area in front of the house, the Harley was gone.

CHAPTER TWELVE

As DENNY SLOWED the pickup and signaled for a left turn, Christine anxiously leaned forward in her seat, straining in the dusk for a glimpse of Clay's house. The gas station farther along the highway had turned on its signs for the evening, and she could see oblong TV screens glowing through the curtains of her neighbors' homes, but even from a distance the beach house looked dark and cold. Expertly Denny whipped his truck across the path of an oncoming car and pulled up to the curb next to Clay's driveway. The garage door was closed and locked, and there was no sign of light in the rear of the house. Christine sank back against the seat. "He's not here," she declared.

Lib, squeezed between Denny and Christine, said bracingly, "You've beaten him home, that's all. He's probably just out riding around somewhere. You know Clay when he's steamed. He'll be back after he's cooled down a little."

Christine stared at the black windows and shook her head. "No, he won't. You guys told me once that you were afraid Clay might hop on his motorcycle some night and never come back. That's what he's done. I've driven him away."

The Abramses glanced at Christine, then at each other. Under her breath Lib whispered to her husband, "What are we going to do, honey? I don't want to leave her alone in this state."

Denny nodded, scrubbing his beard with his palm. "Let me think." After a moment he suggested heartily, "Look, Christine, sometimes when Clay's feeling bugged about things, he goes down to the marina and works on the boat. Why don't I drive over there and take a look? Lib can stay here with you, and when I find Clay, I'll make him give you a call."

Christine smiled wanly. "That's awfully sweet of you, Denny, but I hate to put you to so much trouble, especially after I already dragged you two away from the party."

"Hey, what are friends for?" the big man said dismissively. He waited until his wife and Christine had disappeared through the kitchen door, and then he revved the pickup and sped out onto the highway.

Inside the house, Christine wandered around, switching on lamps. Light reflected the eggshell gleam of the freshly painted walls and picked up the subtle colors in the oriental rug on the living-room floor. Lib looked around her with approval. "You two have been fixing up the place, haven't you? It looks very nice."

"Thanks," Christine murmured. "We're redecorating a little. I've put my house in Mill Valley on the market, and after it sells, we'll have to move my furniture in here. Clay thought we ought to spruce up things. He actually offered to hang floral wallpaper in the bedroom, even though he hates it...." Her voice trailed off into a sob. "Oh, God, Lib, what have I done?" she cried, sinking onto the couch. "Clay thinks the reason I won't marry him is that I don't love him!"

Lib sniffed. "That's a damn fool thing for him to think," she said flatly. "I've always figured Denny and I are about as romantic as it's possible for a couple to be, but when I see you and Clay together, sometimes I feel downright jealous." She paused, eyeing her friend curiously. "Not that it's any of my business, of course, but why don't you want to marry Clay? Except for Denny, I can't think of any man who'd make a better husband."

"But what kind of wife would I be?" Christine rejoined. "I don't want to hurt him by shackling him to a sick woman. I need to be a hundred percent certain I'm cured. Suppose we got married and the cancer recurred—"

"Suppose you *don't* get married and the cancer recurs?" Lib shot back impatiently. "Do you honestly believe Clay would suffer any less? Do you imagine his feelings for you are so shallow that the absence of a marriage license will somehow lessen his pain?"

Christine blinked. "No. I guess not," she admitted in a tiny voice. She looked up at Lib, and her tone grew firmer. "Certainly not."

Lib huffed. "Amazing. At least you're beginning to see the point I'm trying to make." With ironic compassion she studied the emotions playing over Christine's face, then she said, "Tell you what, hon—I'll make us some coffee. I'm sure that after—"

She was interrupted by the jarring electronic buzz of the telephone. Both women jumped. "I'll get that," Lib announced, striding back to the dining room. Christine's gaze followed her. She watched Lib pick up the receiver, listen silently and then carefully replace the handset in its cradle. When the older woman returned to the living room, her expression was stony, her mouth set. Seating herself beside Christine, whose eyes were round with foreboding, Lib told her quietly, "That was Denny, dear. He's down at the marina. He found Clay's motorcycle parked next to the Institute slip, but the boat is gone."

CHRISTINE PACED back and forth across the oriental rug, her relentless steps compressing the soft wool fibers into a shiny path barely detectable in the waxing light. Gesturing nervously, she demanded, "But, Denny, he's been gone all night. Why *can't* we get the Coast Guard to mount a search-and-rescue mission?"

Denny, sprawled uncomfortably on the sofa, lifted his head and blinked irritably. Only his wife's stern glare prevented a testy retort. Swallowing his annoyance, he cleared his throat and repeated, "For the tenth time, Christine, there is no reason whatsoever to assume that Clay is in any trouble. He's an expert sailor in a seaworthy vessel. He's also an adult. If he chooses to drift out on the ocean all night, brooding about your argument, then he has a perfect right to do so."

Pausing in midstride, Christine pressed, "And he doesn't have to answer your radio calls if he doesn't want to?"

"That's right," Denny said, pushing himself upright on the couch. He stretched his cramped limbs stiffly. "If Clay's in the kind of mood you've described, he's probably not monitoring the radio at all, the way you might unplug the telephone if you didn't want to be bothered. Of course, at this hour it's much more likely he's just asleep. That boat does have several bunks." He paused, watching her agitated movements with sympathy. "Christine, please, why don't you try to get some rest? It's nearly dawn, you're exhausted, you're imagining things. The next thing you know, you'll be telling me you're worried that Clay's been eaten by a shark."

Christine gazed silently at her friend, wondering what Denny would say if she told him that she had in fact been worrying about sharks—just as she'd also worried that Clay might fall overboard, or commit the cardinal insanity of skin diving alone. Perhaps he'd been trapped by the tentacles of a giant squid, like John Wayne in some late-night movie she'd watched as a girl. Christine had no idea she possessed such a vivid—and morbid—imagination. But with Clay out of her reach and at risk, suddenly no danger was unimaginable, no terror unreal. She wanted him home where he belonged, safe in her arms. She wanted him home *now*.

Christine walked to the front window and lifted the curtain to stare out across the empty highway toward the invisible beach. The rising light was only just now beginning to touch the uppermost fronds on the crowns of the tall palms on the other side of the road. She remembered the first night she spent with Clay, when the storm had littered the ground with palm branches, broken and in shreds—the way her life had seemed at that moment. She supposed it would be supremely, unbearably ironic to lose Clay after spending months obsessed with the prospect of her own death. For the first time she began to appreciate how precious and fragile *all* life was—far too precious to squander even a moment worrying about the future. If anything happened to Clay, she'd have no future. She wasn't as resilient as her mother, devastated by the loss of her first love, then brought back to life, phoenixlike, by another. If anything ever happened to Clay, Christine knew, there would be no Jeff Silvas for her, no new love to replace the one she'd lost. If anything ever happened to Clay, there would be nothing.

She let the drape fall back into place, and she turned away from the window. She gazed fondly at her friends, her dear, wonderful, tolerant friends, whose loving support had been almost as important to her during the past stressful months as Clay's. Denny was struggling to fold his ursine body into something approaching a comfortable position on the lumpy, too-short couch, while Lib sat upright in a chair, her eyes stretched unnaturally wide, near zombielike with fatigue. Christine suggested gently, "Hey, you guys, there's a king-size bed going to waste in the other room. Why don't you two use it to get some real sleep?"

Lib yawned prodigiously. "But what about you, Christine? You're tired, too. Will you be all right?"

"I'll be fine," she insisted. "I want to stay near the phone, and if I decide to rest, it won't be the first time I've slept on this sofa. So go on, scoot, both of you, right now."

"Yes, ma'am," Denny said, levering himself to his feet with a swallowed groan and a chorus of creaking joints. He glanced wryly at his wife. "We're getting too old for this sort of thing, babe," he grumbled, taking her outstretched hand.

Lib smiled sleepily. "Speak for yourself, Dennis Abrams." Tossing her long grayish braid over her shoulder, she led her husband down the hallway.

Christine's expression was full of yearning as she watched the couple depart. She had to admit that there was something poignantly appealing about the idea of sharing your life with one person, trading private jokes, becoming so accustomed to each other's little quirks that at times you were almost telepathic, slipping quietly into middle age together, growing old....

Wrapping the mohair afghan around her shoulders, Christine kicked off her shoes and settled back to wait for Clay's call. When he returned from wherever it was he'd disappeared to, she decided as she propped her elbow on the arm of the sofa and nestled her cheek in her palm, if Clay still wanted her, she'd marry him right away, even if he insisted on eloping to Reno. She could endure five hours clinging to the saddle of a speeding motorcycle, if that was what the man she loved truly wanted.

As long as he still wanted her.

As long as he came home.

THE TELEPHONE rang before eight o'clock. When Christine leaped up to answer it, an adenoidal voice informed her that a freighter heading out of the Golden Gate at dawn had spotted a converted trawler adrift in the sea lanes; when the Coast Guard sent a cutter to investigate, they discovered the Institute's boat dead in the water, out of fuel, its batteries drained. The dispatcher who telephoned Christine told her that the single passenger had asked the Coast Guard to relay the message that he was unharmed, but for further information Ms. Dryden would have to wait until the boat was towed into San Francisco, the port nearest the point of rescue. Christine thanked the caller, hung up the phone, then ran down the hall to pound on the bedroom door.

Delayed by early-morning commuter traffic on the Golden Gate Bridge, the pickup reached the wharf almost at the same moment the cutter and Clay did. Alongside the Coast Guard vessel, the Institute's trawler looked like an oversize bathtub toy, an impression emphasized by the towrope attached to the prow of the boat, and the way the smaller craft bobbed high in the water. Denny wheeled the truck into a parking space, and he and the women bounded out just in time to see a sailor tie off the trawler's mooring line, while Clay, swathed in a blue blanket, climbed down from the fly bridge and jumped across to the dock.

Denny and Lib dashed toward him, Denny's powerful legs carrying him ahead. When Clay saw his friend charging at him, he held up his hands and exclaimed in a rush, "All right, all right, I admit it! Of all the idiot stunts I've pulled in my life, this takes the cake. I headed out to sea without even checking the fuel gauges, and then ran down the batteries trying to start the engine again. It was stupid, it was dangerous, but I'm okay and the boat wasn't damaged."

Braking to a halt, Denny regarded Clay narrowly. "Nobody cares about the damned boat, man," he said, "but you've got a lady who's been awake all night worrying herself to death about you, and I'm willing to bet you're not going to be okay for long if you don't come up with some brilliant excuses real fast.''

Lib caught up with her husband. "Clay, you have no idea what you've put Christine through," she admonished him. "It broke my heart to watch her."

Clay glanced past his friends and spotted Christine standing at the far end of the dock, holding back as if reluctant to face him. She'd pulled on a cardigan, but even from a distance he could see that she was still wearing the same white jeans and pink top that she'd donned for the party. His mouth compressed. "I know I'm a selfish, inconsiderate jerk," he said gruffly. "I'm just glad she had you guys with her. Thanks." Handing the blanket to Lib, Clay squared his shoulders and began the long, deliberate walk to his woman.

Her face was an ivory mask, still and unreadable as she watched him approach. She studied each footstep with painstaking attention. When he stood directly before her, shivering in the misty morning air, her eyes slipped over him comprehensively before returning to meet his gaze. Stretching on tiptoe, she touched his lips with her fingertips, then quickly she drew back. When her palm trailed down the sleeve of his leather jacket, he captured her hand in his, warm and reassuringly solid. Christine said, "I thought something had happened to you. I was afraid you might be hurt. I was ... afraid."

Clay inhaled raggedly. "I'm sorry, darling. I behaved childishly. I had no idea I could still be so immature."

Christine's lashes fluttered. "It wasn't entirely your fault," she reminded him. "You were upset."

He grimaced. "That may be true, but I had no right to worry you. You have enough problems without me taking off like a spoiled brat." He paused. "If it's any consolation, I just spent the most miserable night of my life on that boat."

One corner of her mouth lifted fractionally. "Good," she told him. "I hope you were cold and hungry and scared."

Clay nodded. Candidly he conceded, "I was all those things. This jacket is great for the bike, but it isn't terribly useful for keeping out the damp, and the only food I could find was a stale chocolate bar squashed in the bottom of one of the lockers. As for being scared, well, it's a hell of a long way to Hawaii, especially when you don't have any power."

His grip tightened around Christine's hand. When he spoke again, he sounded weary and utterly vulnerable. "Of course, what's really remarkable is that being cold and hungry and scared wasn't the worst part of the night. The worst part was being without you...." His voice faded. Then suddenly Clay groaned, "Dear God, I don't ever want to be without you again!" and with a growl of passion he dragged her against him.

She could taste salty teardrops on his mouth, but she did not know whose tears they were—his, hers, theirs. Clinging to him fiercely, she could feel Clay tremble. He cried, "I'm so sorry, Christine, so damned sorry! Forgive me for saying the things I did. I was selfish and arrogant and cruel. You're the bravest woman I've ever known, and you've never backed down from anything—not cancer, not even blood-stained bikers who look like they're about to shoot up your pretty little restaurant. Faced with courage like that, I must have been out of my mind to think I could browbeat you into marriage. If your independence means so much to you, I'm not going to try to take any of it away from you. As long as we can be together, I'll settle for whatever you're willing to give me."

Sobbing, she choked, "But I want to give it all to you, my love, my life—even my hand, if you're still interested."

Clay grew very still. Lifting his head to stare intensely at her, he asked quietly, "Do you really mean that?"

She sniffed and nodded. "I've done some thinking, too, darling. You were right from the beginning—whatever the future holds, nothing matters as long as we're together. I'll marry you today, if you ask me. I love you. I want you to have everything you want."

Clay's lips quivered. "I'm a greedy man, Christine. I want everything, period."

"Then it's all yours," she vowed, and they kissed until they were interrupted by a young Coast Guard ensign who apologized sheepishly and then presented Clay with the bill for towing his boat into port.

"ADAM SILVA, get off that motorcycle right now and come here!" Meg called to her son, who straddled the gleaming Harley and made vrooming noises while he fiddled with the throttle. Reluctantly the boy climbed down from the bike, taking care not to disarrange the flowers and streamers dangling from the handgrips. Removing the black safety helmet that was much too large for him, he set it on the saddle next to Christine's smaller blue one, then he trotted dutifully across the grass to the French doors of the room where his mother was helping his sister dress.

Stretching his thin neck uncomfortably to relieve the pressure of his tie, he announced with a pained sigh, "Here I am, Mom. What do you want?"

"I want you to stay off that motorcycle," Meg said. "After all the trouble Clay's friends went to to decorate it, I don't want you to mess anything up."

"But Clay *told* me he'd let me have a ride on his bike," Adam reminded his mother, sounding grieved.

Meg shook her head impatiently. "Well, he certainly didn't mean today," she snapped. "Now please go locate your father for me—I think I saw him and Henry Berlinger walking down toward the bluff a few minutes ago—and after that, you're supposed to be helping Samantha with the balloons." Meg stood at the window long enough to ensure that her son was following her orders, then she returned her attention to her daughter, who was slithering into a slim white cocktail-length gown. "Don't mess your hair, dear," Meg warned severely.

As Christine's lustrous head emerged through the beaded neckline of her dress, she grinned at her mother. "Hey, Mom, why don't you lighten up on Adam, okay? He's just a kid and I want him to enjoy the wedding. For that matter, while you're at it, why don't you lighten up a little on yourself, as well? The whole point of today is for everybody to have fun."

"Didn't you know? It's a rule—the mother of the bride *never* has fun," Meg drawled ironically as she began zipping the back of the dress. At the waistline she frowned. "Oh, my, this is a little snug. You'd better suck in, dear, I'm going to have to tug a bit."

Christine inhaled, and her mother jerked the zipper tab the rest of the way to the top. When the dress was securely fastened, Christine relaxed and observed mildly, "Thanks. I guess I've put on weight since my last fitting."

Meg froze. Searching her daughter's face, she asked, "You aren't pregnant, are you, dear?"

Christine smiled benignly. "Too soon to tell," she quipped. She paused. With her gaze focused on the corsage pinned on her mother's smart suit, Christine ventured carefully, "If it turns out I am pregnant, how would you feel about it?"

Meg's gray eyes glistened. "Oh, Christine, I can't think of anything in the world that would make me happier," she breathed. Before she could say more, Lib bustled into the room with the florist's box containing Christine's bouquet.

The ceremony was conducted on the grassy slope behind Dr. Berlinger's farmhouse, where the lush green lawn, still spangled with morning dew, swept down toward the ocean. At the top of the knoll a small altar had been erected, draped with white and covered with flowers and seashells; a purple plush walrus peeked from behind a spray of orchids. To each arriving guest Christine's little brother handed a heart-shaped helium balloon, while Samantha Harris, plump and giggling, helped people write their good wishes on slips of paper that were then tied to the balloon strings. By the time the minister and Clay assumed their places at the altar, along with Dr.

Berlinger, Clay's best man, the air danced with float-
ing hearts, a carnival of valentines.

Hester and Frank McMurphy, beaming at their son,
walked arm in arm down the center aisle to take their
seats at the front of the congregation. Meg, escorted
by Adam, followed after. Then Denny Abrams, re-
splendent in a ruffled Guatemalan shirt, rose to face
the audience. Clasping his hands, he threw back his
bushy bearded head, and in a high, clear tenor that
floated with aching purity across the hills, he began to
sing a Hebrew wedding chant.

At the house Lib heard her husband's voice, and she
glanced at Christine, who was standing next to her
stepfather. "That's the cue, hon," the older woman
teased, "your last opportunity to cut and run."

Christine shook her head. "Not a chance, Lib, not
a chance."

Lib grinned. "Funny, somehow I thought you'd say
that." Smoothing her long caftan, she picked up her
matron-of-honor's bouquet and hurried through the
French doors.

Inhaling deeply, Christine tightened her grip on her
own flowers and glanced at Jeff Silva, tall and distin-
guished in his Air Force uniform. "Well, Colonel,"
she bantered, "I guess it's time for us to report to
duty."

"I guess it is, at that," he agreed, crooking his arm.
As Christine curled her fingers around his sleeve, Jeff
said fondly, "You look very beautiful today, Christine, more beautiful than ever. I wish your father was
here today to see you."

In Christine's mind flashed faint images of a long-
ago summer day, a picnic and a three-legged race and

a hearty laugh that had been silenced too soon. Wistfully she gazed at her mother's husband, who had brought life and hope and joy back into her family, where before there had only been sorrow and despair. Squeezing his arm, Christine told him quietly, "But my father *is* here today, Jeff. I thought you knew." Together they marched out of the house and across the lawn to the man who was waiting for her.

As soon as Christine saw Clay, the rest of the world disappeared. Her friends in the congregation—Tish, the chefs from La Courgette, her old college roommate—everyone vanished from sight, along with Denny and Lib and Dr. Berlinger and even her family. The minister reciting the familiar words was a disembodied voice. In all the world there was only Clay—Clay, with his glowing blue eyes and whimsical smile; Clay, incredibly handsome and endearingly ill at ease in an elegant gray suit; Clay, who had swept into her life like a knight on a charger, scooping her up behind him on his saddle while he battled the dragons that threatened to devour her; Clay, whom she loved, who loved her.

"For richer, for poorer," the minister said, and Christine knew that although the two of them would probably never be particularly rich in material things, their life together was going to be a treasure house of laughter and adventure and passion.

"In sickness and in health—" Already their love had been tested in the furnace, and it had emerged bright and new-minted, tempered, unbreakable.

"For as long as you both shall live." And beyond. Amen.

"Husband and wife," the minister intoned, and tenderly Clay framed Christine's face with his hands. As he lowered his face to hers, she closed her eyes, lost in the wonder of the moment, too stunned by the feel of his mouth, the taste of his love, to realize that the entire congregation had risen to its feet to applaud them.

Then against Christine's lips Clay whispered, "Open your eyes, darling. Look up." Dazedly she lifted her lashes, blinking back the brightness. She glanced heavenward. Overhead sea gulls whirled and danced against the shining sky, and the balloons floated upward to greet the morning sun.

Following the success of WITH THIS RING,
Harlequin cordially invites you to enjoy the
romance of the wedding season with

BARBARA BRETTON
RITA CLAY ESTRADA
SANDRA JAMES
DEBBIE MACOMBER

A collection of romantic stories that celebrate the joy,
excitement, and mishaps of planning that special day
by these four award-winning Harlequin authors.

**Available in April at your favorite Harlequin
retail outlets.**

"GET AWAY FROM IT ALL" SWEEPSTAKES

HERE'S HOW THE SWEEPSTAKES WORKS

NO PURCHASE NECESSARY

To enter each drawing, complete the appropriate Official Entry Form or a 3" by 5" index card by hand-printing your name, address and phone number and the trip destination that the entry is being submitted for (i.e., Caneel Bay, Canyon Ranch or London and the English Countryside) and mailing it to: Get Away From It All Sweepstakes, P.O. Box 1397, Buffalo, New York 14269-1397.

No responsibility is assumed for lost, late or misdirected mail. Entries must be sent separately with first class postage affixed, and be received by: 4/15/92 for the Caneel Bay Vacation Drawing, 5/15/92 for the Canyon Ranch Vacation Drawing and 6/15/92 for the London and the English Countryside Vacation Drawing. Sweepstakes is open to residents of the U.S. (except Puerto Rico) and Canada, 21 years of age or older as of 5/31/92.

For complete rules send a self-addressed, stamped (WA residents need not affix return postage) envelope to: Get Away From It All Sweepstakes, P.O. Box 4892, Blair, NE 68009.

SWP-RLS

"GET AWAY FROM IT ALL" SWEEPSTAKES

HERE'S HOW THE SWEEPSTAKES WORKS

NO PURCHASE NECESSARY

To enter each drawing, complete the appropriate Official Entry Form or a 3" by 5" index card by hand-printing your name, address and phone number and the trip destination that the entry is being submitted for (i.e., Caneel Bay, Canyon Ranch or London and the English Countryside) and mailing it to: Get Away From It All Sweepstakes, P.O. Box 1397, Buffalo, New York 14269-1397.

No responsibility is assumed for lost, late or misdirected mail. Entries must be sent separately with first class postage affixed, and be received by: 4/15/92 for the Caneel Bay Vacation Drawing, 5/15/92 for the Canyon Ranch Vacation Drawing and 6/15/92 for the London and the English Countryside Vacation Drawing. Sweepstakes is open to residents of the U.S. (except Puerto Rico) and Canada, 21 years of age or older as of 5/31/92.

For complete rules send a self-addressed, stamped (WA residents need not affix return postage) envelope to: Get Away From It All Sweepstakes, P.O. Box 4892, Blair, NE 68009.

© 1992 HARLEQUIN ENTERPRISES LTD.   SWP-RLS

"GET AWAY FROM IT ALL"

Brand-new Subscribers-Only Sweepstakes

OFFICIAL ENTRY FORM

This entry must be received by: April 15, 1992
This month's winner will be notified by: April 30, 1992
Trip must be taken between: May 31, 1992—May 31, 1993

YES, I want to win the Caneel Bay Plantation vacation for two. I understand the prize includes round-trip airfare and the two additional prizes revealed in the BONUS PRIZES insert.

Name _____

Address _____

City _____

State/Prov._____ Zip/Postal Code _____

Daytime phone number _____
(Area Code)

Return entries with invoice in envelope provided. Each book in this shipment has two entry coupons — and the more coupons you enter, the better your chances of winning!
© 1992 HARLEQUIN ENTERPRISES LTD.   1M-CPN

"GET AWAY FROM IT ALL"

Brand-new Subscribers-Only Sweepstakes

OFFICIAL ENTRY FORM

This entry must be received by: April 15, 1992
This month's winner will be notified by: April 30, 1992
Trip must be taken between: May 31, 1992—May 31, 1993

YES, I want to win the Caneel Bay Plantation vacation for two. I understand the prize includes round-trip airfare and the two additional prizes revealed in the BONUS PRIZES insert.

Name _____

Address _____

City _____

State/Prov._____ Zip/Postal Code _____

Daytime phone number _____
(Area Code)

Return entries with invoice in envelope provided. Each book in this shipment has two entry coupons — and the more coupons you enter, the better your chances of winning!
© 1992 HARLEQUIN ENTERPRISES LTD.   1M-CPN